# WHAT DOESN'T
# KILL YOU

# WHAT DOESN'T
# KILL YOU

## AIMEE HIX

MIDNIGHT INK
WOODBURY, MINNESOTA

FIRST EDITION
First Printing, 2018

Acquired by Terri Bischoff
Book format by Bob Gaul
Cover design by Shira Atakpu
Editing by Nicole Nugent

Midnight Ink, an imprint of Llewellyn Worldwide Ltd.

**Library of Congress Cataloging-in-Publication Data**
Names: Hix, Aimee, author.
Title: What doesn't kill you / Aimee Hix.
Description: First edition. | Woodbury, Minnesota: Midnight Ink, [2018] |
  Series: A Willa Pennington, PI mystery; #1
Identifiers: LCCN 2017029389 (print) | LCCN 2017038985 (ebook) | ISBN
  9780738755151 | ISBN 9780738754437 (softcover: acid-free paper)
Subjects: LCSH: Women private investigators—Fiction. | Missing
  persons—Investigation—Fiction. | Murder—Investigation—Fiction. |
  GSAFD: Mystery fiction.
Classification: LCC PS3608.I95 (ebook) | LCC PS3608.I95 W48 2018 (print) |
  DDC 813/.6—dc23
LC record available at https://lccn.loc.gov/2017029389

Midnight Ink
Llewellyn Worldwide Ltd.
2143 Wooddale Drive
Woodbury, MN 55125-2989
www.midnightinkbooks.com

Printed in the United States of America

I dedicate this book to my beloved daughter.
Precious Girl, remember, if fear rears its ugly head,
look it right in the eye and spit in its face.

# CHAPTER

## 1

**COP FACE SETTLED DOWN** onto my features. Impassive, in control, unflappable. Involuntarily, my hand went to my holster, finding nothing. Old habits were hard to break, and apparently four months off the force wasn't long enough.

I should have been surprised to see Joe Reagan staring back at me, I just wasn't. I'd known this favor was going to end up biting me in the ass. Didn't they always? I was told he would be out of the house when I arrived to help his live-in girlfriend, Violet Horowitz, move out. So it was less than ideal that he was there, especially since he was sporting two holes in his faded t-shirt and lying in a pool of blood just inside the back door. At least he wasn't going to show up halfway through moving her out and pitch a fit. The only other silver lining I could see was that *I* wasn't going to have to fill out the paperwork.

I looked back down through the window at his body, hand flung out toward the refrigerator. It was obvious he hadn't much cared about appearances. Short, poorly cut hair framed a face of slack features, but he'd been decent-looking. A solid seven when his blood had been inside his body and not all over the cracked, yellowing linoleum. The t-shirt and stained jeans were more evidence that bowing to society's obsession with appearance had not been high on Joe's list of priorities.

Pulling the sleeve of my hoodie down over my hand, I gave the knob a gentle twist. Locked. I hurried down the steps and around the side of the house to the front porch. There was a good, solid wood door like all houses used to have before subdivisions started popping up like candy from a Pez dispenser. With no windows, it was secure as hell and also locked. Pressing the doorbell, I listened to the ring strangle into a rattling noise. Of course.

Blistered, peeling paint and signs of ill maintenance were everywhere. The front of the house looked even worse than the back, if that was possible. There were stains on the concrete stepping stones, the edges rounded and chipped from age and mistreatment. The fall grass was overgrown and untidy.

I walked down the uneven wooden steps riddled with splits. Standing on the gravel walk, I looked up to the windows of the second floor but nothing moved. Not even a twitch of the curtains. I returned to the back of the house where I'd parked. I took another long look at the back door, this time for signs of forced entry or a hasty getaway. Nothing appeared out of place, but I knew it wouldn't. I'd have noticed while knocking my knuckles raw just a few minutes ago.

A breeze ruffled through the few dry leaves still left on the dormant trees, highlighting how quiet and removed the house was from the rest of the neighborhood. The overcast November day was eerie enough without stumbling across a body. I suppressed a shiver as I eyed the wooded lot to the side of the house. There was no menacing figure in a hockey mask. Not that I saw. The scene was certainly set for a horror flick, though. Deserted house down a quiet lane, a dead body. And me without my usual badge and gun. Not that those ever seemed to stop psycho killers in the movies.

So, no masked killer and no Violet Horowitz in some kind of fugue state, clutching a smoking gun after killing her allegedly abusive boyfriend in what any crappy television lawyer would argue was self-defense. I really hoped she wasn't dead in the house too, because I was not up for telling her grandparents that piece of bad news.

Maybe Violet came home to find Joe dead and she rabbited. It was a possibility. I doubted, given what I knew about her, that she'd have been able to pull herself together enough to drive off after something like that, though.

Most likely, Violet saw Joe was where he wasn't supposed to be and backed out of the drive before he noticed that she wasn't where she was supposed to be either.

Lowest on the list of possibilities was that Violet had shot Joe. I didn't know the girl well but if I couldn't picture her leaving Joe, dead at someone else's hand, and heading back to the mall, I really couldn't imagine her gunning him down a la Dirty Harriet. If that girl even knew how to hold a gun I'd be stunned.

I pulled my phone out to make the call to 911. As I unlocked the screen, my eye caught sight of a depression in the mud next to the bottom stair. I bent over and took a picture of what looked like a boot print. I glanced around the property again while I dialed, this time looking for any other signs of the boot owner. It could have been Joe's footprint for all I knew. My view of his body hadn't extended to his feet.

"911. What's your emergency?"

"I've got a 10-61 at 114 Jennings Circle. Last entrance, a tenth of a mile past the hydrant."

"Badge number, please."

I sighed. "I'm not a ... I'm a former LEO. My name is Willa Pennington."

"Dispatching cars, Ms. Pennington."

I pressed end on the keypad and dropped the phone into my hoodie pocket, then got in my car and cranked the engine to get the heat going.

It was less than ten minutes before an ambulance pulled up with the promised Fairfax County Police Department car behind, both in full waffle-mode, lights and sirens blazing. I mentally crossed the fingers on both hands that the uniforms in attendance were ones I had a good rapport with. I hadn't stepped on too many toes when I was on the force. I'd made only one actual enemy—Tony Harrison. And he hated everyone, so I was less an enemy and more just one person on a long list.

So, of course, good ole Tony exited the driver's door.

Dead guy, strike one.

Perpetually angry former colleague, strike two.

I cut the engine and got out of the car. Harrison spotted me and narrowed his eyes. He looked like he wanted me to try something so he could wrestle me to the ground and handcuff me, and not in a sexy way. His antipathy toward humanity in general ran even deeper for women in authority, which I had been the last time I'd come into contact with him.

The other cop, a rookie just out of the justice academy when I'd turned in my badge in June, ambled over, hands hovering over his shoulder radio and holster. Still greener than lime Jell-O. I kept my hands in full view and tried not to make any sudden, alarming moves.

Just in case. Maybe my day would improve if Barney Fife Junior shot me before Harrison even opened his mouth. The kid would probably just shoot himself in the foot, but a girl could hope, right?

Harrison eyeballed the house and then me like he was trying to decide what to do first—check out the dead body or harass me. My plan was to only answer what was asked so I kept my mouth shut. Let him find it on his own like I did. He chose the house and the wrong door.

I watched Harrison come back from the front of the house, his lips a tight line. He tripped over the edge of a buckled out stepping stone, catching himself before he face planted. I barely maintained my serious *I just found a dead body* expression. He managed to glare at me harder, an impressive feat on such an overcast day. He motioned with his head to the rookie and pointed at me.

"Ma'am? Miss Pennington?" His voice was as soft as his eyes, and if those eyes were any indicator, this kid was not cut out for regular police work and, for certain, not murder. He needed to be on crosswalk duty. Maybe directing traffic out of a church parking lot on Sunday. Officer Friendly doing the elementary school circuit.

"Do you want me to tell you what happened today, Officer?" I asked.

"Oh, yes. I'll need to get out my notebook first."

I had a feeling he'd be joining me in the former-cop ranks sooner rather than later. I hoped it wasn't boots first.

"I arrived at just about eleven forty—"

"This morning?"

I had to push down the urge to school him on the cardinal rule of witness statements: Just let them talk. Real life wasn't like those cop shows where you had forty-two minutes and you needed to cut out all the bullshit so Detectives Pushing Retirement and Hotshot Ladies Man could solve the crime before the final commercial break. Chatty, nervous, rambling witnesses were a cop's best friend, second only to the neighborhood busybody.

"Yes, eleven forty this morning, Officer."

He nodded. I wondered if I'd be able to get through a full sentence before he interrupted me again.

"I arrived this morning at approximately eleven forty to help my neighbors' granddaughter move out."

"Of this house?"

I nodded and looked around trying to see what was keeping Harrison. I would never have believed it if someone had told me that one day I would look forward to talking to him.

"And then what happened?" He was patient, I'd give him that.

"I knocked on the door for a bit but no one answered. Probably because the only person home is deceased."

"And you didn't see anyone?"

"Other than the dead guy? No. Not a creature was stirring, not even a mouse."

I heard another set of car tires crunching on the gravel drive. The cavalry had arrived. I was freed from the purgatorious clutches of both the uniformed officers on scene. The ambulance crew looked relieved too. Detectives on scene meant they could clear out instead of just sitting on the sidelines as a corpse grew colder.

A tall, imposing woman stepped out of the newly arrived unmarked. It appeared my luck had turned. The boxy jacket, a few years out of fashion, and the signature low bun told me that the senior investigator on the case was Det. Jan Boyd. The role model for my career before everything changed.

Detective Boyd approached us. Considering that Joe Reagan wasn't getting any deader, it was the smart move.

"Officer Pennington, I didn't know you were on scene," she said.

"I'm not with the department anymore, Detective," I said.

She lifted an eyebrow but said nothing.

I saw Harrison barreling toward our little group. Boyd waited until he had stomped the whole way from the house before directing him to take High School Cop back to their car to await the evidence collection team. He opened his mouth like he wanted to argue but didn't make a sound before turning on his heel and walking back to the black-and-white. I doubted his silence was due to actual deference to Detective Boyd's skills but more a personnel file thick with complaints, especially considering his stiff gait.

"Did Harrison give you any trouble, Willa?"

Holy shit! She knew my first name. Of course, rule number two of interrogation was to build a rapport, get the person feeling comfortable, like you were on their side, so she might have just been playing me. But even if it was just a technique, I felt more comfortable than I had been before she arrived. Harrison had that effect on … well, everyone.

"I am sure that was on his agenda, but he must have run out of time. Although, and it pains me to admit it, he's a decent enough cop when his personality doesn't get in the way."

Boyd nodded. "And you were a better-than-decent cop."

I saw the hook and the bait and merely shrugged. "Personal reasons," I said and continued on with relevant information. "The victim's name is Joe Reagan. I'll bet you'll find he has a rap sheet heavy with small-time busts."

She looked at me again. Boyd had the best kind of cop face—blank and intimidating—which was great for the cop but not so much for anyone they were talking with. A notebook appeared in her hands while I tried to avoid confessing to Reagan's murder, the Beltway Sniper shootings, and the Lindbergh kidnapping. She was damn good—I hadn't killed Reagan, I was thirteen when the sniper shootings happened, and my grandparents hadn't even been born in 1932.

I gathered my dignity back up, hopeful Boyd hadn't noticed my nerves, and continued my statement. "I'm here because I agreed to help my dad's neighbors out. Their granddaughter, Violet, lived with Reagan. She had accused him of abusing her. They had pictures—finger marks on her arm, bruises on her hip, a bite mark. The usual abuser bag of tricks. Allegedly, I mean."

Her brown eyes sparked angry for a second before the blank mask settled back on her features.

"My parents are on a cruise, so the Horowitzes asked me to help her move while Joe was at work. I think they were worried she'd back out."

"Or that he'd show up and teach her a lesson?" Boyd asked. "This is pretty isolated from the neighbors. Anyone on the road on the way in?"

"Not since the parkway. These houses aren't a subdivision, not as close to schools, no community areas, lots of land, so pricey enough. Probably an older demographic."

She looked around again at the rundown property. "Walk me through it, please? Start when you pull into the drive."

"I pulled in slowly. There was no one on the lane after the initial clutch of houses and no cars in the driveway. That surprised me. I was early, so maybe Violet hadn't arrived from work yet. I pulled around the back of the house and backed my car in."

I felt Boyd turn to eye me.

"Just in case we needed to get out quickly. I left enough room to maneuver the car if someone tried to block me in."

She turned around to look at the car behind us. "Good plan. Are you carrying?"

She sounded nonchalant but I knew it was anything but an off-handed question.

"No. I have a permitted weapon, but it's at home."

"I wouldn't have blamed you if you'd brought it." Her voice had that soft, wheedling quality meant to induce me into contradicting my statement. Fat chance.

"You're welcome to search me and my vehicle. I'll even consent to a GSR." I hadn't touched a gun since I'd handed in my badge and service weapon the day I resigned. I pointed to the back door. "At five of noon, I decided to check the house. You'll notice the back door has no landing, just a top step and then the door. I stood on the fourth step and knocked. When I got no response, I got on the top step to look into the house. I saw Reagan's body instantly."

I paused, expecting her to go look at the scene, but she motioned for me to continue.

"I headed to the front of the house to see if I could see anything. The front door is solid with no sidelights and there are no windows except on the second floor. I rang the doorbell and got no response."

"Do you think she could be in there with him?"

I looked at the old house, with its aura of defeat and oppression. "I think Violet drove up, saw her boyfriend was home, and turned right around."

I'd answered the question she asked, but I knew what was really on Boyd's mind. She'd have to consider it no matter what her gut told her. If she was even considering me as a suspect, Violet had to be number one with a bullet. Pun intended.

"I'm curious to hear your opinion of Violet Horowitz."

I shrugged. "She's a few years younger than me—maybe twenty-four?—and I only met her once when we were kids. From what her grandparents shared, she's been pretty coddled most of her life. An only child of wealthy helicopter parents from Northern California. She would have been good mark for a guy like Joe Reagan."

At the question in Boyd's eyes, I held up my hands. "I don't know anything other than what I've been told. This was just a neighborly favor."

"I'll bet you're regretting that now," she said.

"I have a general rule about not doing favors, but the Horowitzes have always been good to me and my brother."

Boyd was all business suddenly. "Gut feeling, please. Did Violet Horowitz do this?"

"Nope. The scene is too clean for him to have gotten violent and she fought back. He's got two to the torso in a decent placement. That's a confident shooter, not a panicked young woman."

"Any other scenarios occur to you?"

That was an odd question for a witness.

"Like …?" I mean, I had, for a second, considered that Violet might have gotten fed up with being smacked around and *planned* to take out her boyfriend, but it was a passing thought.

"Could it have been one of the grandparents, knowing you'd find the body and provide deniability for the granddaughter?"

My mind boggled at how cynical that thought was.

"David and Susan Horowitz have been a part of my life since I was in grade school, Detective Boyd. David is a retired pediatrician and Susan a nurse. They introduced my dad to his wife, Nancy. No, I don't think either of them had anything to do with Joe Reagan's murder."

She opened her mouth, but I held up my hand to forestall the question I knew was about to come.

"No, they didn't hire this. They're not killers and if for some bizarre reason they suddenly were, they would not have sent me to find the body."

She handed me her card. "If you think of anything else give me a call. Oh, and Willa—I know it's pointless to tell you not to talk to the grandparents, but you need to limit it to talk. Am I clear?"

I nodded. Nobody deserved to be murdered, but I didn't have to stand for Joe Reagan. One of the perks of handing in my badge. But even if it wasn't my job, I couldn't help but wonder what the hell had happened to Violet Horowitz.

# CHAPTER

## 2

As I trudged up the front walk I saw Susan's face peek out the living room window and knew I couldn't delay any longer. My stomach soured at the worry on her face. David had the door open before I took another step, his expression a mirror of Susan's.

"Violet's not with you, Willa." It wasn't a question.

I met David on the landing and looked him in the eye. "Joe Reagan is dead, Mr. Horowitz. I don't know where Violet is."

I heard Susan gasp inside the house. I motioned toward the open door. "Maybe we should go in and sit down. I'm sure you both have questions."

He stepped out of the doorway to let me in. I looked around at the Thanksgiving decorations already up, three weeks early. David ushered me into their tidy living room with the window Susan had peeked out when I arrived. She was perched on the edge of an armchair. She didn't look at me when I came in. She was staring at a picture of a dark-haired girl about six wearing a purple princess costume.

"Violet?" I asked.

Susan nodded and placed the frame on the console next to her chair.

This was worse than any of the notification calls I'd had to make when I was a cop. At least then I hadn't known the family and I had some answers even if they were unpleasant. The kindest thing, for all three of us, would be to just be as straightforward as possible.

"When I arrived at the house this morning to meet Violet, no one was there. I knocked for a few minutes but no one came to the door, so I stretched up to look in the window. That was when I saw Joe's body. He'd been shot twice."

Susan let out a little sobbing noise.

"How do you know Violet wasn't there?" David asked. What he really wanted to know hovered in the awkward silence.

"Based on the scene and my experience … my instincts are telling me she wasn't there, that she's most likely safe."

I gave them a minute. Their suburban life hadn't prepared them for dead felons or missing granddaughters.

"So what happens now, Willa?" David looked me right in the eye.

"You both need to understand that the police are looking for Violet. She's going to be officially labelled a person of interest. They have two scenarios in mind. One is that she's a victim and in need of assistance. The other is that she's involved in Reagan's death. They will be coming here to talk to you very soon. Just be honest with the detective.

Her name is Jan Boyd and she's the best option you've got for getting Violet home safe. Boyd's fair, a good cop."

"Should we call an attorney?" It was just like David to get to the thorny details quickly.

"A third party who is looking after your interests, and Violet's, is not a bad idea. This isn't a television show so the cops aren't automatically going to assume you're stonewalling them or that you or Violet are guilty. A family attorney should be fine at this point, but you will want a criminal attorney later. When Violet is found, or returns on her own, the district attorney could attempt to file charges."

Susan gasped. "But if Violet's innocent…"

"Mrs. Horowitz, charges are filed and dropped all the time. Filing charges gets the person in custody to answer questions in a more controlled setting. Sometimes it's done to protect the individual. Sometimes the DA's office is just cranky that someone isn't being as cooperative as they'd like. We'll cross that bridge if we come to it, okay? I just wanted to warn you."

David patted her hand. "It'll all be okay, dear."

I stood up and immediately David popped up out of his chair too. I'd forgotten how old-fashioned he was. That would go over well with Boyd.

"One last thing. If Violet calls, you need to convince her to come home. The sooner Boyd can talk to her, the better for Violet."

Susan glanced at the photo again. "Violet's been feeling a little overwhelmed lately."

I looked back and forth between the two of them. I wasn't sure what that meant since from their description Violet struck me as the kind of girl who got overwhelmed by too many lip gloss options.

"What Susan is trying to say is that Violet's pretty upset with us. We had a fight last night when we told her you'd be helping her move out. She stormed out during dinner."

"Just do your best to impress upon her the seriousness of her situation. And even if you can't convince her to come home, you have to tell the police she contacted you. That protects the two of you."

I could see Susan gearing up to argue with me.

"If you're in jail, you're no good to her. This is a murder investigation. Boyd would jail both of you for obstruction of justice if she found out."

David walked me to the door. "Willa, I hate to ask, but ... " He let the question hang in the air.

"Mr. Horowitz, I'm not a licensed private investigator yet, and even if I were, it's illegal for PIs to investigate murders in Virginia."

He nodded, looking dejected, and I felt like shit. My hands were tied. He closed the door behind me as I walked down the steps.

I hadn't asked them if they knew where Violet was because I had assumed they weren't just acting concerned. One of the first lessons you were supposed to learn as an investigator was not to make assumptions.

———

I had barely gotten the kitchen door at home shut behind me when I heard Ben call out, "Will, you've got to come see this video. A guy timed up *The Big Lebowski* with his dog's mouth moving."

It sounded hilarious. I needed some hilarious after my very unamusing murder scene.

"Will! Seriously, it's the funniest thing. You have to see him do the line about the rug."

15

I headed into the living room where I found my teenage brother sprawled, all 6'3" of skinny arms and legs, on the couch, a tiny smartphone cradled in his massive hands.

"A dog doing *The Big Lebowski*? Aren't you a little young for The Dude?" I teased. Of course, I was the one who'd shown him the movie when he was seven. Mom grounded me for two weeks for exposing him to bad language and violence. I was glad she never found out about me letting him watch *Fargo*.

I ruffled his hair because I knew it annoyed him. He flicked it back into place with a jerk of his head. I flopped down next to him, nudging him out of the way enough to squeeze in between him and the arm of the couch.

"Okay, show me this dog video." I leaned over his shoulder to peer at the phone screen but he grabbed the TV remote control.

"I'll just fling it up to the TV. I put a little something together this past weekend since Mom won't pay the 'exorbitant fees they want for those things.'" His impression of our mother was dead on. The little tech genius was always upgrading something. I couldn't keep up with how his brain worked. None of us could.

"You're trolling dog videos on the Internet. Mom still hanging tough on not getting a puppy, sport?"

His eyes rolled. "Ugh! Her latest argument is that I'm leaving for college soon and the poor thing—her words, not mine—would be so lonely."

The whole family was adamant that Ben go off to college, get his degree in something technically obscure that made a ton of money, and then cure cancer or something else equal to his intellect. Ben, on the other hand, wanted nothing more than to be a private investigator like Dad. And me now, I guess.

"Besides, I told her I'm going to stay home and go to community college for the first year."

This kid was going to give our parents ulcers with his stubborn refusal to accept their dreams for him. He wasn't lured in by any sexy portrayal of a PI in a movie—shootouts and bedding the bad girl with the heart of gold. No, he just thought our dad was the coolest, most awesome grownup on the planet. He was right. That still didn't mean it was the right life for Ben.

"I thought we'd agreed you were going to apply to the colleges your school counselor said wanted to give you scholarships. Remember, keeping your options open?"

He shrugged. Pushing would only cause him to dig in deeper. He was almost as stubborn as me.

"Dude, do whatever you want. Mom would love to keep you home with her. Remember how hard she cried the day I applied to the academy? And I still lived at home."

He'd gotten a funny look on his face. I could play him like a video game.

"I've got some time before I head out with John. I guess I could fill out the Common Application to make Mom happy. Most of the schools she's excited about use it."

I nodded like it hadn't been my idea and headed to the door that connected the family room to the room over the garage, Dad's office, as nonchalantly as I could. Just because I couldn't officially investigate didn't mean I wasn't curious. It wouldn't hurt to poke around a bit and see what was up with the dead guy. Had been up. Whatever.

"Let me know if you need any help, bud." I ignored his snickering. I consoled myself that even if I wasn't the smartest kid in the family, I was still the coolest.

Dad's office had only been shut up for a week, but it had already taken on that disused, empty smell. I cracked the window open a bit. I am sure Dad thought he'd left his desk tidy. Ben had gotten the slob gene honestly. And undiluted, it seemed. There were papers stacked in some fashion but Dad's organizational skills didn't seem to fall into any recognized form of order.

I slid the laptop out from the pile it was buried under and turned it on. Crap. Password protected. Dad must have written it down somewhere since I doubted he was able to keep a password in his head. And he probably hadn't hid it anywhere too clever. I leaned back in the chair and looked around the room, trying to think like my dad. I picked up the Rubik's Cube. Dad hated puzzles. I ran my hands over it, feeling for any anomalies in the surfaces. One of the squares was a little askew. I grabbed the letter opener, wedging it in the space, gave a gentle twist, and the whole cube popped open. Dad's cheat sheet fell out into my lap.

I scanned the list and found his log on and skip trace database passwords. Heh. *Nice try, Dad.* Once the computer was done coming to life, I opened the skip trace program and entered in Reagan's data, guessing that his first name was Joseph, and threw in the address on Jennings Circle. And hello, all the information I could possibly want on Joseph Lyndon Reagan. Were his parents under the impression he was going to be president someday, saddling him with that moniker? Maybe they should have spent more time teaching him to not be a criminal.

I scanned the information on the screen and then hit the print button. No harm in making a hard copy. For learning purposes. I had been right in my assumptions about his history with the law—chronic petty criminal. The most serious charges were for Distribution and Sale of Stolen Property, but he had a laundry list of Minor Possession, Drunk and Disorderly, Simple Assault—all self-control issue crimes. He hadn't been making it a career. He'd just been an immature dumbass.

"Will?"

I heard Ben calling from the main house. I checked the time and saw that I had been at it for a half hour. Ben could have finished his college application form while I had been hunting down Dad's passwords and running Reagan's rap sheet. I had no idea how easy or complicated the forms had gotten in the decade since I'd done my own.

"Hey, Will."

I looked up from the screen to see Ben leaning against the door frame. He looked nervous.

"What's up, Benj?"

He bit his lip and he looked five years old again. "So I was filling out the form and I got to the demographics portion. You know, name, date of birth, race..." He trailed off and just stared at me.

"And you know all that stuff, smarty pants," I said.

He nodded, his eyes darting all around the room refusing to meet mine. "I was checking Caucasian, non-Hispanic and I thought... I've never... we haven't... whatdoyoucheck?" He'd blurted the words out so fast I almost hadn't deciphered the breaks between them.

*What do* you *check?*

Sonofabitch. He was nervous about asking his own sister what box she checked on a stupid form. "No, we've never really talked about it. I assumed that was just because you had no room in your brain for anything other than gigabutts."

"Gigabytes," he said.

I snorted a laugh. "I know, dork. I was teasing. I usually check both Caucasian and African-American. Until they come up with a better way to ask, I'll just choose both. Because I am. I'm not more one than the other."

He started chewing on his thumbnail. He looked even more like five-year-old Ben doing that.

"It's just genes. Hair color, eye color, skin color mean shit, okay? It's just a stupid question on a stupid form that they use to create pie charts and crap for their annual report."

He looked like he wanted to say something but was holding back. Then he smiled and turned to leave. "Mom's right. You cuss too much."

# CHAPTER

## 3

"Hey, Sunshine."

That voice through the phone caused the hair on the back of my neck to prickle. I'd picked up the unknown number thinking this might be an update regarding Violet. Tears stung the back of my eyes before I could stop them. I cleared my throat.

"Seth."

I didn't know how else to greet him. He sounded happy and part of me, the bitchy part, begrudged him that. I knew Seth adored Michael and grieved the loss of his younger brother deeply, but it was hard to get past my own grief. It had only been a few months. Plus, things had never been easy between us. If asked to label our relation-ship I'd definitely have to choose *it's complicated*.

"I heard you were back in town and was hoping we could get to-gether."

I glanced around my dad's office, as though looking for a hidden camera. Was this a prank? I wasn't sure how to take the invitation. The last time I'd laid eyes on Seth Anderson I was putting back on my mourning clothes and doing a stealthy walk of shame out of his apart-ment.

"I, uh … I'm busy," I said.

He laughed. "I didn't say when yet. You're busy for the rest of your life?"

He sounded so breezy and light and I felt my sadness at being re-minded of Michael harden into the hollow anger I had gotten used to.

"I'm busy right now, Seth." I kept my voice as neutral as possible. Let him take that whichever way he wanted.

"Sure," he said. "It's just that Matt's Pool Cue is reopening—"

"Matt's reopened? That's amazing," I said, interrupting him. Un-expectedly happy memories of Michael, my best friend, replaced the grief for an instant.

"Well, it's reopening in a few weeks, Sunshine, but they're doing a dry run tonight. I figured you'd want to go."

"Hell, yes."

Which is how I found myself walking back into Matt's after more than a decade. The new location's parking lot was fairly full, a relief. I still wasn't sure how I was going to handle seeing the oldest friend I had in the world at this point. One who I could count on the very short list of people who'd seen me naked. Seth's list was not nearly as short as mine, which was always our problem when we got right down to it. Pun very much unintentional.

Still, I couldn't resist the lure of revisiting the restaurant that figured so largely into my youth.

"Kid, you grew up on me," Matt said as he enveloped me in his large frame. As sneak attacks go, I've had worse.

I looked up into his smiling face. "Sorry, Matt. You know how difficult I've always been. I grew up just to spite you."

He laughed and released me. "No joke, kid. You turned into a beautiful woman. I see the dumbass finally wised up." His eyes slid over to Seth standing at the bar chatting with Pam, Matt's wife.

Crap. Had Seth said something to them? He told me about the reopening, but I'd hung up shortly after. It's not like we arrived together.

"No, we're not ... it's not like that. I actually haven't seen him since Michael's memorial service." My face flushed hot and pink from having to bring up a subject I knew was going to garner a condolence.

Matt looked down. "Pam and I were heartbroken when we read that he'd been killed."

I nodded, swallowing down the hard lump that I knew contained all the tears I'd refused to shed since the day the Colonel had called my dad with the news.

Again, he looked over at Seth. "And *you* two never dated? I mean, you and Michael, no way, but ... "

I shook my head. Oh, hell no, I was not about to admit that a few swigs of tequila and two hours of repressing a nervous breakdown I richly deserved was all it took before I humiliated myself by hopping into bed with *Seth*. That was going to my grave if I had any say in the matter.

The flush in my cheeks ramped up and I struggled out of my leather jacket. Matt took it from me and walked over to Pam and Seth. To avoid staring at the group and allow myself some time to regain my composure, I glanced around the restaurant. It was bigger than the old location with more separation between the different kinds of tables. You could still eat and play if you wanted, but the tables ringing the perimeter of the pool room were bar-style—smaller and taller, so they didn't interfere with a shot, always a problem in the old place. All the old art, if you could call it that, was up on the walls.

I ambled over to one grouping of photos and was gutted to see Michael's beaming face. It was a shot from the final pool tournament before the original location had closed. I knew the exact reason he was smiling so brightly, because I had taken the picture. Michael was holding a trophy. Even though I couldn't read the placard, I knew it said *Worst Player*. That trophy was currently sitting on the shelf in my closet.

I hadn't realized I was shaking until a warm hand closed on my hip. The scent of cold air and soap told me it was Seth. His thumb gently caressed the bare skin where the edge of my shirt had ridden up over the waistband of my jeans. Of course it was Seth. He was the only person who dared to walk right past all of my boundaries. He draped his other arm around me and held me loosely. I stiffened momentarily then leaned back into his chest, eyes still on the photo. It managed to be comforting and make me uneasy at the same time.

The three of us were a past that was hard to forget, no matter how much I wanted to. Memories that made me cry as easily as they made me laugh. Sometimes at the same time. A different lifetime. Not for the first time, I felt older than I should. I could only imagine how Seth felt, comforting me over the death of the brother he'd spent a lifetime watching over and protecting.

I wasn't much of a hugger, never had been. Michael wasn't either and had wriggled out of the surprisingly long embrace I gave him before he left for Afghanistan. I would give anything and everything to go back in time and extend that last hug. Seth, though, had always been much more comfortable with touch. His body wasn't much like

Michael's either. Seth was all solid muscle and coiled energy where Michael had been lanky. Michael had been non-threatening, calming, a still pool. Seth's emotions poured off him and being near him was like being sucked into a riptide. Part of me wanted to get dragged under and buffeted around, helpless. I wanted to melt into him and let him take over. The rest of me knew how dangerous that would be and had worked hard to keep a certain wall between us. I'd let it come down just for one night after Michael's death, and now I had to rebuild it. To stay sane enough to have dinner with him, at least.

I gently, casually, pushed away from Seth's chest, and he dropped his hands. I gave myself another moment before I turned to look at him. We stared at one another longer than was probably appropriate until I chickened out and broke eye contact. He seemed content to stand there silently so I looked him over, taking in his well-used work boots, worn but clean jeans, and chambray shirt. He was scruffy but still annoyingly handsome. Not an elegant bone in his well-toned body and girls had always flocked to him. At least the ones that liked the manual labor, rough hands but gentle eyes type. And who didn't, really?

For the second time that night, I willed the blood to stop rushing to my cheeks. And other body parts. Not that it would have helped. Years of evolution has ensured that the male of the species drew that kind of reaction and even my own considerable ability to mask my feelings couldn't override biology. Deep cleansing breaths and I could, perhaps, control the traitorous swirl of emotions running through me. Emotions were the easy part; memories and hormones had a mind of their own.

He broke into a smile that bordered on his usual arrogant smirk and I had to resist the urge to smack him. He'd done a nice thing letting me know about Matt's reopening; the least I could do was not assault him. To be safe, I shoved my hands in my back pockets. He mimicked me, a habit he didn't notice but I had, years ago. It wasn't his only tell but it was the biggest. He was nervous too. Good.

Matt's voice boomed across the music and chattering guests. "Cue Pizza for Willa."

I rushed over to the window to grab the tray with the pizza and two icy bottles of Mexican soda. "You remembered, Matt."

"I remembered the pizza but Dumbass brought the soda. Maybe he's not so stupid after all."

His habit of referring to Seth as *Dumbass* always amused me. Matt adored Seth, but it was in spite of Seth's efforts to make himself eminently likeable. Seth looked like a bruiser but he had a sophisticated mind and he knew how to get most people to react the way he wanted. The varsity cheerleading squad and the girls' volleyball team included. He saved his genuine self for very few people.

I saw Seth had set up at one of the bar-style tables in the back and brought the tray over, sliding it onto the tabletop.

"Thanks for the sodas, Ace. It was a rare nice thing for you to do for me," I said, jumping straight into the verbal abuse that had served me well with Seth for most of our lives.

He grabbed his own and took a swig. "I thought I was pretty nice to you the last time I saw you, darlin'. You seemed pretty pleased, anyway."

And there it was. Tears prickled on the backs of my eyes and I blinked them down. All I wanted to do was forget about that night. I'd known the moment I kissed him it was going to be a mistake, I just hadn't cared. To Seth it was a joke. I wasn't anyone special, just one more on the list.

"Impressive. You broke your own record for the fastest jackass comment, Seth."

The smile never left his face. "Sorry, sorry. You started it."

We were the only people in the back room, the others preferring to eat and reminisce in the dining room proper, but I made sure to keep my voice low. "Look, we were both in a bad place, missing Michael. It happened." I shrugged but my voice was shaky. That day was still too raw in my heart. That night? I couldn't even begin to think about processing that on a level other than *mistakes were made* and *move it along, folks, nothing to see here.*

"I'm sorry, Willa. I didn't mean to hurt you." The look on his face was one I usually enjoyed seeing; the one where he let the girl du jour down easy. Getting it was very different from watching it happen to someone else. I hadn't realized how humiliating it was.

"You didn't hurt me, Seth." It was the truth. I had hurt me. Michael's death had hurt me. "I was hurting before I walked in that room. Nothing you did—nothing we did—made it worse. There wasn't a worse to get to."

Seth took a half step around the table and wrapped his hand around my arm. "No, I mean it. I should have known better. I should have been better. That's on me."

I eased my arm out of his grip and brushed an imaginary hair out of my eye. "So it's decided. We chalk it up to the tequila and we're just friends again."

He gave me a surprised smile. "You'll never be just a friend, Will."

I nodded because I didn't know what else to do.

He picked up the bottle. It was surprisingly sexy, the way he eyed me the whole time he put the bottle to his mouth, closing his lips around the rim slowly, and took a long swallow. He never took his eyes off mine even as he put the bottle back down on the table. My libido threatened to turn lava hot as I watched him lick the last of the soda off his lip, suddenly remembering how his lips felt on mine. That was all it took. My brain told me it was a mistake and my body was just not buying it.

"Just soda tonight, Sunshine. How about we give it another shot?"

Were we joking again? My hormones didn't think so. He was not looking at me like he was joking. I wanted to say yes. I wanted to climb into his lap and press into him. I wanted to crawl into a bed with him and stay for a week, let him make me forget about everything. Even though it was the worst idea.

"I don't think so, Seth." I sounded nowhere near normal. Even my voice was on board with a sequel to *Willa and Seth Get Naked and Sweaty*. My brain was only the body part being reasonable. Thank god my brain was in charge tonight. For a change. "It's been a weird day and I'm not up for it getting any weirder, thanks." That was better. I sounded less like I wanted to climb him like a tree and more like I had a little dignity.

We ate in silence. Blessed, sweet silence. But he kept looking at me.

Seth broke the silence when he'd finished his third piece of pizza. "You know that was a joke, right?"

Thankfully, I was still chewing so I could just nod. I didn't think he'd been kidding. It hadn't sounded like he'd been kidding. The look in his eyes didn't seem like he'd been kidding. I wasn't the best judge since all I could think about was him not kidding and how that would go. Naked was how that would go.

*Bad, Willa. Stop remembering him naked.*

"You said you had a weird day?"

"If you consider finding a dead body weird."

He froze, bottle of soda halfway to his mouth. "What?"

I nodded. "Dead guy, dead serious."

"What happened? Are you okay?" He reached over and grabbed my hand. A normal action under the circumstances, but since I didn't know where we stood I slid mine out from underneath and tried to play it off by swiping the napkin across my mouth.

"Long story short, I went to help the Horowitzes' granddaughter... you remember them? Anyway, she needed to move fast and when I got to her place I found the boyfriend shot. As for being okay... yeah... I mean, I wasn't there when it went down."

He shook his head. "I meant emotionally."

I'd known what he meant. I just hadn't wanted to answer it. I wasn't okay. I hadn't been for a long time.

"I'm... fine. I'm always fine, Seth. You know that."

# CHAPTER

## 4

**MANY HOURS LATER I** lay in bed thinking over the previous night. I still hadn't gotten any closer to figuring out what was going on with Seth. I'd had plenty of time to mull it over too since I hadn't gotten even a decent night's sleep going on five months.

I stretched and was getting up when my phone beeped.

LAST NIGHT WAS FUN, SUNSHINE. I'VE MISSED HANGING OUT WITH YOU.

Anxiety churned in my stomach, sour and hot. I wasn't ready for round two with Seth. The previous evening had taken all my mental energy.

I tried to put him to the back of my mind while I showered and almost succeeded. It had been good to see him again. Playing pool and joking around had been like old times. It had even been almost fun despite the awkwardness. He'd been oddly flirty with me. I'd spent a few hours chewing on that too. As the sky lightened from dark blue to gray, I'd almost decided that he just wanted to do what he thought Michael would have wanted—be friends even without Michael as a buffer and connector. Almost.

Beep. LUNCH?

I turned the phone face down on the nightstand. Avoidance was an art form. I would answer him but not until it was too late. I had things to do and I needed more time to figure out just what was going on with him and what I wanted to be going on with him.

First stop was the mall. Susan had told me that Violet worked at an accessories store there. The cops would have already done their interviews to try to trace Violet's movements around the time of Reagan's murder, so I could be nosy without getting in any trouble. I was still just shadowing the cops for the investigative experience.

I shoved my phone in my jacket pocket and headed out.

There was tons of parking since it was a weekday and the mall was just opening. I looked over the giant You Are Here map. How were there so many accessories stores? Who needed that many cheap bracelets?

The store where Violet worked looked like a modern candy box. All sleek white molded plastic walls and fairy lights in bright colors. Katy Perry blasted out at a soothing, window-rattling level. When I stepped over the threshold, it cranked down several hundred decibels.

"Sorry. The night crew leaves the music on loud when they close up. Can I help you find anything?"

The offer was made in a bland drawl that matched the look on the girl's face. She leaned dispiritedly on the glass case filled with sparkly cell phone covers. I had no doubt I would have lost my mind if I'd had to work there. Bored seemed the best-case scenario.

I walked over to the counter as she eyed me suspiciously. Fair enough. I didn't look like her standard customer.

"I was hoping to ask you some questions about Violet Horowitz."

She straightened up and smoothed down her smock. I tried very hard not to wonder about why she'd need a smock to sell five-earring sets for twenty-five dollars, each set seven dollars if purchased singly.

"They said they might come back with more questions. The cops, I mean. You, I guess," she said. She was nervous. That worked for me.

I nodded. *They might come back with more questions.*

"I'd like to just ignore your statement from yesterday, if you don't mind. Sometimes it helps you remember more if we start fresh."

It would also help me because I didn't have her statement from yesterday.

"And there's no need to be nervous. Just think of this as a friendly chat."

Her smile didn't reach her eyes. Mine did. Interrogations were fun and no statement was designed to make people feel more nervous than telling them not to be.

I flipped open my notebook and dropped my smile. "Your full name again."

"Um, Angela Martin. Celeste. Sorry, Angela Celeste Martin."

"Great. So how did you meet Violet Horowitz, Miss Martin?"

"Oh, um, we met at Killian's."

Killian's was notorious as a rough bar. I'd been once in college. That had been enough. A raised eyebrow was all it took for Angela to flush.

"It's gotten a lot better than it was," she said.

It would have had to since it couldn't have gotten worse. I'd seen enough inter-department briefs on the latest fight or parking lot stabbing. That substation wasn't the most popular, partly because of Killian's.

"Violet approach you or … ?"

Angela flushed deeper. "We met in the bathroom. There was a fight. Um, a televised MMA thing with a cover and the crowd was pretty packed."

So Killian's hadn't gotten better so much as they'd learned to charge more for the damage. That certainly explained how it managed to stay open. Squeaky wheels got greased.

"So you two bonded over not enjoying grown men beating the stuffing out of each other?" My tone was conspiratorial.

"The testosterone was a little high. We just needed a break. My boyfriend is a bartender there. He's the reason she met Joe, actually."

Wow. We got there a lot faster than I had hoped. Angela's eyes got wide.

"I can't believe Joe's dead. He wasn't the best boyfriend but he really loved Violet."

I wasn't the best judge of it but I figured abuse was an automatic disqualifier from the title. As for love, the bruises negated that too. Sure, that was a matter of opinion but it was a pretty widely shared one.

"And your boyfriend's name?"

"Why do you need that?" Angela frowned.

What was that about? I scanned her face again more carefully. I didn't see any evidence of abuse, not even well-covered, but some men were craftier than Joe Reagan and made sure no one saw the bruises. Then again, just because the boyfriend knew Reagan didn't mean he was an abuser too. It just made it more likely. That whole birds of a feather cliché.

"Well, he knew Joe and hooked him up with Violet, so naturally that's an avenue we'd like to explore."

*We* meaning me, myself, and I.

"Oh, he didn't know Joe exactly. He just introduced them at the bar. Like, literally, introduced them as the winners of the raffle."

Killian's was holding raffles? For what? Ice packs for after you got stomped for looking at some meathead wrong? Gift cards for the emergency room? Free physical therapy?

"Still, as the bartender there that night he might have some information that could be—"

"He's not really good with cops. He's an ex-con."

Of course he was. At least I only chose emotional bad boys so I felt justified in being judgmental.

"I promise I'll be gentle with him," I said.

"Dave Barker."

I scribbled some detailed, time-consuming nonsense to keep her off-balance. It was a cheap trick but one that was effective. In police notes you're not allowed to delete anything; if you have to cross something out, you're allowed one strikethrough. Your notebook can always be called as admissible evidence. But I wasn't a cop anymore and my notes were protected under client privilege. Or they would be if I had a client. Or a license. Which reminded me I needed to get out of the store before a real cop caught me. Like, god forbid, Boyd.

"Just one last question, Angela. When was this?"

"Um, August seventh."

"This past August?"

She nodded. Jesus, did no one take the time to get to know someone before moving in with them? That was barely three months ago.

I closed my notebook and thanked her for her time. It looked like I was headed to the bar tonight.

———

After lunch (coffee), helping Ben with his AP calculus homework (him pretending I was helping when I had no idea what any of the words meant or even if they were in English), continuing to ignore Seth's texts, and dinner alone (more coffee and a brownie) since Ben was out with his best friend John, I headed out to Killian's.

It was a fair haul from my side of the county because despite the roads that ran directly across and directly through and directly around, there weren't any that really ran directly anywhere else. I cranked the radio loud enough to ignore the annoying, hollow drone of my car's twenty-year-old engine and the thoughts I didn't want to think about the man I didn't want to think them about. At least I succeeded in drowning out the engine for the duration of the trip. The thoughts were more stubborn.

I brutally shoved down my uncertainty over Seth and walked into the bar. It was already crowded despite the early hour—lots of people drinking their dinner. The crush of people made the air feel heavy and thick. Testosterone overload, indeed. The crowd was mostly men, mostly manual laborers, mostly drunk. I felt the crawl of Bad Idea all over my skin, my instincts kicking into high gear.

I was dressed a lot more conservatively than some of the other female clientele and, as such, garnered a few glares from them. I met all of them with the look I practiced in the mirror in high school, the one that said I'd kick their asses if they didn't put their eyeballs back in their overly made-up heads. It worked on all but one and she gave me a curt nod. She had at least thirty years on the other women here. She was the head bitch. I pushed easily through the crowd that was drunk enough to be loose, at least with a sharp elbow here and there.

Standing in front of her, I took my hands out of my jacket pockets.

"I don't know you." Her voice was flat and lacking an accent. Another native, if I'd had to bet.

"No." You either had to make friends with the head bitch or stare her down. I kept my gaze even, hands hanging free, just in case.

"Do I want to know you?" she asked.

I shrugged. "Maybe."

She lit a cigarette while I eyed the bar area looking for Dave Barker. Him being a con had worked in my favor since I could look up his info, but if he was on duty tonight it wasn't yet. I didn't have time to wait. I had to get home to pretend to supervise Ben.

Head Bitch it was.

"My friend Violet told me about this place. Said she met her guy here. I split with mine a few months ago."

She pulled a stray piece of tobacco off her tongue with her ring finger. No ring. No indent. Nothing to do on a Tuesday night but a bar? You were discouraged from making judgements as a cop since it affected how you directed your reporting. You miss something in a report and the detective getting handed the case was handicapped. Luckily, being a PI meant it was just me and I could indulge my natural judgmental side.

"You ever meet anyone here?" I asked.

She eyed me up and down, taking in the outfit I had carefully selected so as not to appear too out of place.

"You're a little upscale for this place, hon."

I had, of course, been selecting from my own wardrobe, so I wore my sexiest jeans with my lowest cut t-shirt and highest-heeled boots. The trashy version of me was still too fancy for Killian's. I'd have to let Leila know that the next time she fussed at me for not putting on my face, as she referred to it. *Southern ladies always do their faces, even going out to get the mail,* I'd heard more than once over the summer. I had pointed out time and time again that I wasn't Southern and I sure as hell wasn't a lady.

I mimicked her shrug. "I just moved back from out of town and half my clothes are still in storage."

I saw a guy eyeing us from about a yard out, pushing his friend and giving the least subtle nod that I'd ever seen. He was shorter than my companion, if you could call her that, which meant a good four inches closer to the ground than my five-seven, and built like a fighting dog. His companion was a taller, doughier version with dead blue eyes. I shifted back to Head Bitch and wished I knew her name so I could call her that in my head. I was starting to feel bad thinking of her like that because she was being nice. Nice-ish. Well, not hostile.

"You moved from the beach here? Heading to winter? Are you stupid?" She said it all with a smile and her face changed. She wasn't pretty. It was too soft a word for her. She was attractive, with dark green eyes. They were an unusual shade and that reminded me of Seth and his pale green eyes and stupid nonstop texts. He'd texted half a dozen more times throughout the day. He'd even sent me knock-knock jokes.

The beach? Why in the hell would she think… Ah, yes, my "tan." But, much to my parent's chagrin, I wasn't a tenth-grade biology teacher and it wasn't my job to give a lecture on the vagaries of human genomes. I was trying to track down a murderer, so I played along.

I laughed. "Hell no. If I'd lived at the beach I'd never leave. I was in the Southwest. Santa Fe."

"A lot of wetbacks there. At least there's no niggers. They don't like the Mexicans, either."

My stomach went hot. This had been a mistake. Playing at PI was stupid.

She must have seen the look on my face because she smiled again. "Sorry, hon, I forgot we're all supposed to be PC nowadays, right? Forget I said anything."

# CHAPTER

## 5

"Hey."

The slightly slurred almost-greeting came courtesy of the guy who'd been eyeballing me.

"Hi." I kept my voice neutral. The evening had gotten out of hand. Now I just wanted to extricate myself and go home. It wasn't the first time I'd heard the N word, obviously. It wasn't even the first time someone hadn't realized they were talking about me and half of my family. Just because it wasn't the first time didn't mean I'd gotten used to it. Or over it.

The guy tried to hand me a highball glass. I didn't reach my hand up to take it.

"No thanks."

He kept the glass up, pushing it toward my face. "I'm not good enough to buy you a drink, is that it? You think you're too special for a guy like me?"

Great, he was more than just a little drunk and had little man syndrome. No matter what I said he was going to stay pissed. It was his default setting. He was looking to be offended.

"Sorry. I don't take drinks I didn't pour or open myself. Bad experience at college." I tried to ease the refusal with a bright, empty smile.

"You accusing me of something? You think I gotta drug a woman to get her to go home with me?"

That went well.

Head Bitch looked at him hard. "Shut the hell up, Ed. The girl said no and it ain't about you, so slide your ass back over by Mark and cool off."

"She's a snotty bitch because she went to college."

"She's a woman that doesn't want your drink and she doesn't owe you shit. You want a woman, get a clue and change your routine. And shower after work." She pushed him hard, making him spill the drink all over his white t-shirt. He glared at her but moved back.

"Sorry about Ed. He's got a chip on his shoulder because he's short. And that makes him an asshole. Then he blames women because they don't want an asshole. Who's short too."

"I appreciate it. He's not going to try anything with you, is he?" I was genuinely worried for her safety. The guy was only going to get more drunk and his friend had a creepy aura about him.

"Oh, he wouldn't dare even if he talks big. He's my sister's kid. She'd beat him raw if he raised a hand to me. And women gotta stick together. There's too many like Ed who think we're just supposed to drop to our knees and suck them off for buying us a drink."

Ew. Accurate but gross. She was a racist feminist. That was a new one for me.

"Well, I think I'm going to leave now. Violet's boyfriend wasn't that big of a prize anyway."

I slid my phone and car keys out of my pocket and texted Seth as I walked out, trying to look purposeful and off-limits. Seth was acting odd but he was light years better than the losers who'd been licking their chops over the new meat dropped into their cage. Besides, I hadn't planned on ignoring him forever. I was cranking the engine when I saw Ed watching me from the doorway. Over the course of the night I was sure the story would change from me refusing him to me begging him to do me in the bathrooms. I shuddered and pulled out of the parking lot.

The phone rang and the display lit up with Seth's number. I punched accept and speaker, taking my eyes off the road for only a second.

"Killian's? What the hell are you doing there, Sunshine?" His voice was agitated. I'd be pretty pissed too if someone had been dodging my texts to hang out in a dive bar.

"It was for a case. I needed a witness but he wasn't there."

"What case, Will? Your dad is on vacation and you don't have a supervising investigator."

He sure knew a lot about private investigator apprenticeship rules all of a sudden. Which I mentioned.

"I took a look on the Internet today in all the free time I had not getting a reply to my texts."

I laughed. "You didn't waste all your time looking up bad jokes?"

"You on your way home?" he asked.

I turned onto the exit for 495. "Give me fifteen minutes and meet me at my place? I'll buy you a drink to make up for hurting your girly feelings."

"I'm happy to bring tequila." I heard the smirk in his voice. It didn't annoy me as much as it usually did.

"One beer then I'm kicking you out, Anderson. I'm a responsible adult with legal authority over an impressionable child." I punched the button to hang up, still smiling.

Seth was parked on the street behind Dad's truck so I pulled in front of the Horowitzes' house. He stepped away from the motorcycle as I shut off my lights and in a few long strides had managed to get to the car door and open it for me. He'd always been gentlemanly. That part wasn't even a ploy to get girls to like him. He hadn't needed it.

"When did you start riding?" I'd never seen him on a bike before. I'd never even heard him express any interest in motorcycles.

"Just expanding my horizons."

One of his famous non-answers. I was reminded why I'd snuck out of his bedroom at dawn, hungover and ashamed—he held everyone at arm's length. Emotional bad boy, indeed.

"Right. You and your horizons have always been so limited. Well, good for you. I'd hate for you to not be able to donate organs in your early thirties when they're still so undamaged."

"I'm more worried about you in that rattletrap." Another deflection. He smirked again but dropped it when he saw my face. "What? What did I do this time?"

I shook my head and locked my car door. I walked across the grass that separated the two yards with him almost on my heels. He grabbed my arm, gently, and spun me to face him. He was close and even in my heels he was still half a head taller than me. He could have leaned down a fraction and touched my face with his. I took a step back.

"You never answer the question I ask. You answer but it's a side step. And it's annoying."

He looked confused.

"I asked when you started riding and you gave me some crap about horizons."

He rubbed his forehead. "You don't let me get away with anything."

I almost countered. I almost reminded him that he'd let me get away, that I'd walked right out of that apartment and heard not one word from him for four months, but I knew it would sound wounded and I wasn't about to give anyone that.

"It's not about … You extended an olive branch last night, Seth. I'm just trying to get to know you again." I turned back to the house.

"The next weekend. We had the memorial service and we … did what we did and then I stayed drunk for a few days and then I went and got the bike."

I looked back at him over my shoulder and he had that weird look on his face again. The one I had seen the night before.

"What are you just standing here for? I told you I'd buy you a beer, didn't I?"

He grinned, caught up to me, and we walked the distance to the house side-by-side.

In the kitchen he peeled off his jacket and gloves, laying them atop one another on the table. It reminded me of days of playing in the snow, long after we were all too old to be doing so, and coming inside to warm up with hot chocolate Mom always had waiting.

"Hey, do you remember … "

It was a story I suddenly didn't want to bring up. We were both trying to move on from Michael and I needed to leave that past where it was. I'd had enough maudlin memories the night before.

"Remember what?" Seth asked.

I shook my head. "Forget it." I busied myself getting the beers out and opening them, avoiding his stare. I headed into the living room and set the bottles on the coffee table.

We sat not looking at each other while we awkwardly drank our beers in silence. Mostly. I stole looks out of the corner of my eye because he looked amazing. Still. Always.

"So, how about those Redskins?" he asked then laughed.

I didn't because it occurred to me that I wasn't sure what we were doing or what I wanted us to be doing. And I couldn't let that linger in the unknown. Bull. Horns. I put the bottle back down onto the table. "Okay, so this is weird. It's going to be weird until it isn't or it's never going to stop being weird and we're going to have to admit that we can't figure out how to be friends now," I said.

"Is that what you want? To be friends?" He put his bottle down too and turned toward me.

I nodded, my mouth suddenly dry. I had this buzz in my head like a dead phone line and the quietest little voice dared me to admit that I did not want to be friends, that I wanted to do some very friendly things to him but that *friends* was not how people usually classified those things. Not unless *friends* was followed by *with benefits*.

"Just friends?"

I wanted to nod. I could even picture doing it. I just didn't.

He leaned closer and tilted his head to one side slightly. It was a move that turned the junior varsity cheerleading squad to puddles of girl goo. For good reason. He smelled amazing, like soap and his leather jacket.

I glanced down at his hand resting on his thigh. He was worrying his thumbnail on the denim. It made me feel better that he was nervous. It was nice that I wasn't the only one. Less than a beer gave neither of us an excuse. Whatever we said or did was on us only.

"I told you that we'd never be just friends."

I looked up and found him staring at me. His eyes kept flickering down to my lips. I knew he was going to kiss me. I didn't stop him.

I remembered kissing him the night of Michael's memorial service. Sitting on the floor, the bottle between us. We hadn't had that much to drink before one of us (me) said we ought to just see what we had been missing all those years. See if it was that big of a deal or if we'd just made it into something bigger because we weren't doing it.

It was that big of a deal. I remembered staring at him when he'd pulled away from the first kiss. I remembered seeing his eyes looking lost and sad and happy all at the same time and wondering how that was even possible. I remembered him reaching up to touch my face, running his knuckles over my cheekbone gently, before leaning in to kiss me again.

Just like that night, it started out searching and unsure but by the time we heard the front door, Ben coming home, we were in a full makeout session like teenagers.

We both jumped up and started reassembling our disheveled clothes. I wasn't ready to answer any questions so I pushed Seth into the office. When I returned Ben was smirking at the two beer bottles and the smushed couch cushions.

"Hey, Benj, how was your night?"

"Clearly not as good as yours," he said.

"Yeah, well, I think it's time you got to bed. Rest, study, get into a good college, save the world."

"Will, I've pieced together that you've got a guest."

"I guess we can't fool him," Seth said, reappearing. He and Ben did some elaborate male-bonding handshake ritual that made me want to smack both of them.

"We could have tried. You could have stayed where you were hidden until after he'd gone to his room so we could have avoided embarrassing questions."

Ben hitched his backpack up again and backed out of the room. "You never saw me. Continue doing the embarrassing things you don't want me to ask about."

I closed my eyes, leaving them shut even when I felt Seth slide his hand over the small of my back.

"I hate to do this but I have to go. I have some stuff I need to get done tonight."

I nodded. "This was probably a bad idea anyway."

He leaned down and kissed me, reigniting what I thought had turned to cold ashes when Ben opened the front door. Then he pulled back. "It was a great idea. One I'd like to revisit very soon. And often."

He'd slipped out of the house, grabbing his jacket from the kitchen, before I'd finished feeling fuzzy-stomached at his *soon and often* comment. Smiling like the idiot I clearly was, I grabbed the beers and dumped the almost-full bottles down the drain. Flipping the kitchen lights off, I went around the house making sure the doors were locked.

I headed down to my bedroom, looking forward to going to bed for a change. Even if I couldn't sleep I had something nice to analyze for a change. I brushed my teeth and got undressed, then remembered that I needed to write up my visit to Killian's. I'd leave out the parts I knew would hurt Dad's heart, but it was important to get even the few details about the case into a proper report.

I pulled on a pair of running shorts over my underwear and didn't bother with a cover up over my tank top. Ben was likely not coming out of his room again for the night but I still wasn't tempting fate and possibly emotionally scarring the kid. I shook my head to settle down the voices in my head giving me conflicting opinions on getting physical with Seth again. It had been easy, one voice argued. Its counter provided that it had been too easy. The fact was I'd known him more than half my life—all my important years—and I trusted him as much as I trusted anyone. He'd never knowingly hurt me, but neither one of us were ever going to be easy-going enough to let it be anything other than *it's complicated*. The families would be over the moon if they found out we were involved, which was why they *couldn't* find out. Hence trying to hide him from Ben earlier.

In the dark and in my distracted state, I bumped into a dining room chair, stubbing my toe. My quiet cussing and hopping around didn't fully mask the sound of something off. I felt my whole system slam into alert despite my throbbing toe. My eyes flew to the interior door. Someone was in Dad's office. It could have been Ben, but he wouldn't have left the light off.

I crept through the rest of the dining room and pressed myself up against wall next to the mostly closed door into the office. Seth had definitely left that open when he came out. There weren't any valuables beside the laptop, and the only weapon in there was in a lockbox. A lockbox that was about as secure as a hammer, screwdriver, and a swift whack would take to overcome. I had no weapons handy and I was not about to go in there unarmed and braless. It just didn't feel particularly authoritative, and my unsecured boobs were not enough to distract anyone sufficiently.

I heard the rustle of papers. Whoever was in there was either fascinated by Dad's stacks of papers and folders or he was looking for information. It wasn't unheard of for someone to try to get over on the PI that had been hired to catch them doing whatever they were doing, but Dad hadn't left any open cases before he and Mom went on vacation. The problem was that someone was messing with my business, and that wasn't okay. Unarmed and braless was going to have to do.

I reached in and flipped on the light, pushing the door open and stepping into it, hoping the surprise was enough to scare the intruder.

Seth stared back at me. "Shit."

I had no idea what to say. He looked down at my chest and then back up to my face, his cheeks bright pink.

The little voice in my head, the one that had reminded me it had been too easy, laughed at me. That pissed me off more than Seth standing in my dad's office, going through my files and ogling me.

"Looking for some light reading before bed, Seth?"

He opened his mouth and closed it again. "I said 'shit' already, didn't I?"

I pushed the office door shut again so Ben didn't hear us. I was going to start out civil, but I was sure this was going to become a heated discussion quickly.

"Do you want to tell me what the hell you're doing here, in my office, going through private business files?"

"Can't."

I nodded, my lips a tight line. "Can't?"

"Nice unicorn jammies."

I tried to stay calm. Anger forced you to negotiate from a position of weakness.

His eyes flicked back to my chest again as my breasts pressed up higher and perkier than before by my arms crossed tightly over them.

"If you look at my boobs again, Seth, I will become extremely violent. What are you doing, and don't say you can't tell me."

He sighed. He showed me the file in his hand—Joe Reagan. "This is why I'm here."

I took a second to breathe in and out a few times. Calming, deep breaths. It didn't work. "That is a *what*, not a *why*." I'd said it in a nice reasonable tone instead of the sarcastic, bitchy tone I really wanted to use. I was proud of myself.

"What were you doing at Killian's earlier?"

More sidestepping. I was getting whiplash from the way this night was yanking me back and forth. "That's not an answer to why you are sneaking in and reading that file."

"Quit being stubborn, Will. Why were you at Killian's? It's a simple question."

He'd gotten the hard set to his jaw that always made me clench my fists. I was not going to explode at him. I still wanted to believe he had a reasonable explanation. If he gave it to me, I'd believe him. "So is that why you're here reading my business files in the dark."

He dropped the file on the desk. "It appears we're at a stalemate."

I laughed. It was actually funny. He was talking like we were in some movie, business rivals after the same account, talking tough, wearing fancy business suits in a penthouse office.

"A stalemate? Like a Mexican standoff? Except, you broke into my goddamned house less than a half hour after I watched you walk out. We generally call that breaking and entering."

He shrugged. "I'm a family friend checking on you and your little brother while your parents are out of town. I found a door open. I was concerned."

Obnoxious, goddamned, overbearing, mother—

"And because I'm a good guy I, of course, came in to check and scared you. I'm sorry." He didn't sound sorry. Not even a little.

"Nice story. Now tell me the truth. Why are you here reading the file on Joe Reagan's murder?"

He looked away, up and to the right, and I knew he was about to lie to me.

"I was concerned about you when I heard you'd been at Killian's."

Even if he hadn't looked like a lying liar pants with his shifty lying body language, no one would have bought that story. Not even Ben, who had believed in Santa long after all the other kids and he was a certified, with corroborating test results, genius.

"You were concerned about my safety because I was at a dive bar earlier so you rushed off only to come back after I went to bed and then broke in to snoop? Really? You're really trying to sell me that line of bullshit?"

He shrugged, all studied casualness. "It's the truth, Sunshine."

"You're just concerned for my well-being?"

He nodded. "You shouldn't be looking into a murder. You could jeopardize your license application."

"I'm doing a favor for a family friend. And it's none of your damn business. If you're done shining me, you know where the door is."

"You're mad at me."

I nodded. "And I was worried I was being too subtle."

He started to walk to the exterior office door I was now sure he'd unlocked when he'd been in here earlier.

I hadn't yet blurted out the question my brain was screaming at me—was that what he'd really been after earlier on the couch? I had my pride.

"Is this what you meant by *soon*, Seth? I'm interested to see what *often* will be."

Okay, I didn't have my pride. I was hurt and confused. And embarrassed.

He turned back to me, his hand on the knob. "I would never lie to you about that, Willa. I thought you knew me better."

I watched him walk out the outer office door and then down the stairs to the driveway. I locked it again and didn't take my eyes off him until I was sure he was really gone. I thought I had known him better too. I didn't understand what I knew anymore.

# CHAPTER

## 6

I HATED RUNNING. THE feeling of sweat rolling down my spine, the end of my ponytail brushing against my neck irregularly until I could get in a good rythym, the way my shorts would bunch up in the back because I hadn't bought any new ones since the academy and the ones they gave out were cheap and mine had been too big. But it was free and it exhausted me and sometimes I didn't hate it. Sometimes I could even stop thinking and things would get quiet in my head.

The nights I was able to sleep took exhaustion or alcohol, and I knew I couldn't solve missing Michael by drinking. I was barely hanging on. Something had to give and I was afraid it was going to be me. I knew how easy it would be to sink into oblivion, to give up on everything. Michael would have hated that but he didn't really get a vote anymore.

I felt like stubbornness was the only thing holding me up at this point. Like if I refused to give in, eventually the darkness would give up, stop circling, looking for the crack it needed to get inside and go away. That I'd wake up one morning and it wouldn't hurt so damn much. And I wouldn't feel so damn guilty. And I could take a deep breath again without feeling like I was breathing in glass and razor blades and gasoline. All I had to do was survive until that day.

That's why I usually ran at night. After Seth left, after I tossed and turned all night, after I'd beaten myself up for hours, after I couldn't stand it anymore, I threw on my running clothes and slid out of the house before Ben's alarm even went off. I needed to run off the confusion and anger. The pain. I needed to run myself empty again.

I ran the several blocks from our house to Michael's parents' house slowly, trying to get a good pace, trying to ensure I didn't wind myself by starting too hard, too fast. I needed to make sure I could push myself a little more on this run. I had no idea how far it was to the old house anymore. I had driven there the past few times and those had been years ago, before Michael joined the Army. I should probably let it go. I was a grown-up and it was a stupid thing we did when we were kids. But I just needed to see it once more. I needed to escape into the past for just a little bit.

The Anderson house was perfect, as always. The solar-powered lights were still on as dawn was barely breaking and there was enough light to see the precision lines that edged the lawn. The bushes against the house had been cut into perfect rectangles, like coffins settled under the kitchen windows. God, where had that morbid thought come from? I shouldn't have been surprised. I had always liked the Andersons in a formal, at-arm's-length kind of way, but they were rather rigid. They'd mellowed some after the Colonel retired, but we all still called him the Colonel so that was a hint right there. They were loving, if not excessively warm. I hadn't ever really gotten my head around how my dad and the Colonel were best friends. They were so different but Dad had been thrilled that they decided to move a few blocks away when the Colonel's last assignment was at the Pentagon. Michael and I had been twelve, instant friends despite our genders and puberty. He knew every single thing about me from awkward preteen to high school girl searching for her identity through college and then the academy. We shared everything, even his brother—as long as it was just sharing him as a brother. Seth had been fifteen, older and more exotic, but I'd felt an instant pull with him. All the closeness I had with Michael—more, actually—but none of the calm, and after all the turmoil with Leila, I craved calm. Seth scared me emotionally before I understood what there was to be afraid of, while Michael had been the human equivalent of a blanket fort. When Seth went away to college, Michael and I spent most of our time just the two of us, and we both stayed home for college. Never more than two blocks away from each other as we grew from young teens to adults. Until the day he told me, casually, that he was leaving for Georgia, for Officer Candidate School.

I could see Barbara through the window in her robe. She was making the Colonel coffee and breakfast, of course. I didn't need to look at the watch I didn't wear to know the time. Food was on the Anderson table the same time every morning and every night, rain or shine, winter or summer, dead child or live one. That was just the way they did things. A time for everything under the sun, a time to be born, and a time to die; a time to kill, and a time to heal. And a time to eat.

Staring at the Colonel and Barbara while they ate breakfast without their sons wouldn't make me feel better. Watching the people who'd raised the men I was trying to get out of my head wouldn't make me empty. I started to run again. Seeing the house I had avoided for so long, despite how close it was, stirred up feelings I didn't want to feel. Looking at them, seeing them the same as they had always been. Like Michael's death had changed nothing for them. Not one damned thing. Except a new arrangement on the mantel to make room for an urn full of ashes that once upon a time had been the best person I had ever known.

I shut it all down and just ran. The houses were getting farther apart. The trees closer together, standing taller, older. This was the oldest part of the neighborhood. A few more minutes and I'd see the marker. The sweat began to run down my back, making the sweat-shirt humid and heavy, weighing on me, dragging me down. I slowed long enough to strip it off my body and over my head, almost missing the sign that lead me into the wooded area and over the easement the storm water ran through and then into the woods proper. I tripped over the roots that were higher and knottier than a decade ago. I side-stepped the rocks that had sat so long the dirt crusted up the sides of them, the summer rains sinking them deeper until eventually the earth would reclaim them.

Young trees had grown up in the years that had passed and their sprouting limbs whipped me as I ran, forcing me to slow down. It was even darker here in the trees, much darker. There would be no light to guide me. My eyes adjusted to the deep bruising dark of the trees, away from the lights on the neighborhood streets. I knew I should turn on my phone's flashlight app, but I was afraid it would break the spell I wanted to evoke in these woods. Time travel. Back to the past for a few moments. Where Michael's spirit might still be for a flicker of a breath.

I finally cleared the deepest part of the woods and skirted over to the lane that barely showed anymore. We never figured out what the lane was for since it started in the woods, which were hundreds of years older than the house. There was no driveway. There may have been a path for a horse and cart once upon a time. Michael and I had run through possibilities reasonable and absurd. A hermit, a deaf couple, a witch. Whoever had lived there had abandoned their home long before we'd found it as gangly, coltish young teens. That had been part of the game. Who and why.

The first of the day's weak light crept through the tree line, gray and pale orange, like the dying remains of a campfire. I rounded the last corner at a slow jog.

And there was nothing. The house was gone.

I turned and looked back the way I'd come, confused, wondering if maybe I'd gone the wrong way. Turned left instead of right. But the view behind me was just as I remembered.

There was a raw wound in the trees to the left of where the house had been. I walked slowly over. I felt my stomach start to churn, a sour taste under my tongue. I took a deep breath and quickened my pace. I could see a sign at the start of the new path, muddy and churned with tracks. They had ripped down our house and were putting in thirteen luxury homes. More trees would soon be gone. They would gut the woods for a pool. The old was discarded for the new and improved, shinier and better than an old house tucked into a defensive ring of towering old oaks. A little voice inside me marveled at how long it had lasted, how long those trees had hidden its existence, keeping our secrets.

I stared at the yellow construction trucks neat in their row waiting to eat more dirt, more trees, more memories. My chest squeezed a little bit as I tried to catch my breath from the run and the loss of our special place.

I turned and ran. There was nothing left here for me. Another change. Another loss. *Doors closing, windows opening* they had said to me. It was all so much bullshit. Life just pounded you. Bad things happened to you not because you were bad but because random bad things happened to people. Like Michael's Humvee hitting an IED a week before he was set to come home. One week. He should be safe at home right now, getting ready for his bored stiff federal contracting desk job. Instead he was in an urn on his parents' mantel next to his picture and a folded American flag. The other guys in the truck had survived. One goddamned week.

I didn't know what was worse, the anger or the helplessness. The grief hit me whenever it wanted, punishing blows to my heart, sucking my equalibrium from me. Nothing I had tried made it stop. I barely slept. The nighttime was the worst. I had no one to pretend for in the darkness. It was just me and the rage. Six days and he would have been safe. And he should never have been there to begin with. If he hadn't listened to all that hooah bullshit his dad and his brother had spouted. Family tradition, they talked about. The Colonel came back from Vietnam and the Gulf Wars fine. One hundred forty-four more hours. Seth came back from two tours in Afghanistan without even having caught a cold. Just another hundred and forty-four hours and Michael would have been on that plane back home. I could picture it so clearly. I could see his face light up when he saw us standing there. And I could hear the applause as the people in the airport saw returning service members. Just eight thousand six hundred forty minutes more and my best friend wouldn't be dead.

I hated that everyone around me said they understood what I was feeling, because no one really did. Dad had missed the Vietnam War by two years. He was out of the military by the time the Gulf War hit. Mom made me see a therapist. She said that grief counseling wasn't anything to be ashamed of. She said many police officers sought assistance to deal with the heightened day-to-day tension and uncertainty. The therapist had talked about PTSD and that any traumatic event could cause it. She talked about me having PTSD like I'd had to live inside the horror that Michael had endured. I couldn't even imagine what that had been like. I picked at the pain like a scab, trying to get under and over and through to it, and I never could. And every moment of every day, under my breath, I prayed to gods I didn't even believe in that his death had been instant. That he hadn't suffered. That he hadn't been afraid. That his final thoughts had been of hope and soaring wings of freedom. Like we had talked about those summer nights in that old house, with candlelight making shadows on our faces and it was safe to talk about our secrets.

And it was gone now. They tore the house down, cleared the fields around it, wiped the past away like it was chalk, impermanent, unowned. But we had owned it. Michael and I. It was our space.

It was all gone now. All of it. I just wanted to be empty. Why couldn't the universe just stop kicking me in the chest? My feet pounded the pavement faster and faster until the only sound I heard was the slap of my feet on blacktop and my breath in my ears, the frantic whoosh like waves pounding the shore. It tripped out of me like it was trying to escape. I ran until my lungs hurt. I ran until everything hurt. Except my heart. I didn't feel that anymore. I wouldn't feel it anymore.

If I didn't feel it, then I didn't think about it. I didn't think about Michael being trapped in a burning vehicle, metal crushed in on him, glass exploding, pain consuming him. If I didn't think about it, then I didn't have to ask myself why Seth had stirred it all up, acted like he cared if I got my feet under me again only to push me down again.

He'd said he wouldn't lie about that, but I didn't know what he'd lie about anymore. Maybe I never had.

It was better being empty. It was better than how it felt when they looked at me trying to find the scar. I was good at hiding it. I could show them what they wanted to see. I could keep it to myself and if I had secrets, so what? Everyone had secrets. I wasn't hurting anyone but myself. I could take it. It was the least I could do. And if they stopped watching so carefully, so much the better. They could feel like they were doing what they needed to help me get over it. They didn't worry then. They didn't have to know about Seth and the humiliation of being in his bed, knowing what I'd known about him. I could hide it all. Every day the mask fit a little better, settling on my skin and then under it. I knew it was going to be permanent eventually. For now, I could run.

# CHAPTER

## 7

I WAS STILL EXHAUSTED but I wasn't covered in sweat anymore when I stumbled into the kitchen to make Ben's lunch for school. Instead a hot cup of coffee was shoved into my hands and I was guided to a chair. I was really sucking at this guardian gig. Although I had managed to make it out of bed before the bus for once. But I'd left him alone in the dark house to get himself up, so I was pretty sure that left me back at zero. I squinted up at him, his lanky frame backlit by the under-cabinet light as he spooned oatmeal into his mouth. What teenage boy chose oatmeal? And not that stuff in a packet either. Real homemade oatmeal cooked in a pot on the stove.

"Thanks for the coffee, sport."

He ate more oatmeal while looking at me. His face was thoughtful as he swallowed. "Have you thought of going to a doctor for the insomnia, Willy Bean?"

I grimaced. That godawful nickname. It had been cute when he was five.

"Yes, and she told me exercise was a great remedy. I have just been out for a predawn run." I smiled at him, sunny and fake. Who was the pretend grown-up here anyway?

"And what's going on with Seth?"

"Why do you want to know?"

He didn't reply. Just looked at me while he ate. No expression, just the mechanical spoon in and chew routine. Like I didn't know what he was doing. I rolled my eyes at him.

"Ben, that doesn't work on me. I know all of Dad's tricks."

He pouted while putting his spoon and bowl in the sink. That didn't work either, but I knew if he thought he'd gotten what he wanted, he'd leave it be.

"Fine. Seth and I have a complicated relationship. We're trying to figure it out."

He smiled.

Great. *Trying to figure it out* clearly meant getting married and making him an uncle in his mind.

"I meant it when I said *complicated*. Don't get your hopes up."

He just continued smiling at me. Fine. When nothing more came of it, he'd get over it.

After the bus drove off, I went back down to my room and slid a junk food breakfast pastry out of my secret stash. The booby-trap hadn't been disturbed, so I knew Ben hadn't found it. I wasn't worried he'd eat them; I didn't want him to throw them out. He'd been brainwashed by Mom that foods full of fake ingredients weren't good for you. Stupid doctors and their scientific studies. I took a big bite of carbs and fake strawberry jam and chewed in defiance.

My mind flitted back to Seth. I couldn't stop thinking about it. Why was he coming around now? What was he up to? I still could not believe he'd gone through my papers. His explanation made no sense, yet nothing else I could come up with did, either. Had he really only been concerned about me? Why wouldn't he just ask me if he was worried? But how did Seth even know about Joe Reagan? I'd told him I found a dead body but not the name. At least, I didn't think I said a name. So how did he know what to look for?

Seth could have been a friend of Reagan's. Weirder things had happened. Joe Reagan hadn't come across as a guy with tons of redeeming qualities, but a person didn't have to be a saint to enjoy a beer with. The cops would have notified next of kin and Seth could have found out from them and then put it together from that.

I retrieved the file Seth had left on the desk and pored over the printouts. I didn't see anything I hadn't seen the last time. But Violet had to know more about Joe Reagan's life. And David and Susan would know more about Violet. Time to head back next door. I could pump them for information without implying that I was going to investigate. I had found a body while doing them a favor. They would feel indebted.

David met me at the door wearing pressed khakis and a plaid flannel shirt. He looked like the kindly pediatrician he'd been until a few years ago. When I saw him I instinctively expected to be handed a lollipop.

"I'm sorry to bother you so early, Mr. Horowitz. I was just wondering about some things … after yesterday." That was nice and vague.

"Can we do this over at your house? Susan had a restless night last night and she finally fell asleep an hour ago."

He trailed me across the lawns, up the stairs, and into the kitchen where he took a seat. I poured him a cup of coffee and, after setting it down in front of him, sat down too. I had my notebook open, ready to run through the questions I had when I noticed him twitch as he brought the cup up to his mouth. It shouldn't have been anything. It should have just been stress and fatigue. But it wasn't. It was nerves. I knew what he was trying to hide. He didn't have the experience to lie well enough. And I was a trained observer and, frankly, a damn good one.

"You know where she is, don't you?"

He startled, spilling the coffee on his dark blue plaid shirt. He didn't respond, but he didn't need to. That twitch and then startling was all the answer I needed.

"How long?"

He placed the cup gently down on the place mat. "Willa, I'm not sure why you think—"

"I'm not going to buy it so you might as well tell me."

He rubbed his hand over his eyes. "She called last night. To tell us she was safe."

I got up and made my way over to the coffeemaker to pour myself a cup and take a moment to rework my plan. I knew they hadn't called the cops because Boyd would have been here already. She was that kind of cop plus she would be desperate for leads since the first forty-eight hours were almost up.

"I said I couldn't help you and I can't, really." My interrogation of Angela and visit to Killian's were decidedly unhelpful. "But I can give you some advice: You have to let the cops know she called."

"She's my granddaughter, Willa."

I sighed and cursed my own moral compass. "This is not a question of loyalty. This is about what, in the long run, is going to end up hurting all of you. The cops likely already have a warrant for your phone records. They are going to know she called. At minimum all three of you will end up charged with Obstruction."

He just stared at me. I saw that being reasonable was not getting through to him. I hated having to do it, but he needed a shock to his system. I took a sip of my coffee. "How well do you think Susan's going to sleep in lockup?"

That got his attention.

"You know that I am right. You know this is exactly what my dad would be telling you right now. Call the cops, David." I'd never called him by his first name before, but I hoped it would help get my message across.

He nodded and got out his wallet to get Detective Boyd's business card. I pointed him to the landline on the wall. I zoned out a little bit while he gave Boyd the details of Violet's call. He only took a few minutes to relate the facts. She was probably pissed that he didn't call her right away, but it was still early morning. She could assume he wasn't trying to hide anything but rather falling back on manners in a tough situation. I hoped. Either way, she couldn't prove anything.

He sat back down at the table and looked at me, disappointment evident on his face. I refused to feel guilty. I was helping them even if it didn't seem like it.

"You're going to have to be extra careful with Boyd now, you know. She's suspicious that you didn't call her right away." Now that I'd done what was right, I wanted some information to ease my own mind. "Tell me what she said. Let's talk it out and get it straight before Boyd gets here."

He nodded then, with a shaking hand, picked up his coffee cup and took a sip. I waited. This was the easy part. Waiting for the words to tumble out. Just like that rookie cop should have been waiting for me to spill my guts. I gave it time for my words to sink in. He nodded again, as if to himself, and I knew I had him.

"Violet said she arrived home about eleven thirty. She saw a truck in the driveway. A big silver pickup. She didn't recognize it. No one was standing at the front door so she knew whoever it was, was inside the house. She assumed that meant Joe was home, so she left. She went to a friend's house."

I jotted down the time and the truck description. The truck had to be in the front if she saw both the truck and the door.

"So where is Violet now?"

He just shook his head. I shouldn't have bothered asking. I didn't need to know but I couldn't quell the drive to investigate.

"Okay, how about an easier question: Why didn't Violet come to you night before last? Or did she, and then seeing all the activity she took off again?"

He just looked at me, sad and conflicted. Fair enough.

I had roughly a ten-minute window when I knew the killer had been on scene. I'd never be able to get a time of death from Boyd. Even if I did it wouldn't matter, since we'd have no idea how long the killer had been there before Violet arrived home. But it was something. A place to start.

I sent David back home with the request to think about telling me where Violet was. His eyes had betrayed him when I asked if he knew where she was; of course they knew where she was hiding. They were going to gamble that Boyd wouldn't be able to prove it. I hoped he was right.

My mind kept circling back to Seth. I wasn't going to be able to drop it until I knew how he was involved. I wanted to believe he was just worried about me, but that didn't feel right. I wanted to believe he was a friend of Joe Reagan's, but that didn't ring true either. I couldn't just let it be despite my deep desire to do just that; to put the pizza and the making out to the back of my mind, let it all go. I just couldn't. Finding Reagan's body and Seth calling me up the same day didn't feel like a coincidence. My gut—something that I had been both encouraged to trust and admonished not to trust too much as a cop—told me that Seth knew more about it than he was letting on.

How I was going to figure that out was still an unknown quantity. I had databases I didn't really know how to use and less resources, less training, and less experience than Boyd. All I had was a ten-minute window when someone with a large silver pickup had been at Reagan's house. And that Seth knew something. Piece of cake.

I poured another cup of coffee but couldn't remember if that made two or three … maybe four. I really needed to get a handle on the caffeine. There had been a suggestion or two that my trouble sleeping could be related to my overconsumption of coffee. I should probably start listening. Later. I needed all my faculties right now.

I wandered into Dad's office and tried to focus. Did he have software for collecting case data? He must. They use case management software at the police department, so some enterprising private eye must have developed a civilian version. And Ben wouldn't let Dad get away without having something for organizational and billing purposes. I pulled up my phone and scrolled through to the picture of the passwords then booted up the computer.

It occurred to me, belatedly, that I needed to let Dad know what had happened. I had to make sure I downplayed it enough that he didn't get it into his head to cut their vacation short and come home early. They'd been saving for this vacation for years. I wasn't about to let some dumbass getting himself killed ruin it for them, even if the police thought the prime suspect was their dear friends' granddaughter. And that his best friend's son was also, maybe, somehow involved.

And, you know, that I had found the body. I was really going to have to spin that one hard.

I also needed to tell Ben something. I should have done it yesterday.

I was too scattered lately. It felt like my brain was on time delay. I was sure some of it was fatigue and I knew Mom wasn't wrong that I was suffering some emotional trauma, but I had been getting by well enough. And then Seth walked back into my damn life.

I opened the case software and created a new file for Joe Reagan. I took my time and did a timeline to the best of my ability, starting with the first contact with the Horowitzes asking me to help Violet to this morning's conversation with David. I added the details I knew, like the times, the truck Violet saw, and Seth's surprise appearance. Then I remembered the shoe print. I saw there was an option to add photos to the case file and I uploaded that too.

I looked at the scant information in the file and felt a wave of frustration sweep through me. I needed more. I pulled up the database and ran the searches on Reagan's priors again. I don't know if I thought something was going to be updated about his murder or just hoped that there would be a Click Here to Find the Murderer button. Nothing.

I narrowed my focus to the newer charges and printed out all the details of each arrest in the past year. I would see what I could learn about his known associates. Those would be the best bet for someone mad enough to put two bullets in his chest. It was a stretch, but it was better than nothing.

Knowing that a good investigator follows any lead no matter how remote or bizarre, I made myself do a search on Seth Anderson, prove to myself that I had merely invented something to worry about. He could have had a friend on the force. That made more sense than him knowing Reagan and not mentioning it. So he talked with a cop buddy and decided to get on his horse and ride to my rescue. That totally gibed with my experience with Seth. He was an infuriating ass but one with good intentions.

I found nothing, which wasn't a surprise. I saw one speeding ticket from the week before Michael's death. His juvenile record was sealed years ago, so I hadn't expected to see that anyway. A memory whispered at me, of the night he'd gotten busted for underage drinking. Seth, a high school senior, his white knight complex having started very early, had seen the sweep of the headlights from the cop car pulling into the park's lot and insisted Michael and I run. But I couldn't. I got tangled in the roots of a tree. Seth, realizing I couldn't get clear in time, strolled over to the cop car and confessed. The fake ID he'd used to buy the beer had been run through the system before the cops got his real name.

I ran the alias, Seth Andrews, through the database, expecting another dead end. Instead I found a pending charge for Accessory to Murder. His pale green eyes stared out from the mug shot, so there was no question of mistaken identity.

As much as I didn't want to think it was possible, the oldest friend I had left in the world had just become my number-one suspect in the murder of Joe Reagan.

I pushed away from the computer and grabbed my phone off the desk.

"David? I need to talk to Violet. Not tomorrow. Not later. You've got ten minutes or I'm telling Boyd you know where Violet's at and I will have her throw your ass in jail. Right now."

I didn't waste any time feeling guilty about yelling at him. This case had been a nightmare from the beginning. Now Seth was in the mix. This had shot past *not good* straight into *hell on earth*. My heart was pounding so hard I wondered if I was having a panic attack. I was too young for a heart attack, no matter how much junk food I ate. The nausea was the result on that snotty little voice reminding me that a potential killer had his hands all over my body last night and that not too long ago it had been much more than just his hands.

I picked up the sticky note Seth had left the day before with his number. Maybe he was on drugs. The pending Accessory to Murder charge could have been an overdose that Seth didn't help in time, or maybe he'd served some driver too many beers before they plowed into someone. You never knew how the district attorney was going to indict. Was it wishful thinking that I didn't want him to be a bad guy? Yes, it was. But I wasn't going to let that stop me from indulging in some serious rationalizing. It was the only way I was staying sane at the moment.

I started to enter the number when my phone rang. Right. I had blackmailed and threatened someone's grandfather. I was going to hell. I clicked Accept.

"Willa Pennington here. I do not want you to say your name."

"Uh … okay."

The voice was soft and girlish. And scared. I fought back the urge to reassure her. It wasn't my responsibility to make sure she was emotionally secure while she was on the lam.

"I need you to tell me about your boyfriend's friends. I need names, phone numbers, addresses, any and everything you have."

"I don't have any idea who his friends are. Were."

"Seriously? You lived with him and you don't know anything about any of his friends? Not even a damn first name?"

And she promptly dissolved into whimpering little sobs. The tiniest shred of sympathy I had for her was gone, but I wasn't getting anywhere with her being my usual charming self.

"Look, I know I'm being harsh, but I need your help. I need information only you have, Violet. Help me help you."

It wasn't a lie. Any exculpatory evidence I found would go straight to Boyd. Unless that evidence pointed to Seth and then … then I'd deal with it when I had to.

"He was friends with a guy named Mark. I didn't like him. He was mean. He gave me the creeps."

I had to wonder what qualified Mark as mean if she loved a guy who smacked her around. Nothing I was comfortable with came to mind.

"Mean? Mean to you?"

"To Joe. Joe didn't like to have his friends over much. And after they left, he would get mean too. He wasn't always mean, you know. Sometimes he was nice."

Defending her abuser even though he was a dead man or defending herself for staying with him even though he hurt her? I didn't care. It made sense that feeling small around Mark would have made Joe treat Violet even worse. I had never understood men like that—I'd seen too many examples of real men, who didn't need an ego boost from smacking around someone smaller and weaker.

"Did Mark drive a big silver pickup truck?"

She gasped softly. Had she really thought her grandfather wouldn't tell me?

"The one time Joe had his friends over I stayed upstairs while they watched a football game downstairs. Joe told me to keep my mouth shut and stay out of their way."

It would have been a little too convenient to be able to wrap up the case like that. Silver truck at scene, Mark drives silver truck, ergo I have not had sex with a multiple murderer. He'd just committed the one murder. I don't know why I thought that would be any better.

"I heard Joe was doing some kind of manual labor. Was he working construction or as landscaper, maybe?"

"I'm not sure. He didn't come home too dirty."

So Joe wasn't working one of the few jobs he was qualified for. Another dead end. Did this girl know anything about the man she'd been sleeping next to?

"Can you tell me anything that might help us find who did this so you can come home?"

Her voice was still soft but I heard strength in it too. "I want to help. I do. I just … I know lots of stuff but I'm not really sure if I know anything useful."

"How about this? How about you go through your memories of any time he talked about his friends or his work. Any time he mentioned something about people he knew. Any mentions of what happened during his day. Write it all down, even if it seems unimportant. It could be the tiniest piece of information that makes a difference."

"I can do that." Her voice had grown stronger during the call. I wondered if everyone had been underestimating this girl. "Okay, I have to go now. My friend says—"

"No." I stopped her before she could give me more information than I wanted to be responsible for. I hadn't lied to Boyd yet and I didn't want to start. "I don't need to know. You're safe and that's all that matters. Call me at this same time in two days and give me your list okay?"

The hesitance was back in her voice when she answered, "I will."

Mark was a good lead but I couldn't let her off the phone without asking her what I desperately needed to know.

"One last question. Did Joe know a man named Seth?"

"Oh, yeah. Yeah! He came by the house once when Joe was out. He was nice."

"Light hair, green eyes?"

"Yes, that's the guy. He had a nice smile."

So, to recap, Seth had broken into my office to read my case file on a murder he shouldn't have known about, a pending charge for Accessory to Murder (which, let's face it, was just a legal term for *we have slightly less evidence than we'd need to prove he's an actual killer*) under an alias I knew was his, and I could place him both at the scene of a second murder and having known the victim.

Well, at least Violet thought he had a nice smile.

Shit.

# CHAPTER

---

# 8

I PULLED UP OUTSIDE the work address I found for Seth's alias. The sign on the painted cinderblock building read ANDREWS MOTORCYCLE REPAIR. Seth's alias owned a motorcycle repair business? That hadn't shown up in any of the records. I thought Seth had gone the federal contractor route after leaving the service like most people in the area. Michael had been deployed so my contact with Seth the last few years had been holidays and family get-togethers. He'd been vague when people brought up work but that wasn't unusual for contracting. Even in a boring desk job that involved pushing papers, the papers pushed were usually stamped CLASSIFIED. It had been easier to fall back into watching movies, bantering—small talk would have just exacerbated the awkward tension—and using Ben as a buffer. Why was Seth running a garage, under an alias no less? He said he'd only had *his* bike for a few months. And romancing me then breaking into my home?

No other cars sat in the shallow lot sandwiched between the road and the front of the building. I got out of the car and looked around. There was no entrance that I could see. I walked to the side of the building where a rutted dirt lane ran past. There had to be a door into the place somewhere.

As I rounded the corner, I saw that there were bays along the wall of the building and past those was a metal staircase up to a door. None of the bays were open even a sliver and I couldn't hear any noise coming from inside. I wondered how wise it was to walk into a situation I had no information on. The little voice in my head—which had been getting quite a workout the past two days—shouted, *Not smart at all!* Then she started listing off different scenarios I could be exposing us to like a movie trailer for *Slow and Painful Ways to Die*. I told her to shut the hell up and quit being a wimp.

I was debating the best way to get into one of the bays when the door at the top of the stairs banged open against the railing and an angry man stepped out. His head bent, he stomped down the metal stairs, heavy boots causing the steel to sing and creak with each step. He was so caught up in his thoughts he didn't notice me until he was a few steps away. I flattened myself against the bay door.

He stopped in front of me and glared. His red face was shot with veins across his nose and cheeks. A sickly sweet smell poured off him so strongly my stomach flipped. It was obvious years of alcohol abuse had taken their toll on him. "What the hell are you staring at, girly?"

Smart me kept her mouth shut. Dumbass mouthy me couldn't resist. "Nothing. I can't see a damn thing through the fumes." I pushed past him and sauntered off as casually as I could with smart me chastising me for turning my back on a man I had just insulted.

The door sitting open at the top of the steps seemed promising. I walked up the stairs as quietly as I could. Stealth seemed to appease the part of my brain that had been urging me to run home like a good little girl since the second I'd arrived and was currently cowering after the exchange with the stranger. I continued to ignore it like I had been for the past twenty-some years and concentrated on sneaking up the really loud stairs. Failing to be ultra-quiet, I just hoped the person was preoccupied. Or people.

I got to the top and stopped before the landing to poke my head around. My training officer had drilled into me that stepping full into a doorway without looking was a good way to end up with an honors guard funeral. The room was empty. So the red-faced man had been mad he couldn't talk to whoever he was looking for. Was that Seth? I was so confused. These were the parts of an investigation I'd never seen as a cop; I got to see the beginnings and the endings. Apparently, being a PI was all about the middles.

I stepped up to the landing and into the office, shooting another glance down the stairs. I was alone. I walked into the room and looked around. I moved toward the large plate glass that framed a view of the whole ground floor. There were mechanics working on motorcycles. It appeared to be exactly what the sign said.

"What the hell are you doing here?"

I spun around. Seth was standing in the doorway I'd just come through. Obviously he knew how to sneak into a room, but he'd proven that last night.

"Jesus, Willa, how did you even find this place?"

The minor nerves I'd refused to indulge in on the drive over broke free and I couldn't remember any of the pithy remarks I'd prepared. He didn't look like a killer. He looked like Seth.

As he closed the door, Seth looked over at me. "Get away from the window."

Without thought, I took a step toward the back wall as requested then stopped. "Seriously? What the hell am I doing here? How did I find the place? After last night, that's what you have to say to me?"

"Willa, please, step away from the window."

I stayed in the middle of the room. "No, you tell me what's going on. How you knew about Joe Reagan. How you have an alias and that alias owns a business. What the hell you were thinking coming on to me last night."

"I can't give you the answers you want." He glanced over at the window. "Did anyone see you when you arrived?"

I paced around the room, staying away from the window and surveying it covertly. I'd never been in a garage office before but I didn't see anything out of the ordinary, other than its barrenness. The room wasn't quite the length of the building, maybe three-quarters, with battered metal desks lining the glass wall. The whole place looked unused. There were no papers or objects on any of the desks. Industrial gray was the color scheme. At least it was clean. From what I'd been able to see of the four guys working down in the bay they did seem to be actually repairing motorcycles, even if they looked the opposite of law-abiding.

"Again, you're saying you can't. You can, you just won't. Do you even care that I'm thinking the worst things about you? That I've been trying to come up with rationalizations for your actions? How have you been charged with murder, Seth Andrews?"

At the mention of his fake last name and the murder charges, he pressed his lips tightly together, the cords in his neck standing out prominently against the tanned skin.

There was no information about him in the room we were in. I saw a door that had to be for a closet or storeroom. I wondered what I'd find in there. I wondered what Seth would do if I tried to open the door. I walked away from him and turned the knob. I found a small storage with a few stacked boxes, a cot, and half-bath facilities.

"You want to turn out my pockets too, Willa? There's nothing here for you. You need to go. Now. Do not come back."

"Seriously? That's all you've got?" I didn't bother to conceal my annoyance with him. It wouldn't have helped anyway. He always knew when I was mad at him. Probably because I wasn't good at hiding it. Other emotions, definitely, otherwise the little dance we had been doing most of our acquaintance would have ended up in a bed a hell of a lot sooner and with a hell of a lot less tequila. But I wanted some damn answers.

His eyes darted over to the window. "Keep your voice down."

My eyes narrowed. He was too concerned with who had seen me or who might hear me. He clearly had more secrets he didn't want me digging in.

"Nice business you've got here, Mr. Andrews," I said, motioning to the view below. "A fine crew of mechanics you've got down there too. Quite a few changes for you since you left the Army. Preppy clothes gone, motorcycle, criminal record. Anything else you want to make me dig up on my own? You know what I can come up with in less than a day. You sure you don't want to just come clean?"

"I know what you think you've come up with, Willa. It's all stuff I can live with."

"You can live with me thinking you're a murderer?"

He nodded, jamming his hands into his back pockets, and rolled his neck to loosen the muscles. But he wasn't okay with it. He was a clean poker player but in life, he had three tells. That neck roll was one of them just like rubbing his thumb nail and mirroring my body language.

"Really?"

"What? You can't imagine me not giving a damn? Oh, Sunshine, you overestimate your appeal. You were a decent lay, I will give you that, but it was any port in a storm that night. Plus it was easy. All I had to do was apply a little liquor and I knew you'd drop your panties."

The pulse in my throat jumped. "You bastard."

"Acting like you were so much better than me. Being a tease all those years. Admit it, you'd been dying for an excuse. You didn't even have to admit you wanted to spread your legs for me. Michael biting it gave you the perfect opportunity."

I didn't even realize I had slapped him until he started laughing. "Is that the best you've got? Good thing you ditched the uniform, Sunshine. I've got to know though: Did you keep the handcuffs? You must have because you sure loved it when I held you down. If you're up for a go right now, I'd be happy to oblige. I've got a cot in the back or I can bend you right over the desk and make your day, but then you've really got to go."

Sonofabitch. The slap hadn't gotten his attention, but the second time I used my fist and his head rocked to the side. My dad had taught me to throw a great right hook and I put my whole body into it. I had no idea how he hadn't seen it coming because I'd telegraphed the damn thing all the way from my hip.

"Better, Sunshine. Always lead with your best punch." His hand whipped out and grabbed my wrist tightly before I could hit him a third time. He pulled me into his body and the collision made me bite my tongue.

I yanked my arm back trying to dislodge his grip, but he held on. "You can go fuck yourself sideways with a red hot poker, Seth."

"I'm not playing with you anymore, Willa."

My stomach turned into a hard ball of nerves, but I wasn't letting him win. I swept his leg and we tumbled. Seth refused to let go of my wrist and dragged me down on top of him in a tangle of limbs and solid muscles. We were not a graceful heap, all artfully arranged like on television. I banged my elbow on the concrete floor.

Before I could register the pain shooting down my arm, Seth had me rolled over on my back, his weight pressing me into the floor. Real and true panic blossomed as I lay there pinned. His hand came up over my mouth, covering it, pressing the meat of his palm up against my nostrils.

In my panic, all I could register was that this was not the man I once knew; the one I'd gone camping with and who'd taught me how to fish, always baiting the hooks for me because I couldn't bear to hurt the worms. The one who'd sacrificed himself to keep me and his little brother from getting caught drinking at fifteen. That guy would never have talked to me like I was trash. He would have never laid a hand on me in anger. This was not my Seth.

For a second, I saw regret and shame in his eyes. He started to roll off me and I pushed up hard, scrambling to my feet, haste winning out over grace.

I stared at him, trying to regain any semblance of control over myself and the situation.

"Charms and lies have worn off so you have to resort to insults and force, Seth? You've lost your edge," I said. It probably would have been a more effective slight if I hadn't been snorting air like a bull.

The only sound in the room was me panting. I desperately wanted to rub my wrist to ease both the ache and the indignity from being manhandled. I resisted and slowed my breathing. I refused to show him any fear. Or pain. I had assured him the last time I saw him that he wasn't capable of hurting me. I was living the lie.

The best defense is a good offense. "Who in the hell do you think you are? Or don't you know anymore? Seth Anderson, Seth Andrews. War hero, garage owner. Killer. Let me tell you who you're not: You're not someone who will ever put his hands on me again. Take that to the fucking bank."

I headed for the door and turned back, rage and fear combining in an almost overwhelming adrenaline cocktail, my fingers in a minor tremor, all pins and needles.

"I mean it, Seth. I'll keep your secrets. Your parents have been through enough, but if you come near me again..."

I trailed off, not even sure what I could threaten him with. He outweighed me by at least seventy pounds and had changed in ways I couldn't even fathom.

"Sunshine?" The mocking tone in his voice burned my cheeks. "Stay away."

I turned the knob and dashed out for real as full-blown shaking began in my hands. It took three tries to get the keys in the ignition and I had to pull over a block from the shop. I rubbed the pain away from my wrists until my fingers stopped tingling.

The voice in my head mocked me by replaying Seth telling me last night he'd never lie about his feelings for me. If I believed what he'd said today, he'd been lying for a long time.

# CHAPTER

## 9

My phone beeped, startling me. I checked the display and saw it was a text from Dad.

Is your brother keeping you on the straight and narrow?

Ever the comedian.

I tapped out a brief recap of the last few days and asked him to call when they got into the next port. That I needed a few minutes of his time for a consultation. I also snarked at him that he needed a better hiding place for his contraband password list. I deliberately left out the part where *I* had found the body and Violet was on the run from the cops. Or that her grandparents knew exactly where she was and were keeping it to themselves. Or that Seth was possibly a murderer and had kind of assaulted me. I bit my lip waiting for his response, my stomach tying in knots. I really didn't need the added stress of my dad freaking out and trying to cut their vacation short. I had to hope I'd been casual enough. And vague enough about the details I knew would cause him to call immediately and use his loud voice.

Do I read you correctly that VH is a suspect in a murder?

I typed back the three letters for person of interest. Then thought better and added, *only*.

Will call tomorrow. Time unknown. Be available.

And he bought none of my vagueness. He was going to call tomorrow and I would have to give him enough so that I would get the advice I desperately needed but not so much that he caught the first transatlantic flight home. Or I had to convince him that it was totally under control. Convincing myself first was key, of course.

I got back to the computer and started searches for the names on Joe Reagan's criminal court proceedings. Even the cops. Especially the cops. I knew some of the arresting officers and I was sure I could get them talking about the cases for a beer or two. Letting drop that I'd found Reagan's body would be all it took. And I wanted to know more about any confidential informants listed, information I could only get from the officer on record, if he'd give that information up. Cops were notoriously close-mouthed about their CIs, even with coworkers. For good reason, sure, but that didn't help me, so in a burst of optimism I marked it down as part of my plan.

I really needed two plans—one for Dad and a real one. I was cooking the books on my own father. I hated lying to him. Actually, I didn't. I wish I did. Truth be told, I was pretty okay with lying. Not the most noble of personal values, but people who said they were always honest were lying to themselves more than anyone. Lying made things easier; that's why we all did it. I don't mean the big ones—*No, honey, of course I'm not banging your sister*, or *I have no idea where those school kids got that crack, Officer*. I'm not a sociopath. I mean the lies that we use to hide the things that hurt the people who love us. Like telling Dad that everything was under control and I could handle a murder case that I wasn't supposed to be investigating anyway.

Plan of action for Dad: Simple background searches and an alternate theory to present to the cops via the Horowitzes' duly hired attorney. Nothing that could get me in trouble—or rather him, since I wasn't a licensed private investigator, merely his apprentice.

Plan of action for real: Bust a murderer by any means necessary short of getting anyone else, least of all me, killed. Even if that murderer was Seth. Yeah, that was a plan I definitely needed to be keeping to myself. Mostly because it was light on actual plan and more of a mission statement. I just needed to be methodical and think things through.

I picked my phone back up from the desk and called David. When he didn't pick up I left a message detailing that I didn't want the information I'd asked for earlier—no need to incriminate anyone in case the cops got a warrant for the phones and voicemail too—but that I did need different information. Like about Joe's recent employment. I needed to nail down that boot print. Seth's boots could have made the print, but those boots were everywhere. I didn't think about how much nerve it took to ask him for anything after I blackmailed and threatened him. This case was going to end up with a bunch of burned bridges and me holding an empty box of matches. Justice would be served, but I might end up with a lot fewer friends. I had so few to begin with.

My phone was still in my hand when it rang. The display showed Government Center. I tapped the screen to accept the call.

"Pennington."

"Willa, it's Detective Boyd."

I heard the clacking of keys. The department really needed to replace those crappy old keyboards.

"I wanted to thank you for the call I got this morning. I assume you're the reason David Horowitz called me."

"I just reminded him that making sure the police had all the information would make it all run much more smoothly for his granddaughter. He's a good man and just needed a little reminder to do the right thing."

"Uh huh. Not so good that he would tell me where she was," she said.

"If it makes you feel any better, if he does know where Violet is, he didn't share it with me, either."

"I'm actually calling because I wanted to review your statement with you. As the only witness we have, it's critical that I make sure everything you know and remember is in the file."

I tried not to infer that I had deliberately left anything out or forgotten a critical detail. Like the boot print. Whoops.

If I got back on scene I could try to spot any subtle evidence of Seth being there now that I knew to look for him. Could I get Boyd to let me in by telling her I had a vague memory of something tickling in the back of my mind? Would she buy that? I had nothing better to do at this point but find out.

"Now that you mentioned it there's something just ... bothering me. Something hovering. You know what I mean?"

She paused for what seemed like too long. *Bite the hook already, dammit. I need back on that scene and you need a murderer. We work together, even if you don't know about it, and we can get this case closed.*

"I do indeed know what you mean, Willa."

She was still calling me by my first name. That had to be a good sign. Time to go in for the kill.

83

"Maybe if I could go back to the scene to look around a bit. I got a good view of the yard, but my view of the body was limited because of the positioning of the steps."

I let out my breath slowly. It wasn't unheard of to let a witness back on scene to clear up a statement. It wasn't common, either. Mostly because people didn't want to go back to the scene. But I wasn't an average witness. I was a trained observer and even if I didn't wear a badge anymore, Boyd had to know that this was her best shot to get more information out of me. And as she said, I was her only witness.

"How about this afternoon? Three fifteen. I've got an hour."

I tried not to hyperventilate as she ended the call. She was giving me an hour on the scene. A full hour. That was amazing. I might actually be able to help her catch this killer (hopefully, not Seth) and have something to tell Dad tomorrow when he called me. The day was starting to turn around.

———

As I paced on the gravel drive leading to Joe Reagan's house, I ran over and over my conversations with Seth. I knew I wasn't in the best frame of mind for meeting with Detective Boyd, but I had to pull it together.

I'd made sure to park as far up the drive as possible to avoid any issues with the crime scene designation. I didn't see any tape except the seal on the front door, but I refused to take any chances pissing off Boyd. I checked the time on my phone and wondered how far I could push for information. I reasoned that the more I pushed the less she'd believe I knew Violet's whereabouts.

Had I been so blind to my assumption that Violet wasn't the killer that I hadn't properly considered her guilt? Was yesterday even when Reagan had died? A time of death late yesterday morning didn't rule her out, but if it was as far back as the night before last, there was no way the cops would consider her anything other than a suspect. I pictured the scene. No, my first assumption had been correct. The blood on the body was dark but not dried. Joe Reagan had to have been shot sometime yesterday morning, probably no more than an hour before I arrived. Relief washed over me and I kicked myself for the last-second doubts. I knew in my gut that someone other than Violet had shot and killed Joe Reagan. I didn't have the luxury of doubts. I had to focus on the facts and my instincts.

The crunch of tires on gravel alerted me to Detective Boyd's arrival and I made sure I got the hell out of her way. She pulled way down on the drive, directly in front of the house. I hurried to meet her.

"Why the hell did you park so far back, Pennington?"

"I wasn't sure how far the crime scene extended, Detective, and the last thing I want to do is unintentionally damage your investigation."

She smiled at me. It seemed genuine, but what did I know? I was overtired from a couple months of not sleeping and I'd just come off an encounter that would have screwed me up even if I just left a hypnotherapy session eating a chocolate ice cream cone and wearing new shoes. Damn Seth.

"Willa, can I be honest with you?"

I nodded. I didn't know that I believed she would actually be honest with me, but I could pretend. In the spirit of honesty.

"We've got nothing on this case. And no one thinks the girl or her grandparents are responsible. Not even Harrison, who we can both admit pretty much hates women. I want to close this and I could use all the help I can get."

So it was quid pro quo. She'd give as long I gave. And since I wasn't in this for the cash or the collar, striking a deal didn't cause me any heartburn.

"What about the footprint? Did you guys get anything from that?"

Her expression went back to cop face in an instant. And from that I gathered that the footprint was news to her.

"What footprint?"

"I didn't mention it yesterday?" I knew damn well I hadn't. I had forgotten all about it by the time she'd arrived. That didn't make me feel great about my detective skills but, in my defense, I wasn't on the job. I was the civilian.

"No, I don't believe you did." Her voice was controlled, but I knew she was angry. My not mentioning it wasn't great, but it wasn't as big of a problem as no one on her team noticing and logging it. Someone was going to get their ass handed to them. Senior uniform on scene, most likely. Harrison might be on crossing guard duty by tomorrow.

"I am sorry, Detective Boyd. I really did forget about it. I've never found a dead body before." That was true. I'd seen them but I'd known to expect them. Finding one out of the blue was a jarring experience.

She nodded, the motion clipped. "This is why we like to review statements."

I pointed to the backyard area. "It was next to the back step. It looked fresh."

She shot her eyes over to the side yard. "Show me."

I walked her around to the back of the house and squatted next to the area where I'd found the footprint. Since she was already mad, and mostly not at me, I figured confessing to getting a shot of it would probably get me another point in her favor.

"I got a photo of it too."

She nodded again and looked away from me quickly, turning a tight circle on the walk, taking in the whole property. I doubted she was looking for any other missed evidence and guessed she was instead trying to figure out how a simple homicide had gotten so far out of hand.

I stood up and gestured to the back door.

"You don't think Violet did it because the only way the shooting makes sense is if the perp was on this back walk shooting up into the house. And there's no reason for her to have done that. The only way Violet being the shooter makes sense is in self-defense, and shooting someone from outside the house doesn't line up. Plus the killer had to have been a pretty good shot; Violet has no experience with guns."

Boyd looked at me, this time with appraisal in her eyes. She shook her head and pressed her hands her to eyes. She looked more tired and older than I remembered from even when she arrived.

"The best cop on the scene yesterday didn't even have a badge, forgotten-but-photographed boot print aside. Why in the hell did you … Never mind. When did you figure it out?"

I shrugged. "The shooter being on the walk is the only thing that the lack of evidence supports. Is a look around inside the house out of the question, Detective?"

She turned on her heel and with her measured, sure steps walked to the front of the house. "Call me Jan," she said, over her shoulder.

I followed behind her, feeling a bit like a kid who'd just gotten a wink and a nod from her favorite teacher. I may not have a badge anymore but to Boyd, it seemed, I was still on the side of right. That felt good. Better than anything felt in a long time.

Boyd opened the front door. Down the hallway to the back I saw the dried blood that had pooled where Reagan had fallen. The house was laid out oddly, at least for any house I'd ever been in, shallow and wide. The staircase to the second floor ran against the right wall of the house, leaving all the living areas situated to the left. The floor plan gave me a sense of being off kilter, like the house was weighted wrong and could tip over at any moment. It took me a moment to recognize that the layout of the house mimicked the position of the house on the property.

Boyd stayed at the front door. She was really going to let me tour this scene. And she was going to let me do it on my own. I took the dozen steps I needed to be standing over the spot where Reagan had died. I let my head space just sink into cataloging the house. I thought back to the view from the window yesterday morning, looking down at Joe Reagan's body on the floor.

I could see the blood was smeared a bit where I thought his legs had been. I turned back to Boyd to find her watching me carefully. The hair on the back of my neck prickled belatedly.

"The blood is smeared here. He didn't die instantly, I assume?"

"Medical examiner says not immediately but probably only a few moments."

Her words were clipped. That prickle on the back of my neck returned. I hated that sensation because, lately, it was always too late to stop me from doing something stupid. I fought back the impulse to blurt out again that I hadn't killed the guy. I knew she was just waiting to see my assessment, but her stare was unnerving.

"Could it have happened when the ME's team removed the body?" She shook her head.

"Then the killer touched the body after. Maybe looking for something in Reagan's pockets?"

She just looked at me. I was beyond unnerved now. "Can you please stop looking at me like I'm about to confess or take a run at you?"

She laughed. "Sorry, force of habit. I swear. Yes, I think the killer searched the body. Probably his pockets."

I took a deep breath and pulled the fear back in to let it regain its strength for another day. Maybe a nightmare. Those were always chock full of heart-pounding terror. "Looking for what? Cash? Drugs?"

I'd said it quietly but aloud. It wasn't a question for Boyd and she didn't take it for one. She kept her eyes off of me and let me think.

"A note? His phone?" I mused.

Aha. A cell phone could be both useful to the killer and something to get him caught.

"Reagan have a cell phone on him when his effects were catalogued?"

Boyd smiled and shook her head.

Detective Boyd gave me the full hour to roam the house, looking in closets, under the bed, through books. It was a bust finding anything that wasn't already listed on the evidence log, which Boyd had considerately handed me a copy of before reminding me that while letting me into the crime scene wasn't strictly prohibited, giving me the evidence list definitely was—so keep my damn mouth shut.

———

Sitting back at Dad's desk armed with a highlighter, I marked the items I found interesting. Like fourteen thousand dollars in a lockbox. Along with an unregistered gun. I bet Joe wished he'd had that when whoever killed him drew on him.

The money poked at me. Why would Reagan have that much cash sitting around? If it was pay from a job, even an under-the-table job, he'd be using it for expenses. It wouldn't have been banded in hundreds in a lockbox. Was it cash for a buy of some kind? Was it even his? If he was hiding cash and that was the reason for the murder, wouldn't the killer have gone looking for it? Why would he take Reagan's phone but not the cash? Someone cold enough to shoot a person twice wouldn't have balked at stepping over the body to go find his money.

As much as people liked to believe that life was precious, fourteen grand was more than enough to kill someone over. For a certain type of person, anyway. I had a feeling this one may even have enjoyed it. That worried me and made me glad Violet was gone and safe. If the killer had any idea she'd seen his truck, even if she couldn't identify it beyond the color, she would be in his sights.

# CHAPTER

# 10

**MY CELL PHONE BEEPED,** the display showing my dad's face. I answered in speaker mode. "Hey, Daddy."

"Will, what the hell is going on there? You only call me daddy when you're in over your head."

"It's nothing, Dadd…" I trailed off, elongating the *d* and not fooling either one of us.

Shoot! Was my brain-to-mouth filter going to kick in anytime soon?

"Nothing. Sure. David and Susan's granddaughter is involved in a murder case. Happens every day."

I looked down at the phone, trying to get my equilibrium back a little bit. Talking to Dad about cases always made me feel like a little girl. Badge or not, he still had decades of experience on me.

"Will? Are you okay?"

"Uh, yeah. I'm here. I, uh, I don't want you to worry. It's under control. I've only given them some advice about an attorney and being honest with the cops." For the most part.

"I'm coming home."

The exact opposite of what I wanted. "No, Dad. Just no. You and Mom deserve this trip."

The silence on the other side went on a little too long. "Tell me what's happening. All of it this time."

I forged on as quickly as possible because I knew the roaming charges would be racking up like money in a slot machine. "The other day the Horowitzes came over to see if you would help Violet move because her boyfriend had been hitting her. When they realized you had already left, they convinced me to help."

That earned a chuckle in spite of the dire results of the favor. I ignored it and kept going.

"When I arrived, there were no cars and I thought no one was home. I waited about fifteen minutes and then I saw the boyfriend's dead body through the back door window when I went to knock. Now Violet's in the wind and David and Susan are understandably distraught."

"And you feel responsible?"

I hadn't until Seth showed up at my door telling me to butt out, but I certainly couldn't mention that.

"Not responsible exactly but … they looked to me to fill in for you and I … "

"Feel accountable," he said.

"That's just another word for responsible, but, yeah, I guess I do." That wasn't a lie exactly. I did feel responsible; I was the only one who knew Seth might be involved. I wasn't about to give Boyd that suspicion. Hell, I wasn't even admitting it to my own father.

"All right then, rule number one is always be prepared, and number two is don't ever ask a question you don't already know the answer. Start a case file."

"Done," I said.

"That's my girl. Once the case file is as complete as you can make it with your first-hand experience, you need to run the particulars on everyone involved that doesn't have a badge. That means David and Susan too."

It shocked the hell out of me that he'd even consider them being involved, but I kept my mouth shut and my hand moving, taking notes.

"Since you're not a cop you won't have access to any of the evidence, but if all we want to do is point the cops away from Violet, you shouldn't need it."

"I, uh, I may have gotten back onto the scene and have a copy of the evidence log."

"Willa Elaine!"

"Legally, Daddy. The lead detective, Jan Boyd, invited me back to the scene to review my statement. She gave me the log."

"How in the hell did you charm her into that?" he asked.

"Can't she just like me?"

"No," he said.

Well, ouch.

"I may have accidentally kept a piece of evidence out of my original statement—a footprint. A real accident, I swear. But no one on scene logged it. And I happened to have a photo of it."

Even through the cell static crackling across the Atlantic Ocean I heard him suck in his breath.

"Look, the deal is you're just a private citizen indulging her curiosity by looking some things up. The footprint worked in your favor, but consider yourself out of lucky breaks, baby girl. Stay on the computer and don't get in Boyd's way. She obviously sees you're an asset to her and is giving you some leash—don't choke yourself."

We disconnected after I promised I would call him back if things went badly. *Too late, Dad.* I couldn't deny it. I had to set my own mind at ease or this was going to eat me.

———

"Benjy? You home?"

We really needed to get that boy a car so I'd know when he was home and when he wasn't. Dad's solution to that problem would likely run to GPS trackers and subcutaneous chipping, but considering the kid was more responsible at seventeen than I would ever be, I could convince them to get him some old beater. He spent too much time at home anyway. Especially by the standards I set. Michael, Seth, and I were rarely home as teens. Of course, we didn't have computers to take apart and put back together again. Or apps to design. Or sexting. Thinking of sexting reminded me how grateful I was that there wasn't any evidence of that stupid, horrible mistake I had made sleeping with Seth just in time for Ben to wander into the kitchen and eye me suspiciously.

"What's got you so freaked out?"

I rolled my eyes at him, trying to regain my composure. "Just thinking about an article I read on sexting. You're not into that, are you, mutant? You're not sending some cheerleader pictures of your junk, right?"

The look of horror on his face rescued me from any further need to torture him. It was mean but an effective way to get my mind off thoughts that didn't need thinking.

"Ew! Why would you even ask me that? I can't even ... geez, that's just such a weird thing to ask your brother."

I leaned against the counter and crossed my arms over my chest, trying to adopt a stern expression. "Sexting is a serious problem affecting families in America, Benjamin. People are being charged with possession of child pornography from what started as a simple joke or a consensual relationship. No one is more distressed than I am to have to bring this up, but I wouldn't be a good guardian if I didn't."

He stared at me, his expression growing more disturbed as I'd continued talking. His hands clenched and unclenched and it looked as if he was fighting the urge to covers his ears. "Please stop talking. I'm begging you."

I laughed. I couldn't torment him for too long without breaking. His face was always so earnest. The child didn't have a jaded bone in his body.

"I'm screwing with you, Benj. I know you're not stupid enough to do something that would leave that much evidence. Plus, you can't even talk about sex, so I'm positive you're not sticking a camera down your pants."

He stomped out of the room as much as his gangly legs would stomp.

"Dinner in thirty minutes?" I called after him.

Ben walked back into the kitchen, clearly still annoyed with me. "If you stop saying embarrassing things, I will order pizza so you don't have to try to cook tonight."

"You're a giver, Ben. And don't try to act like it's some big favor to me. You'll order some whole wheat crust thing with organic tomato sauce and locally sourced vegetables and try to pass it off as a real pizza. Also, then you don't have to try to eat anything I've made."

He laughed. I guess I was forgiven for my earlier mention of sex and genitalia. Another wonderful thing about my baby brother was he didn't hold a grudge. Although I was pretty sure some therapist was going to end up making big bucks off him when he was in his thirties. No one was that together, especially not a teenage boy.

"I'll order a real pizza too. One with lots of pepperoni so you can get your daily grease allowance."

"And that's why I love you, Ben. You know me and you don't try to change me," I said.

While I emptied the dishwasher, he picked up the menu from our favorite Italian restaurant, run by a real Italian family and serving authentic food, and perused it casually. Too casually. I continued the kitchen task, one of the few I couldn't screw up, and waited for him to spill what was bothering him. Ben was a talker. He couldn't let silence be unless there was a movie on and then woe to the idiot who talked during dialogue—even movies he'd seen dozens of times before. He flipped the short menu over in his hands a few times too many, cutting his eyes over to me with every flip.

"What's going on with the Horowitzes, Will?"

My stomach clenched. How did he know anything was going on with them? I looked up, hoping my face was as blank as I wanted it to be. "What do you mean? Is something going on with them?"

"Fine. No pepperoni for you then." He put the menu down on the counter and shoved his phone back into this pocket. He was annoyed and was going to attempt to blackmail me with pizza. As if I didn't have my own phone and the ability to call the restaurant myself. I was planning to make spaghetti, the only thing I could make with any consistency, anyway, so the joke was on him.

"Clearly you think something's going on. Would you like to tell me why and I can look into it?"

"I see stuff. I'm not a kid, you know."

But he was a kid. I tried to remember what it had been like to be seventeen. It was only a decade ago that Michael and I were seniors in high school. I had dated a wrestler who hated Michael—not him personally, the mere fact of him. We had broken up because I refused to spend less time with my best friend. It had been such a big deal at the time and I barely remembered the guy's name now.

"Their granddaughter is in some trouble, that's all, Ben. It's nothing you need to worry about. I'm helping them as much as I can."

"What kind of trouble?"

Ben had found a bone to shake and he wasn't going to give it up.

"Help me make dinner and I'll tell you as much of it as I think you need to know, okay?" I pulled a box of pasta out of the cabinet and he took my lead and got out the ingredients for the sauce.

"Are you going to be okay with meat, sport?" I asked, knowing he'd try to pawn off some kind of meatless substitute. "I mean real meat, Ben."

"How about ground turkey?"

It was the best I was going to get so I nodded and he grabbed a package of thawed organic, low-fat ground turkey from the fridge. The fact that it was already thawed tipped me off that he hadn't really planned to call for pizza. The little monkey.

I dropped a dollop of butter into the sauce pan and inhaled the rich, creamy scent as it sizzled and melted. I drizzled in some olive oil and mixed the two before adding the clove of garlic Ben had just chopped. I had about thirty seconds before I needed to add the meat so I busied myself opening the can of tomato sauce—also organic, naturally—and rehearsed the information I was willing to give Ben and the information that I would allow him to pry out of me.

I placed the meat in the pan and allowed it to brown, a process that took no longer than two minutes. I was out of time and had no idea how much information was too much, so I decided to let him in on the whole deal.

I dumped the can of tomato sauce into the pan and lowered the heat on the burner, giving the whole mixture a few swirls.

"Violet had been living with a guy who wasn't treating her very well. He'd been verbally and physically abusing her."

Ben's eyes widened.

"The Horowitzes asked me to help her move out when they realized Dad was on vacation. Long story short, Violet wasn't there but the boyfriend was."

"He didn't hurt you, did he?"

My sweet baby brother.

"No, Benjy. He was dead."

"She killed him?" Ben asked. It was clear I had blown his suburban teen mind.

I shook my head, resisting the urge to laugh. "Also no. She's not the kind of girl who could do something like that."

"How did he … what had … ?"

"He was shot."

His eyes widened and I turned back to the sauce. He needed a moment. And if this didn't push him back to the safety of his computers, we were all in for a long haul. It also gave me a moment to think. Seth was a great shot. Even before he joined the Army, in fact. He could have easily gotten that placement, at that angle, from that distance. After the ugliness at the garage I wasn't having a hard time imagining him doing anything anymore.

"Were you scared?" Ben's voice had gone quiet and low.

I kept my back to him and stirred. "No, not scared. Wary. Unnerved. Annoyed. Which sounds awful, I know, but I hadn't wanted to help anyway and suddenly I had a murder on my hands."

"And it was a murder? He didn't, you know, off himself?"

Off himself. The words sounded so alien out of his man-child mouth. I turned to look him in the eye.

"No. He was shot twice in the torso. And I got to find him because Dad's a PI and I was a cop. I was there because the Horowitzes looked to me to help them in a situation they were unprepared for. That's what this job is like, Ben. You do not see people at the high points in their life."

He nodded and swallowed, hard. "Maybe I should put the pasta in the water now."

I saw that it was boiling rapidly, large bubbles rushing to the surface and exploding. I nodded. "That's a good idea."

We finished up the dinner prep in silence. I used the rote activity to think about Seth's possible involvement with Joe Reagan's murder. I was content to eat in silence too, but Ben, thinking he was changing the subject, wanted to chat.

"So when Seth was here ... I know you said it was complicated ... "

"Yeah." If complicated was code for *I have no idea who Seth ever was and he is possibly a double murderer*, sure. It was complicated.

"And I really don't want to know anything else but ... here's the thing. I've been kind of ... hanging out with him."

I dropped my fork, the utensil glancing off the plate with a clunk and landing on the floor. My lungs burned. I took deep calming breaths that turned into choking on a mouthful of spaghetti I'd inhaled into my throat.

While I coughed up the clot of pasta, Ben grabbed his plate and glass, going for refills. He ate like the food was going to be taken away from him at any moment.

"I see." I clenched my fists and then released them.

"I mean, you were in Santa Fe with Leila and … and … Michael's gone. We've kind of all been spending time together as families."

How had no one told me this? I'd been in touch while I was in Santa Fe for three months. I had texted or talked to Ben every damn day. I wasn't immature enough to be pissed about being replaced or anything, but I was annoyed that no one had told me.

"And I just thought that maybe Seth had given you something for me. A game."

I nodded like that made sense. "A game you've been playing with Seth?" I felt like I was behind on a TV show that had aired new episodes without advertising them.

"Yeah, a computer game. It's called Hearts of Iron. I mean, no, not Seth. I've been playing it with the Colonel."

More nodding. I was starting to feel like one of Dad's bobble heads.

"I mean, it's no big deal. I can just get it from him this weekend when I see him. We're going for pizza on Saturday night."

"Seth or the Colonel?"

"Duh. Seth. I don't even think the Colonel likes pizza." He attacked the food piled on his plate without giving me another look. Which was good because I was pretty sure I wasn't able to hide my shock and horror.

There was no turning back now. I had to find out what Seth was up to before something happened to my baby brother. I had no idea how to stop Ben from seeing him, but Seth was going to have to walk over my cold, rotting corpse to imbed himself any further in my brother's life.

# CHAPTER

# 11

**I SCROUNGED THROUGH MY** nightstand. Whatever I couldn't find a place for got dumped into the drawer over the years, so it was awash with useless crap. But I knew the item I was looking for was in there. I remembered the moment I had dropped the key in, a single metal *W* attached (really an *M* for Michael but I had pointed out to little humor that an *M* was just an upsidedown *W*), sure I would never need it. I doubted when Michael gave it to me "for emergencies," he imagined this was the occasion I would haul it back out for. Maybe he thought I'd need to fetch something of his from the apartment he shared with his brother while he was out of the country, I don't know. I know I hadn't imagined this, but with the key, I was merely entering a home I had been granted unfettered legal access to. That was the argument

I planned to use if I somehow got caught in Seth's home. At least, by someone other than Seth, because I was pretty sure I wasn't going to sell that story to him. And if I did get caught by Seth, well … that was a bridge I'd cross if I got to it. Either way I wasn't letting some hurt feelings stop me. He'd made a big mistake getting Ben involved.

I caught sight of the key through an empty CD case and dove my hand underneath to grab it, promptly jamming a golf tee beneath my middle fingernail. A few colorful curses later, I had the key in my other hand wondering why the hell I had a golf tee. I set my alarm for way too early and tried to get some sleep. I had a busy day ahead of me enacting a halfway decent plan to stake out and then search Seth's place.

———

The best place for a stakeout? Apartment building parking lot. The worst place for a stakeout? Same apartment building parking lot at rush hour. I made sure I was in an inconspicuous spot with plenty of time to spare before I could reasonably assume Seth would be off to work. And then I waited and tried not to nod off and waited some more. I had no idea what time the garage opened (Andrews Motorcycle didn't have a website), so I was out the door before Ben's bus came for the second morning in a row. That gave me tons of time to cool my heels and obsess over my crappy plan and how Seth was involved with Reagan's murder and what the hell had happened to him that he would even think about his brother's death like he had yesterday, let alone say it, and wondering how I could have been so wrong about him for so long and how holidays were going to be super awkward if I put my dad's best friend's son in prison.

That killed more time than it should have and I practiced looking busy and professional and not like a stalker when the denizens of the

Edgecombe community all swept out of their apartment doors and into the lot at seven. Pavlov would have been proud.

As the cars on either side of mine were unlocked and entered, I feigned looking in my bag for some unknown yet essential item. When the lot cleared considerably I felt more exposed. It also gave me a better look at the vehicles I had as options for Seth. While I was certain he'd be on a motorcycle it wasn't out of the question that he might still have Michael's car too. I didn't have a key for that but I didn't think he'd leave anything too incriminating in something so easily searched if he got pulled over.

I squished down farther in my seat and willed myself invisible when the door to his second-floor apartment opened. Clad in another version of manual chic menswear, he pulled the door shut behind him and slowly scanned the area around the motorcycle parking section. He'd always been a careful guy—getting ambushed by a running back upset over the loss of his girlfriend had made an impression—but his body language was too stiff for a longtime habit. He took his time ambling down the stairs and around the landing, eyeballing everything. I had to lean forward to keep him in sight as he crouched down to check something on the bike. Looking for sabotage?

Seth was actively looking for something or someone. I doubted he was keeping an eye out for me looking to exact revenge for his awfulness yesterday. I wanted to regret hitting him. I just didn't. He'd said terrible things designed to hurt and humiliate me, but he'd crossed a line saying I'd used Michael's death. I couldn't ever forgive him for that. Or for being a psycho killer.

After an interminable amount of time checking the bike, he stood, scooping up his helmet, and finally roared out of the parking lot, the bike's engine an animal-like growl.

I counted out the seconds for a full five minutes, adding Mississippis to each count, before I nonchalantly got out of my car and sauntered to the stairwell. I, too, took my time, following Seth's path in reverse and keeping my eye on the entrance to the lot without making it look like I was acting guilty. Or, I hoped I was. Still seeing nothing, I pulled the key out of my pocket and slid it into the lock. Having never used the key before I held my breath, worrying that it would stick or that the lock had been re-keyed. I felt rather than heard the lock click open and let the breath out slowly.

I don't know what I expected but the place looked exactly the same as the last time I'd been there—bleary-eyed, half-dressed in my funeral clothes, frantically looking for the keys to Michael's car so I could escape before Seth woke up and I had to actually look him in the eye. Funny how much worse a hookup looks in hindsight, you know, when hindsight is viewed with the murderer lens.

One last look at the parking lot to make sure I wasn't going to get busted, and I slipped into the apartment. Seth and Michael had spent little actual time as real roommates due to deployments. I had probably spent more time here with Michael than Seth had. I remembered the Coen Brothers movie marathons we'd have so we could bring Ben over to watch them too. And we'd pop popcorn and drink soda—even health nut Ben would have one—and we'd tangle into a pile of limbs and blankets and lose ourselves for hours in movies. And Michael would sneak Ben down to the pool after hours so he'd be wet and smell like chlorine when we brought him home so Mom and Dad wouldn't know we hadn't been swimming with him the whole time. They were happy memories. Mostly. I wasn't quite sure how to have happy memories after someone had died. Maybe there was no such thing as happy memories, just memories of happy times.

I felt a little stab in my heart at thinking of Michael, but I had to shove it down. I couldn't search the place all weepy and grief-stricken. I had a job to do. I reset the deadbolt and vowed to remember to do that when I left. Seth never had to know anyone was here. I'd been here enough to know where the big things needed to land when I was done looking. The little stuff he'd never remember.

I swept the living room left to right. There weren't too many places I could think of to hide contraband, but I pulled out the electronic components and DVDs. And found the first gun. Fully loaded magazine, a round chambered. What was Seth doing that he needed to be ready to shoot while watching TV? I added a check mark to the Guilty as Hell side of the tally. I put the gun back where I'd found it and slid the DVDs back in place. Fireplace mantel was next. I checked the back of all the picture frames but found nothing. That wasn't a big surprise since that was an amateur hiding place. I'd expect better of Seth just for having been a teenager.

I looked under the couch and the space was empty. There wasn't even a dust bunny. No crumbs or coins in between the cushions either. The place was ridiculously clean. Did he have some kind of maid service for criminals? So far this break-in—I mean, authorized and legal entry—was a total bust. One gun didn't make him a criminal even if he'd been storing it a little oddly.

I spotted a laptop on the dining room table but doubted I'd be able to crack the password even knowing him as well as I did. Or as well as I thought I had. I really wanted a look inside.

I moved on to the kitchen and, out of a sense of obligation, checked the fridge and freezer. I was relieved to find nothing unusual, if only so I didn't have to be embarrassed for him. Ditto under the sink. None of the cans were any of those lame *hide your valuables even though the only person you're fooling is yourself with a can labeled Windex* things. The glasses and plates were all neatly stacked, cartoon character mugs with pithy sayings on their own shelf—some I'd given him or Michael.

The dishwasher was free of either clean or dirty dishes. Geez, Seth was the tidiest low-life I'd ever come across. Criminals usually had disgusting homes. My last tetanus shot had come courtesy of a sweep that revealed a rusty knife stuck down the back of a recliner. My thoughts flitted back to the laptop. Password protection usually offered you three shots before it locked down. I could give a few of the less obvious but still relevant options a shot. Nudging aside a pot on a shelf just above my head earned a clunk, and I pulled it down to reveal a second gun. For the eggs and bullets combo platter, clearly. Living room gun, kitchen gun. Did I go for the trifecta of bathroom gun to add to the rapidly expanding pile of overly paranoid weapons stashes or try the laptop first? Since I was loathe to leave any DNA or obvious fingerprints all over what was sure to be, based on the rest of the house, the sparkling washroom, laptop it was.

I opened it up and bombed out with my first three options. Locked. That wasn't a great turn of events, but I had my own computer expert on speed dial.

"Benjy! What's up, baby bro?"

"Uh, study hall, Will."

I kept forgetting about that stupid high school thing. The only reason I'd come back from Santa Fe was to make sure Ben had an adult around while my parents were on their trip, and I wasn't even capable of remembering why he needed that adult.

"Shit. Sorry. So, I just had the quickest question about computers. If I've gotten the password wrong a few times and I'm locked out, what do I do?"

I heard rustling and movement. He was probably going someplace he wouldn't get into trouble for being on the phone. The teachers had been pretty pissy about it when I was there.

"No big deal. I was just fixing Mr. J's phone." Of course. He was probably in the teacher's lounge teaching them how to do their taxes too.

"So you locked yourself out of Dad's computer, huh. You know he keeps the passwords in the Rubik's Cube, right?"

"I'm asking for a friend." Lamest line in the history of lies; it never works, even on the most gullible people.

"Uh huh, a friend, sure. Does this have to do with the Horowitzes?"

"Can you get me in?"

"Not if you don't know the password."

"Don't you have some dohicky that cracks passwords?"

"*Dohicky?* What kind of word is that? No, I don't have a dohicky or a program or an app. Isn't that the kind of stuff you guys don't want me doing, anyway?"

"Well, if you want to be technical about it, yes, this is probably the kind of stuff we don't want you doing but, for practical purposes, if just this once you wanted to tell me how someone would go about it, I—or rather, my friend—would be the one doing it."

"Will, you're not getting past any password. It would take a while. Even with a dohicky."

"I really want in this computer, Ben. What are my options?"

"Can you just take it?"

I considered that for a second and discarded it just as quickly. My goal was to get in and out without Seth knowing anyone had been here. He would definitely notice his laptop was gone and I would be his first stop, without passing Go or collecting two hundred dollars. Too bad there wasn't a card that sent him straight to Jail.

"Not an option."

"I have a thought, something I've been wanting to try. Give me a few minutes."

"Did I mention I'm mildly breaking and entering, Ben?"

"Jeez, Will, this isn't TV, okay? I need two minutes. Kill some time snooping somewhere else. Like the dirty clothes hamper."

"This isn't TV, Ben." I refused to admit it was a decent idea and I shoved the phone in my pocket after putting in the earbuds so I was available when Ben was done. Rummaging through a possible murderer's dirty clothes. I jammed my hand down into the bathroom hamper, ignoring the idea that I was likely going to be coming into contact with underwear, and grabbed the jeans. There was only two days of clothing in the hamper, including the stuff he'd worn for our makeout session. I shuddered and forced myself to put it out of my mind. So I'd screwed a shady asshole. I wasn't the Bonnie to his Clyde, so all I was guilty of, besides breaking and entering, was bad judgment. Which put me in with every other damn person on the planet.

I held the jeans and scanned the rest of the bathroom. So all I'd found was that he was a homebody felon who liked cleaning and laundry? His Internet dating profile had to get the weirdest hits. I searched the pockets and pulled out a scrap of paper with a series of digits on it. I had no idea if it was a code or password so in my pocket it went. He'd never miss it.

"Patch the kernel, mint."

"What kernel, Ben? I don't have any mints. What are you—"

"Will? Shut up, okay."

"I wasn't the one talking to myself."

"Yes, you were, but I wasn't going to ask whose underwear." Apparently, we'd both inherited the thinking out loud trait from Dad. I was supremely grateful I had only mentioned the boxers.

"Okay, I'm going to text you a link. Click on it and the program will download to your phone. Then all you need to do is plug your phone into the computer's USB port. This will let you boot the computer and copy all the files onto your phone."

"Seriously? That doesn't sound possible."

He sighed. "I'm offended. Deeply. I'm hanging up on you now."

"Wait, plug it in with what? I didn't break in with my phone charger, Ben."

"No, but you have one in your car."

"I do?"

"Yes, I made sure you had one because I know you. Anyway, study hall is ending so text me back if you need more help. And you're welcome."

"Thank you, Benjy." But he'd already disconnected. So if I wanted in the computer I needed to go back out to the car. It was a risk but one I was willing to take. I forced down the impulse to scurry down to get the cable and back like a mouse afraid the cat was coming back any second. Acting suspicious looked suspicious. I was just another suburban twenty-something who'd left something in her car. I nodded hello to the few lucky souls who had later schedules. I waved to the maintenance worker picking up debris on the grass ringing the parking spaces.

I checked for the text Ben had promised and followed the link. I tried not to panic at the transformation on my phone. At this point, the only thing I was certain of was that my brother knew what he was doing. It was nice that at least one of us did.

Back inside the apartment, I plugged the phone in and followed the instructions. The screen on the laptop came to life, the password box gone, and a dog's face appeared. That didn't look like Seth's wallpaper so I had to assume whatever Ben had set me up with was working. I dragged the folder for the C drive over to the copy box. A status window showed five minutes to completion. That was more time than I wanted to stick around in the apartment. I'd already been here twenty minutes, which felt like a lifetime. Most of it had been wasted time from a straight search perspective but if I got some useful information off the laptop, it was worth it.

I had nothing better to do while my phone was copying the files so I hit the room that seemed the most promising: Seth's bedroom. I had half expected dirty clothes all over the floor and pizza boxes on the stationary surfaces even considering the fastidious appearance of the public spaces, but everything was military perfect. Even the picture frames were aligned with the edges of the dresser. *Orderly* had taken on a pathological bent. There was a picture of me and Michael at a substation picnic from a dozen years before. We were both fifteen and awkward as hell, just beginning to look like our adult selves, braces glinting. Seth's awfulness confused me even more in light of the fact that every morning he woke up and saw me as the girl he once knew. Fifteen was the year my crush on him had caught Michael's attention and I had been warned that he was not cool with me dating his brother. It was the only time we'd fought.

I shook off the memories and started searching. Gun number three was in between the bed and the nightstand in one of those Call in the Next Fifteen Minutes and Get Two for the Price of One TV commercial remote holders. Clever use for what had always seemed like the laziest of all products. As with the other two, locked and loaded. If shit went down at Edgecombe, Seth was prepared to shoot his way out.

So he had an alias, a new career, a pending conviction for Accessory to Murder, and what one could generously term a small arsenal.

"Hello? Seth?" A woman's voice. I barely had time to be irrationally jealous.

Shit, shit, shit. Who the hell was that? My fingers twitched to grab the gun I had just put back, but that was a worse idea than sticking around so long had been.

I busied myself with pretending like I was finishing making the bed when the woman popped her head in the open bedroom door.

"Oh, I'm sorry. I didn't know anyone was here."

Time for the best acting job of my life. "Hi. Um, who are you and why do you have a key to my boyfriend's apartment?"

Best defense, good offense and all that. I made sure my face showed only annoyance and none of the deep, buzzing terror that I felt. *Please don't let her be his real girlfriend. Please god, don't let her be a wife I've never heard of.* Illogically, I figured she couldn't be because otherwise why was he making out with me the other night? Like somehow being a cheater was beneath him but being a murderer was cool. Logically, I knew she couldn't be a serious connection because the apartment was devoid of any signs of her, but panic does set the brain to spinning in all different directions.

"Your boyfriend?"

Shit, she *was* his girlfriend. Why in the hell weren't there any pictures of her in the apartment? My brain grasped for … Yes!

I wandered over to the dresser and picked up the photo of me and Michael, showing it to her. "Yup. We grew up together. It got romantic just recently."

"Oh." Only disappointment showed on her face. Praise the heavens. She wasn't the girlfriend but she was interested. When she saw his face on the evening news after his arrest she'd be embarrassed that she was ever hot for him.

"And, again, why do you have a key to my boyfriend's apartment?"

"Oh, right. I'm the office manager for the apartment complex. I was just doing a run-through of the apartment before we bring in some potential renters to check the place out."

"Right. That makes sense." I forced myself to laugh. "Since we're moving into our own place."

She nodded, a puzzled look on her face. "Um, right. I guess. Anyway, I'm really sorry. I didn't know anyone was here. You'll be out by ten?"

I heard my cell phone beeping frantically in the dining room and forced another smile. "Just finishing charging my phone and then I'm off to work."

# CHAPTER

# 12

**BUOYED BY MY RELATIVE** success searching Seth's place, I decided to stake out some of Joe Reagan's known associates. I should have taken my win and gone home. I had no idea what I was looking for other than some clichéd bad behavior, but they all either had day jobs or hangovers. One of them had a business truck backed into the driveway but I saw no signs of life at the house, not even when a delivery had to be left with the neighbor.

I gave the three most likely suspects an hour each of surveillance but abandoned the last one just shy of a full hour when I got a call from Susan. My presence was requested. Defeated and feeling stupid, I drove home and trudged across the side lawn that separated our house and the Horowitzes'. I didn't exactly drag my feet, but I wasn't skipping, either.

Susan greeting me with a smile and hug was unexpected, to say the least. "Willa, come in. I just pulled cookies out of the oven. Jasmine tea?"

I had expected her and David to be annoyed, disappointed, angry. I was not going to question cookies and tea.

I sat at the kitchen table, where David had a newspaper pulled up in front of his face. So Susan wasn't on team Willa Sucks but David was still the captain. Fair enough. Time for the mea culpas.

"I just wanted to say how sorry I am that this case is changing our relationship. I've been a little rough on you. I haven't enjoyed it. My only excuse is that I know you both would never forgive yourselves if Violet was even charged for this murder."

The newspaper twitched down an inch, maybe two.

"Don't be silly, dear." Susan placed a teacup and plate of cookies in front of me. The smell of warm snickerdoodles caused my mouth to water. My favorite. And only Susan made them right. I'd tried dozens of different kinds, and they were all worthless compared to the buttery, cinnamony, sugary, crisp-edged, velvet perfection that were Susan's cookies.

As my teeth sank into the first cookie, still warm, I almost moaned. It was impossibly light. The aroma of the jasmine tea was heady combined with the rich scent of cookie. Susan slid into the chair next to me before I started chewing.

"I know there's only so much you can do and that you're trying to help. I don't think I could ever say thank you enough."

Guilt tickled at my heart. Not a punch, just a tickle. I was busting my ass to get their granddaughter clear of murder charges. Okay, I was busting my ass trying to prove that a guy I thought was a good guy was really a murderer, but Violet benefited. And I had just committed a felony in the name of justice. I was a bad ass crime solver. Who was taking a break for cookies. I swallowed and took a sip of the tea.

"I know you both would want me to do anything I could to make sure Violet wasn't blamed for a crime she didn't commit."

*Take that, David.* I wasn't thrilled I had to strong arm him to get the information I needed—the information he should have already given the cops, I might add—but I'd do it again.

Susan patted my hand and pushed the cookie plate closer. "Have another, dear. I know these are your favorites."

I nodded. And a mean thought occurred. Okay, semi mean.

"David, would you like a cookie?"

He had to drop that damn paper now. And he did. Enough to snag a cookie and raise it in the air as if toasting me. And then he put the paper back up again. Well, fine.

The sight of an unattended motorcycle parked in front of my house as I left the Horowitzes' made my stomach clench. I took the side stairs up to Dad's office as a shortcut and spotted Seth sitting at the kitchen table with Ben. A box I assumed was the game sat on the table in between them. Seth looked up and smiled at me. It was not a nice smile. Acid, sour and burning, churned in my stomach.

"Hey, Ben. How was school? Lots of homework?"

He turned to look at me. Based on his reaction, I'd guess my face didn't look friendly. "Um, yeah, I do have some stuff I need to take care of. Later, Seth." He didn't exactly run out of the room, but he didn't linger.

I slid into his vacant seat. "I told you to stay the hell away from me." My jaw was clenched so tight my neck ached.

Seth leaned back in his seat and stared at me, unnerving and intimidating. He'd certainly mastered the look despite how recent his foray into the world of crime had been. I stared back. I didn't feel very threatening but I was willing to fake it.

"Yeah, I did hear you say something like that but then I figured you must have been joking since you visited me this morning."

I shrugged. "You must have hallucinated me. I can guarantee I never want to see you ever again."

He leaned forward slowly, his eyes never leaving mine. "Oh, you know exactly what I'm talking about, Willa. You broke into my apartment this morning and when you got caught you lied that you were my girlfriend."

Dammit! It was a rookie mistake to tell the apartment manager that. I chuckled trying to control the laugh so it didn't waver. "Right. Your girlfriend. Are you sure it wasn't one of your bimbos? I mean, they all look pretty similar to me, which hardly seems like a coincidence now that I think about it. Let me repeat it using short, simple words: I did not break into your apartment." I stood up and crossed my arms. "Now, if you're done with your wild fantasies, I'd like you to leave."

He stayed in his seat. "What were you looking for?"

I rolled my eyes, pretending I was bored, and strode toward the foyer. "I'd love to say it was nice seeing you again, Seth, but we both know it wasn't. At least this time your insults were creative." I opened the front door and stood at it, barely hearing the scrape of the chair being pushed away from the table over the thump of my heart.

He stopped too close, looking down his nose at me. "When I figure out what you were looking for, I'll be back."

I fought the urge to press my back against the wall and away from his body. "Since it didn't take last time … stay away from me, this house, and anywhere you think I might turn up. And definitely stay away from Ben. I may not be a cop anymore but I still have friends who are, and I can make your life pretty damn uncomfortable, Seth."

"You don't scare me, Willa."

I got up in his face, dropping the mask I'd been so careful to keep up with him. "I should scare you, Seth. I have no idea what you want with my brother, but if you do anything to hurt him I will put you in the fucking ground."

He looked startled. "I … what … "

Ben's heavy footfalls sounded from the back hall. "Will, what were you doing this morning? Why is there ATF data in these files you pulled?"

The puzzle pieces rearranged themselves in my head. Seth's behavior, our confrontation at the garage, all the guns in his apartment.

"ATF? You're ATF." I stared at Seth.

He took a step back, looking like he'd swallowed his tongue.

Ben looked back and forth between us. "I don't understand. It was Seth's place? Why?"

Seth dropped his head and laughed, a short, mirthless bark. He turned to Ben. "Can you give us a minute, man? And, um, I need you to stay out of those files."

Ben shuffled off back down the hall and I tried, valiantly, to fight back the anger and disgust I was feeling.

"That's how you knew it was Reagan's murder. You knew before you called me about Matt's Cue. You were just playing me the other night. You wanted to figure out what I knew. And yesterday, I got too close to something so you … you asshole. Would you have actually screwed me too?"

"No. Willa, no."

"I don't believe you. You took Michael's death and used it to hurt me. How could you do that? No, I don't believe that you wouldn't have tricked me into bed if it served your purpose."

He reached for my hands but I jerked back, fisting them. He held his hands up, placating. What he'd done to me—Seth had crossed a line. I understood why now, but that didn't mean I had to like it. I didn't have to accept it, and I didn't have to forgive it.

"Look, I know I screwed this up and I should have told you from the start, but you have to know I wouldn't do that. I would not use you, ever. You mean too much to me."

"That's what you said the other night. And then yesterday you said that I was nothing but a … what was it? Oh, right, any port in a storm. So you'll forgive me if I don't know which lies I'm supposed to believe and which ones I'm not."

"Willa. Yesterday, I had to say that. I didn't want to."

"Yeah, you sounded all broken up. Poor you." I narrowed my eyes at him.

"I deserve that." He rubbed his jaw.

"Oh, and don't expect an apology for punching you. I'm not sure I won't be popping you again, prick."

"Also deserved. Everything you're saying now is justified, but I had my reasons."

"Right. Whatever your case is, I'm sure it's more important than not using your brother's death to put a PI off the track. It doesn't matter. I don't care. Tell me what is going on with Reagan."

"You broke into my apartment. You stole my case files."

"That sounds familiar. Except *you* got caught." My smile was genuine. I took a step back from him. I hadn't realized I'd been slowly advancing on him. I had warned him I wasn't above hitting him again, and I wasn't lying. "You want the truth? I took the key Michael gave me and walked right in. I searched your whole place. And then I boot-jacked your damn computer and took your files. But it was all for a good cause, Seth." I widened my eyes. "I didn't want to. I had to."

"You're mad at me, fine, but I need you to delete those files, Willa. You stole ATF property. That's a federal offense."

I held my hands out, wrists up. "Cuff me, then. You wanted to yesterday. Hold me down, Seth. You know I like it."

"Stop. This isn't a game, Willa."

"And that's another lie, isn't it? I've always been just a game to you."

He punched the doorframe, shaking the wall. All I could do was blink. He clenched his fist open and closed. His hand had to be killing him. Good.

He paced in a circle. "This was a mistake. I shouldn't have come here until I'd calmed down."

"You know where the door is. But before you go, you owe me what you know about Joe Reagan's murder. If you want me to delete the files then give me what I need to clear Violet Horowitz."

"Goddamn it, Willa. I don't know anything about his murder. I don't know who. I don't know why. And if I did, I still couldn't tell you. I *wouldn't* tell you. I'm not jeopardizing a federal investigation or letting you get yourself killed. Reagan was a possible informant, but that's as far as I got. Now I need you to back off."

This time I was the one clenching my fists. Seth had this pathological need to be the guy taking care of everything and everyone. It had been nice when we were kids. It had been kind of annoying as a teen. It was condescending and arrogant as an adult.

I took a deep breath and made sure my voice was low and even. "I'm an adult, Seth. I get to decide what I do."

"Then act like an adult, Willa, and think it through. You'll see I'm right." He slammed the front door on this way out.

I stared at the door for a moment and then grabbed Mom's keys out of the bowl. He'd never think a minivan was following him.

I caught up with him as he rounded the corner out of the subdivision. He'd slowed on his parents' street, which gave me extra time. I stayed three car lengths back like they did on TV. There were no other cars on the road until we got out to the parkway; most of our neighbors were retirees and people with solid nine-to-fives. The parkway was a parking lot. It was easy to keep him in sight and blend in with the other commuting boxes and parents on their way home from picking Junior up at soccer practice. The sky was beginning to darken more as evening took over fast. Daylight Saving Time had given us all an extra hour of sleep and me more cover for tailing Seth.

He turned off into a neighborhood and then, after a few lefts and rights, into a small cul-de-sac. I couldn't follow him in unseen, so I parked along the main road a little too close to a fire hydrant. It was shift change for the cops so I was safe for the next hour. Which is how long he took doing whatever it was. I was about to give up when I saw Seth zip out and head toward the other side of the subdivision. There were more cars now, going more slowly as they turned into driveways, so it was a piece of work to keep my eye on him and stay unnoticed.

He turned left onto a secondary road and I lost sight of him as I waited for my opportunity. The line of cars seemed never ending and I got antsy, slapping the steering wheel. I saw a short space for me to squeeze in and took it. The minivan wasn't great on cornering but it had a surprising amount of pick up and I swept into the line of traffic. No one even honked so it was clearly a common occurrence during rush hour.

Seth was way ahead of me at that point. I had no idea where he'd gone and just hoped he'd stayed straight and hadn't turned at the light I sailed through just as it was turning red. There was a whoop and spastic blue and white lights filled my rearview. I slowed and put on my blinker, but the cop flew past me after the expensive sport sedan that had rushed the light behind me. I flipped the blinker off and continued on a bit slower. I could still catch up to Seth if I figured out where he was going.

A mile up I saw his bike parked in the lot of a fast food restaurant. Considering it was the first time I'd ever covertly followed someone, I'd give myself a solid C. Okay, C minus.

I backed into a spot across from the door with the back of the minivan against a wall. I'd be able to see Seth coming out and get out of the lot easily. Then I sat and waited. And waited. I was about to get out and look into the windows of the restaurant when a tapping on the driver's window let me know that Seth had busted me. He must have taken a very roundabout way to sneak up on me. I turned to see him holding a cup.

"Chocolate shake?"

Sonofabitch. I hit the button and unlocked the doors. He walked around the front of the vehicle and got in the passenger side, handing me the icy drink. I slipped the paper off the top of the straw and sucked up some of the treat. He sipped his own in silence, not looking at me.

"You took a calculated risk running the light. Bad luck about the cop."

I shrugged and stuck my shake in the cup holder. "He popped the Audi instead. When did you see me?"

"When you caught up to me past Mom and Dad's house. It was a good plan to use the minivan, but you didn't have a chance. Especially since I was expecting you to follow me."

"Right."

"I know you better than you think I do, Will. You can't drop it. You need to know—it's just who you are. I'd forgotten that until today. Maybe if I hadn't then yesterday …"

We sat in silence for a few moments. Anyone who saw us would think they were watching an awkward first date or an even more awkward breakup.

"I'm really mad at you, Seth. Like, raging mad. You work for the ATF? When did that start? Wait, you know what? I don't care. God. You know how to push my buttons like they have monetary value."

He nodded. "Right back at you, Sunshine. If you had just stayed out of it—"

"This is my fault? You calling me a whore is my fault?"

"Yes. No."

The look I shot him was pure venom. It definitely was looking more like a breakup.

"I never called you a whore—"

"Close enough."

"Yeah." He looked contrite but he'd also just tried to tell me I was to blame for him doing it, so that mitigated any forgiveness I was willing to offer. He also looked lost. I couldn't help but wonder if he'd thrown himself into his work in the wake of Michael's death. That he'd used it like I'd used Santa Fe. I tried to squash the empathy.

"I wasn't doing anything except some research as training until I caught you snooping."

"And that's why you went to Killian's? For research and training?"

He had me there. I had excused it as training but it was more than that.

"How did you sneak up on me?" He wasn't the only one who could answer a question with another question. "I was watching the door."

"There's another door on the other side by the drive-through. I just walked around."

Of course there was another door. He'd probably picked this specific location for that second door. I picked up the milkshake and sucked morosely.

His smile was resigned. "If I tell you everything I think is safe for you to know, will you drop it? Please."

"Scout's honor."

"You were a Girl Scout for like a month."

"The boys got to do cool stuff and they expected us to sew because we were girls."

"You're impossible."

"Yeah, yeah, make with the sparkly special agent gut spilling now, please." Humor was the only way I was going to get through this situation. That and a determination to forget, for now, all the shit he'd said yesterday. I'd deal with it later.

"About two years ago several Class Three federal firearms dealers on the East Coast reported robberies. Really clean robberies. So much so that the ATF thought the first one was an inside job. Until the second one. And then the third. It was after the third that we knew we had a serious problem on our hands. All totaled there had been over two hundred weapons and peripherals stolen—semi-automatic weapons, silencers, assault rifles."

That was a lot of missing firepower and Class Three was serious business. Not some little mom-and-pop, dime-store operations. They would have state-of-the-art alarm systems. Not many people could get through those kinds of safeguards and get away clean. Clean enough that it looked like an inside job would have been almost impossible.

"That's serious money," I said.

"Hundreds of thousands of dollars. Not to mention guns that can't be traced back to the criminals buying them."

"I can see why the ATF is concerned," I said, putting the milk shake in the cup holder.

"And why I was willing to say the things I said to get you to back off?" he asked.

"Now that you put it that way, what choice did you have? I mean, treating me like a grownup and telling me the truth was clearly off the table. Then you couldn't play the hero and rescue me from having to think big thoughts or make decisions. Thank you so much for reminding me why I'm furious with you." I clicked the button to disengage the locks on the minivan. "Oh, and thanks for the shake, Seth. Get out."

# CHAPTER

## 13

**BLOW DRYING MY HAIR,** I thought about where someone would store that many guns. You'd need to break up the stash and still keep them fairly close for sales. If Joe Reagan was being groomed as a confidential informant by the ATF, that meant he had some connection to the guns, the people that took the guns, or the people buying the guns. I hadn't even considered that he was one of the people who stole the guns. He was a bottom-feeder. These heists were done by people who had unreal smarts, people like my little brother—had he been so inclined and lacking the strongest moral center I'd ever come across, even for a teenage boy.

I hadn't actually promised Seth I would delete the files. I was sure he assumed I would. He was right that the files were federal property. I just didn't see the harm in reading them first. Seth said he didn't know who killed Joe Reagan or why, but that didn't mean there wasn't information in the files that would lead me to the answers both of us were looking for. I was being a good citizen.

Damn, I was good at rationalizing committing borderline illegal acts.

I knocked on Ben's door, cringing as I heard the whir and beep of the machines that crowded the room. I didn't hate computers. I mean, my phone was all kinds of awesome, but it mostly confused me. As did all the other computer stuff. I had no idea how they worked even after years of lectures and demonstrations. But Ben did, and if it had a computer in it, he could make it do what he wanted. Like that neat trick with my phone copying Seth's laptop. I didn't even know how he got the files back off my phone with it still in my pocket.

I knocked again, louder, and then slowly opened the door. With two male best friends in my teen years, I had learned the lesson that you didn't burst through any closed door unless you wanted to see a whole lot you weren't prepared for. My awkward crush had begun after a too-quick swing of a bathroom door and a freshly showered high school senior Seth. The last thing I wanted to see was my naked little brother. The very thought of the possibility of it happening ... I wasn't prepared to even consider that horror.

"Ben?"

I had gotten no response because his headphones were cranked up so loud I could hear the music across the room. Hearing loss had not been mentioned on the list of things I was to prevent while I was "in charge," but I was sure that wouldn't be an argument Mom would accept. I flicked the light switch up and down a few times and watched as panic and terror registered on his face. He ripped the headphones from his ears.

"Are you nuts?! I have backups running. *Had* backups running. Since you just rebooted them four times, I'm sure they're no longer viable."

The attack was one I had gotten before. I wasn't about to apologize. Come on, it was a light switch. He should have expected people to use a light switch to turn a light on and off.

"I guess I assumed after the last time you would have taken something so critical off the light switch, Ben."

He looked like a stubborn toddler. "It's temporary and only because Mom told me I can't rewire the room."

"Whatever. You can back up the Internet later. I have a job for you. One that you can do while you study for your test."

I used air quotes for *study* because we both knew he'd been doing no such thing. He didn't need to. He eyed me with suspicion.

"Like what? Not helping you turn on Dad's computer, right? Or maybe you need to change the channel?"

"I need the files you got from my phone."

"The files you stole when you broke into Seth's apartment? Our friend Seth, who happens to be an ATF agent? Files that must be a part of an ATF investigation that Seth is conducting?"

I nodded. "Yeah."

He fiddled with the cable on his head phones, still spilling out music. "He told me to delete them."

I nodded again. "Yeah."

He began to knot the cable around his fingers. "What makes you think I didn't delete them?"

"If you had then you wouldn't be acting like Angelica Huston in the orange scene of *The Grifters*."

Another movie I probably shouldn't have let a preteen watch. I was a crap older sister. By conventional standards, anyway.

"But if they're ATF files, can't we get in trouble for having them?"

"Yeah, but I doubt Seth is going to turn me in considering he'd have to explain how I got them in the first place."

I was a horrible person. A truly awful individual.

Ben reached into his backpack and pulled out a sheaf of papers. He looked sheepish. "I was going to shred them in the computer lab at school tomorrow."

I took the pages from him. "And the computer files?"

"They're only on your phone. I was remote printing them on the high speed via WiFi when I figured out what they were and then with Seth here ..."

"Okay, listen. What I asked you to do today wasn't right. I can't tell you I don't want you to do PI work and then ask you for help when it suits me. I was caught up in the moment and I didn't think it through."

"The ends don't justify the means."

I smiled. "If you want to be clichéd about it. But here's the thing, I don't actually agree they don't. Not always, anyway. Moral absolutism isn't my strong suit. You have to make choices and you make the best ones for everyone concerned. But you're not everyone, Benjy. You're my brother, and I made a promise to always take care of you. I do that by putting your needs first."

Dammit. I wasn't any different than Seth. I knew if it came down to it, I'd easily hurt Ben's feelings to protect him. Plus I had already decided that the best thing for him was to go to college and use his big brain for something important.

That's some dysfunctional bullshit right there. That didn't make me not pissed at Seth. I was an adult and Ben was not. I shook off the big thoughts I'd admonished Seth for not letting me think on my own and said goodnight to my brother.

I went to my room in the basement. It was cool down there but it felt good. Like maybe I could sleep if everything was just right. My brain could stop thinking about everything. Mom had said meditation would help the insomnia. I couldn't ever clear my mind. There was too much inside my brain. Getting rid of it all was impossible. But I could put it away. Everything but the case. The murder, the guns, the money.

The money in his house. I knew where it had come from now. Reagan had to have been involved in selling the guns regularly. He hadn't just gotten hold of the one. But how did he have that much cash on him? If he was in business with the thieves, they wouldn't have left that much cash with a low-level guy. Unless they didn't know about the cash. Maybe Reagan had been skimming. Maybe he had been killed because he'd betrayed his partners.

My eyes slipped closed once then twice. I was just too tired to think anymore. I dropped my clothes to the floor and crawled into the bed determined to get some kind of sleep. Even an hour or two. Then I slipped into unconsciousness like a stone being dropped into a well.

———

I actually got a decent night's sleep. Better than decent, really. I almost didn't know what to do without the crushing weight of exhaustion pressing in on me five minutes after I woke up. I knew it wouldn't last. I had an hour, at best. I hoped I could extend it with coffee, but maybe the caffeine really was only making it worse.

I found a flash drive and a sheaf of papers lying on top of the ones I'd gotten from Ben last night. I flipped through the pages, skimming information about high-end alarm systems and how to bypass them.

Clearly Ben had read the files and gotten curious about the thefts. So much for the lecture I'd given him last night. If there was any doubt that we were related despite our very different appearances, this was proof.

The only chance I had of getting Seth to agree to let me help on the case was proving that I could carry my own weight. If I could get him off focusing on my personal safety and onto my valuable contributions, I'd have him. He wanted to wrap up this case badly. I'd use that as leverage after letting him whine for a bit about how I'd promised him I'd stay out of it. We both knew I wasn't going to let it go. He'd admitted as much, so he wasn't going to be surprised that I was still in.

I needed to let the Horowitzes know that Violet was mostly off the hook. I wasn't sure how I was going to go about telling them that without giving any actual information, but I knew Seth wouldn't let them twist in the wind too long. The Horowitzes were a nice retired couple trying to help their granddaughter. And if he didn't see it my way, an anonymous call to the tip line letting them know that Joe Reagan had been the subject of a federal investigation might have to happen.

I felt guilty for lying in bed so long even if I was thinking about the case. I could probably get some more sleep if I closed my eyes, rolled over, pulled the covers back up to my ears, and snuggled down into the sweet spot. I wanted to. I probably needed to. But this case was more important. Seth needed to bust this gun ring. The Horowitzes needed the truth about Joe Reagan's death. While he didn't deserve to be murdered, I was convinced he bought and paid for it with his actions. Maybe it was harsh, but he wasn't an innocent. He'd gotten himself into something and if he hadn't been smart enough or moral enough to get himself out of it, well, I wasn't too upset that he'd met his end at the hands of a confederate. Honor among thieves was a concept that had been long outdated even when the phrase had been coined. And Robin Hood had been fictional. Not that anyone could ever convince me stealing and selling high-powered firearms was somehow a benefit to the people.

The anger, righteous or not, spurred me out of bed and into a travel mug of coffee. I sat out on the back deck and went through all the case files. It was cold but the sun kept me warm enough. I was not going to miss the rare sunny fall day even if I was a little chilly. There was a piece somewhere, in my files or Seth's, or maybe in Violet's head, that would solve it all. Just one piece was all we needed. Finding it was the trick. Well, finding it and then knowing it was the right piece.

I reviewed the new information on Reagan's known associates. Apparently Ben had gotten bored with his single assignment and stolen my case files. He'd pulled together an impressive array of data on Reagan, his friends, and even Violet.

From everything I saw, Reagan was a dumbass. How he could have even gotten hooked up with a high-level crew like this was a sticking point for me. I couldn't find a logical connection for him being involved, but he had to have been, otherwise Seth wouldn't have been grooming him as an informant. So he was at least on the fringes and capable of getting useful information for the ATF. That role belied Reagan's intelligence and skill set, if the high school transcripts Ben had dug up on him were accurate. Barely graduated high school even with remedial everything and plenty of vocational courses. He hadn't been good at anything. I mean, I knew the old phrase, God rarely gives with both hands, but in Reagan's case it appeared God hadn't given enough of a damn to give a pinch. What in the hell had Violet seen in the loser?

I must had tipped my head back for a minute to think and let the fall sun warm my face because I startled awake with sticky eyes, feeling groggy. Apparently, I could have slept more. Even with sixteen ounces of strong coffee in me. Once this case was over I was going back to the doctor. I had to admit that I had a problem. *Hi, my name is Willa and I can't sleep, you know, except when my body just decides to shut down like the breaker has been flipped.*

I took my time in the shower. I'd heard that water could boost creativity. Something about negative ions. I had no idea, but Mom told Dad to take a shower every time he was stumped on a problem. She could have just been trying to get rid of him when he was being annoying. I didn't come up with anything new on the case but my hair was deep conditioned and I was a little more relaxed, so there was that. Going a few rounds in a cage match would have been more relaxing than all the obsessing I'd been doing lately.

I had, once upon a time, been a fairly laid-back person. I mean, sure, I had tormented Seth over his bimbos and protected Ben like he was made from spun sugar, but nothing else got me too high or too low. Spending my first nine years on earth with Leila as a mother made such excesses impossible. She was too flighty, too scattered. Someone had to be the grownup, and panicking every time we lost an apartment for unpaid rent or had to move to a new town for another *this is my big break* part would have made it all that much worse. Coming to live with Dad and his new wife allowed me to finally be a kid. I didn't blame Leila and I didn't leave to live with Dad because I didn't love her. I did. I do. I just needed a different life. She had chosen the road and the theater. I chose Dad and school. A normal life. Dad had dived in with joy and a pretty big case of nerves, but he put me first. Always. That was a big relief. Being able to screw up and have a safe place to land is a gift every kid deserves.

# CHAPTER

## 14

SETH DIDN'T TRY TO disguise the annoyance and weariness on his face when I walked in the garage's office door an hour later. He upped and downed my body with his eyes, assessing I didn't know what. He seemed satisfied with what he saw.

"Dammit, Sunshine, do I need to duct tape your ass at home? What part of me telling you that it's not safe for either of us if you're here sounded like an open invitation?"

I looked down at my clothes. "But I got dressed all special to be here." It was the outfit I'd worn to Killian's. I looked nothing like a biker babe but rather the girl who doesn't understand that jeans are not appropriate for family celebrations. Exactly who I was.

"You're just killing me." But he smiled when he said it.

"I wouldn't have come, I swear, but you've been ignoring my texts and I have information you need."

He looked like he wanted to say something more but we heard the clang of footfalls on the steel staircase. Four feet. Two people. Seth looked at me and I saw his face change. He stepped toward me and just before he grabbed me he said, "I'm sorry."

And then his mouth was on mine. I told him to never put his hands on me again. I told him if he ever touched me again, I'd do him harm. But if I'd known he was capable of touching me like this, I'd have threatened him for *not* putting his hands on me. He wasn't sad and grieving. He wasn't a guy taking a chance with a childhood friend all grown up. He was danger and bar fights and car wrecks; fierce, all teeth and tongue, gripping me tightly, holding me roughly, pressing into me, bowing me back with the force of his body. I could only hold on and try to meet him halfway. If he'd asked, I absolutely would have let him cuff me, hold me down—hell, I might be okay with him stealing my car when he was done. I hated to be the cliché girl who got off on the bad boy, but his mouth made me vow to rethink clichés—once I was able to think again. It was like we were reinventing foreplay. My mind fogged to anything but him and his mouth on mine, his hands on my body.

"Whoa. Sorry boss."

He pulled away from me and the tension rushed out from in between us. I blinked a few times, trying to get my bearings. No one had ever kissed me anywhere close to that and if I never got it again … that wasn't okay.

"What the hell do you want? I'm busy." Even his voice was different—rougher, raspier, mean. I wasn't even sure how a voice could convey that much menace in so few words. I realized as awful as he'd been the other day, he likely could have done and said worse. I wasn't ready to forgive him, but perhaps I had gotten off easy in his quest to push me away.

His hands held me in place against him, keeping my back to the men, preventing them from seeing me. It was smart for his cover. It effectively turned me from a point of interest to a non-entity. Just a woman he was sleeping with. And up against him, our thighs pressed together, hip to hip, I was absolutely willing to revisit that specific topic.

The men had slunk back down the stairs as quickly as Seth had started yelling. Undercover Seth was a hell of a lot scarier than the small glimpse I got the last time I'd visited. But then, just like that, he was gone.

"I'm sorry. I just … I'm so sorry." His hands had become gentle again. Like a switch flipped from raw biker badass criminal to sensitive badass hero. It was enough to give a girl whiplash. I couldn't even begin to imagine how he did that. "You told me not to—"

I gently pushed him away from me, mentally restarting my brain. "Buck up, camper. I'm not about to challenge you to a duel. You did what you felt you needed to protect your cover."

He checked that the two guys weren't still outside the door and locked it. When he turned back he made sure he was ten feet away from me. I guess he didn't trust that I wasn't going to make good on my old threat. "You said you have information I needed."

Back to business. Fine by me. I was starting to be a little embarrassed about my nympho thoughts. Not that he knew about them, but that didn't mean they weren't real. And still hovering somewhere in the back of my head. One slipped to the front and I blushed, wondering what I'd need to do to get that side of him to come out again. I shook my head, digging the flash drive out of my pocket and held it out.

He plucked it out of my fingers and backed across the room. "And this is?" he asked.

It was wrong, but I felt the need to tease him. "A flash drive. Some investigator you are."

He muttered something under his breath and I decided to stop being an immature ass. "Some research on breaching high-end security systems like the ones from the robberies."

"You know we've got guys that do this. They have access to all the federal databases and information you can't get on Google."

"Why don't you look at it before you dismiss the information, Seth? Unless you enjoy being Undercover Seth and want to do it for a lot longer. He's a charmer with the ladies." He looked away. If he'd thought we weren't going to deal with that at some point, he'd been put on notice. That conversation was going to be loud. "There are only a few people who can keep up with the constant changes made on those security systems. Those people also know how to stay out of federal databases."

He held the flash drive so hard I thought he was going to bend it. "You didn't delete the files."

I squirmed in my too-high boots as he glared at me. "I figured if you really wanted me to delete them you would have made sure I had. I took that as a sign that you were flexible on the matter."

He shoved the drive in his pocket and began to pace. "I should have known. I don't know why I thought you'd just let me take care of it."

"You mean take care of Violet? She's under suspicion of murder, Seth. She's scared. Her grandparents are scared. And we both know she didn't do it. Look, I don't want to screw up what you're working on, but I'm not going to let this go. All those qualities you hate about me are what made me a great cop. You either take jurisdiction or you take the consequences of me being in your case."

"I could just arrest you for Obstruction."

I knew he wouldn't do that. He knew he wouldn't do that. So I doubled down. "And keep me jailed for how long? What happens to you after you have to explain how I was capable of obstructing? You lose your job, this bust goes down the drain, Violet has to stay on the run. And Thanksgivings are awkward forever."

He shook his head. "You are the most infuriating person. I just have no idea what do with you. None. You're impossible."

I didn't smile. I stood quietly, barely breathing. I owed him the time it took to accept he had no other option than to let me in with dignity. Also, I wasn't entirely sure he wouldn't arrest me just because I'd gotten cocky and pushed him too far.

"You do anything that I haven't cleared and, so help me, Willa, I will drag you off to a safe house and cuff you to a pipe in the basement."

I smiled at him. I couldn't help myself. "That's kinky. You didn't even list that in the options the other day."

He dropped his head and laughed before looking back up at me. "Where did this information come from?"

I hadn't planned to keep Ben's involvement from him. I wasn't happy about it, but I knew a stern lecture from Seth would actually work on Ben. I was counting on Seth blowing two gaskets when he found out.

"Ben."

"Ben? You let Ben read the files? That was so irresponsible. You knew I didn't want you involved because it was dangerous. Ben is—"

"Whoa. Slow down. I asked Ben last night if he had access to the files and he said he didn't. That they were only on my phone."

"He gave you what you needed to steal them from my laptop, didn't he?" Seth's pacing had turn into stomping. If the building hadn't been cinderblock the guys below us would have had drywall dust falling on them.

"Yes. I didn't tell him what it was for but … it was a mistake. I told him I shouldn't have asked."

"But then he read the files, so clearly you didn't make it clear to him. Dammit, Willa."

"I'm mad at him, too, but he left the drive and notes for me this morning. What did you want me to do? It's not like I could go to school to yell at him for interfering in a federal investigation. That seems hypocritical at best."

"I'll to talk to him. Make it clear he's had his first and last taste of acting like you."

I nodded, ignoring the sting that little insult carried. "Definitely. I totally agree. But … this doesn't change our deal, right?" I cringed, waiting for him to start yelling at me.

"You're just killing me. Killing me, Willa."

Okay, not yelling. That was good. "So you already knew what Ben can do?" I asked.

"We've talked a bit. He's been careful to keep it all hypotheticals. I assumed there was more than what he'd alluded to. I am actually a good agent, you know? A nosy PI in my case is an anomaly." He eyed, me. "Anomaly means it happens one time only. Got it?"

I nodded. I didn't want to give away too much because it wasn't my story to tell. "These people—the ones who can do what Ben can do—they can sniff out cops. I don't even understand one percent of it, but it's all IP traces and satellite bounces and routing through public WiFi to a hotspot on a damn cell phone at some goat herder's hut in Dakar. And your guys come blundering with a router named ATF42 and these hackers just scatter to another layer. Like climbing a tree and watching the little kids try to figure out where everyone went."

"But he's safe, right? He's not going to call any attention to himself?"

"The good guys couldn't find Ben even if he was in the same room, and the so-called bad guys are his friends. Or however much you can call a person you only know as Hackopocalypse a friend. He says he's safe and I believe him. Mostly because he's knows I'd kick his ass if he lied about something like that."

"And the actual bad guys. The ones who steal guns?"

"Ben's note said he's compiled data on the most likely options for the tech guy that breached the security systems and that your team can probably figure out who they are IRL."

"IRL?"

"In real life," I said.

"What else is on the drive?"

"Details of how to get through the security systems that are supposed to be unbeatable. Ben says they're designed by guys who are five years behind the curve. Stuff like this really needs to be built by these kids roaming the dark net. Only then would they be unbeatable. Until the next twelve-year-old comes up with a way to tear it all down. It's changing at the pace of a heartbeat, Seth. And these former government wonks just can't keep up."

"So what you're saying is that the security systems are about as secure as a paper bag."

"A wet one."

He rubbed his hand over his forehead. "Tim is not going to like this."

"Tim?" I asked.

"My boss. He's not thrilled about this op anyway. Me."

"Aw, is there someone you can't charm?"

"No, he likes me just fine. It's just me being on this case. And here." He glanced around the office and then looked directly at me. "I'm a little closer to home than he'd like."

"He'd probably find out about the pipe in the basement, in case you change your mind. It's just a thought."

"Will, honestly, I am so far out on a limb with this case that I can't take another step without crashing down. You are a baby step shuffle as long as you do what I say. And, for the record, I don't hate the things about you that made you a good cop. They just scare me. And I finally get why you quit the force."

"Oh?"

"You're too outside the box for a local police force. You had to have been chafing at all the rules and bureaucracy."

Lying to him was an option. I could probably have done it convincingly enough, but he was trusting me so he deserved a real answer.

"Yeah, that wasn't my favorite aspect, but it was more than that. After Michael died I just felt like I was in the wrong place for the wrong reason."

"What does that mean?"

"It means … being a cop was good until it wasn't. It wasn't about the job. It was about me. Everything changed that day."

He looked sad. Well, of course he did. He was in the middle of a case that was beating him down and I had just reminded him that his brother was dead.

"I'm sorry, Seth. I shouldn't have brought it up," I said. "This is business."

"No. It's okay. Sometimes it helps to talk about him with someone who really knew him. They don't get it. They didn't know him like we did."

"Well, that's it. Everything changed. And I didn't. Or maybe I did and the job didn't. I just didn't feel like it would ever be the same again."

"And Santa Fe?"

How to explain that I was afraid to see him again after that night without sounding like a coward? Even if I could admit it to myself, I wasn't about to admit it to him.

"Mom thought it would be good to have a change of scenery. And Leila has a new job teaching and a new husband. He's an accountant, if you can believe that. There was this cool drama festival they put on at the college she's teaching at. So I spent some time not being me. It was easier. For a little while anyway."

"I missed you."

My stomach flipped. I didn't know how I felt about him missing me. Or how I felt about him telling me.

# CHAPTER

# 15

**OUTSIDE THE GARAGE I** sat behind the wheel of my car trying not to
think about how confusing everything with Seth had gotten in just a
few days. I'd had it all under control. I had barely thought about him for
years. We'd done the family stuff and holidays, of course, our two little
families converging. He hey-ed and head nodded in passing, but seeing
him at Michael's memorial service had wiped out all the time that had
passed. I was fifteen again and he was the handsome football star who
grinned at me in the hall and set the girls around me into a tizzy.

I cranked the engine and backed out of the lot to head for home.
The lane was quiet and dark. There weren't any houses on this end of
the road, just small businesses that needed a little property and some

room to make noise like Seth's garage. No streetlights either. Cinder-block buildings here and there. It hadn't been built up, in a stasis from earlier decades, just like the area around Joe Reagan's house. There were little pockets like this all over Fairfax County. The parkway and 66 coursed through and around, making it ridiculously easy to get from point A to point B and ridiculously time-consuming to get from point B to point C. Unless it was rush hour, of course. Then all bets were off.

It wasn't hard to see how some gun runners had made this area their home base. All they'd need is a reasonable cover for moderate comings and goings of no more than five guys. The fewer people involved, the fewer ways the cash would need to be split.

There were no other cars either behind or in front of me and no oncoming traffic. The vast tree line deepened as the road curved and wound around itself. My headlights lit the asphalt only a few yards ahead and the trees arced over the road away from the power lines. It was a distinctly claustrophobic feel. Dark and quiet, as if I were the only person in the world. The hair on the back of my neck began to prickle and stand up. I felt as if I were being watched even though I knew it was impossible.

I finally saw the stoplight for the parkway and my nerves settled down. While the parkway didn't have streetlights either, it was more populated with people coming and going across the county. The sign told me it was eight miles to 66, and I'd be home long before that. The light was red when I got to it, no surprise, and as I slowed and stopped the car gave a faint shudder. I could have sworn I got a whiff of pancakes.

I turned right onto the parkway instead of left; if something was wrong with the car I didn't want it giving out on me in the middle of that wide intersection. I could make a turnaround up at the exit a mile or so on without losing too much time if I needed. Better to take that extra time than stall in oncoming traffic and risk a wreck. I coasted onto the wide dirt shoulder and clicked on the hazard lights.

I pulled a heavy flashlight out of my glove box, grateful for Dad insisting on it the moment I learned to drive. Again, that nervy feeling of being watched had me reaching into the door well to pull out the collapsible baton he'd also insisted on. Dad put Boy Scouts to shame with his preparedness. His motto was always to hope for the best but prepare for the worst. Maybe that hadn't always been his worldview but having a daughter had certainly caused him to consider all kinds of things in a different light. Once that daughter got to be a teenager and a driver, that different light had extended to making sure said daughter was protected even when he wasn't in arm's reach to do the protecting.

I popped the hood and got out. I had no idea what I thought I was going to do. I knew how to perform some basic maintenance—check and change the oil, add more coolant—but troubleshooting damage or repair was beyond me. Had I been thinking clearly I would have just called Seth. He was less than five minutes away and he did know something about cars. I wasn't thinking clearly. And, honestly, part of me still resisted that I needed him to rescue me, even for something as stupid as looking at my car.

I shone the flashlight inside the engine compartment but couldn't see anything obviously wrong. No smoke or obvious fluid leaks. No fire. Which I assumed was good. And I didn't see any missing parts as I moved the beam of light around. I also didn't see the car pull up. The crunch of tires on broken glass alerted me. What should have alerted me was headlights, but the car's lights were off. The hair on the back on my neck prickled again. Call me paranoid but I'd already armed myself for no real reason. The prickle traveled down to the small of my back.

You saw it on the news every day—people gone missing after running out to pick up some milk. Their cars found days later, miles from their intended destinations. No sign of them. I knew that the majority of intentional harm to people was committed by so-called loved ones, but even so, thousands of people went missing every year at the hands of someone they'd never seen before. The ones who found their way home again were called miracles for good reason.

I heard the car door open and shut furtively. I shot my wrist out and the baton snicked open. There would have been no way he'd have missed the sound, but I doubted he'd know what it was. I stepped to the side of the car closest to the road, keeping the baton flush to my leg. I couldn't discount that it might be a friendly person who truly wanted to help. I also couldn't shake the feeling that I was in trouble. Lizard brain was beating logic all to hell.

I took another step, keeping my body slightly turned toward the road. I was now fully visible to whoever had pulled in behind my car.

"Hello, little lady. Car trouble?"

Ick. *Little lady* is not a phrase that should come out of anyone's mouth unless they're channeling the spirit of John Wayne at a séance. I'm serious. That's just gross. And I'm not that little. I'm taller than the average American woman by five inches. I'm pretty solid too. Running has kept me limber and loose. Self-defense classes and police academy training have taught me how to defend myself against a much larger opponent. And I knew that my best defense, was not, in fact, a good offense but rather my opponent underestimating me.

"Yeah. I'm not sure what happened. I'm not really good with cars."

I made sure my voice was a little higher than normal, like the average woman uncertain in what could possibly be a dangerous situation. Like I needed permission to have car trouble or be bad with engines. Like I didn't know this strange man but I wanted to think he had good intentions because that was the kind of shit women dealt with every day. But I wasn't an average woman and I wasn't capable of ignoring the menace radiating off him in waves. The prickle was now a full-blown DEFCON 1. I was vibrating with fight-or-flight. Except there was no flight available. There was road and there was woods, and I wasn't choosing either. Fight it was.

He took a step toward me more aggressively than a person with help on their mind. I pressed the button on the flashlight and swung the beam up into his face. He let out a noise like a bark and rushed at me. The light glinted off something metallic that I realized was a knife. I arced the baton at him, aiming for just above his elbow. The metal connected with a dull thud that I felt rather than heard and he howled. I knew how painful a blow the baton could deliver. Even in training a reminder prod caused pain to radiate down your limb. I hadn't given him a love tap either.

"Bitch."

The slur was a breathy moan. It flashed through my mind to hit him again. I liked *bitch* even less than I liked *little lady*.

"I don't need your kind of help, so mosey along and grab some ice for your ouchie."

I hoped today wasn't the day that my smart mouth got me in deep trouble. With a shaky hand, I leveled the flashlight beam at the ground and stepped away to the relative safety of the woods on the other side of the car. If he was feeling vengeful or just clumsy with his throbbing arm, I didn't want him to run me down. I heard the car door slam. He rocketed off the shoulder and bumped back up onto the road. His dark-ish car was unremarkable, with no license plate to identify it. So clearly I wasn't going to be able to look him up for a later meeting and perhaps introduce him to some uniformed friends so we could all have a chat about the proper way to introduce oneself to a stranger. Like, don't bring a knife.

When I was sure he was gone, I got back in the car, locked all the doors, and called Seth. He was not happy and I didn't give him all the details. Just a quick call to let him know where I was, why I was there, and that I'd made a new friend.

The few minutes I had to myself were spent trying to ramp down my adrenaline and remember any small details I could about the encounter. Both Seth and Boyd would want as much as I could give them. Not that there was much.

Soon the single headlamp of Seth's motorcycle shone through the back window of the car. He arrived in considerably less time than it should have taken, so he clearly hadn't obeyed any traffic laws. I stayed in the car with the doors locked until I saw his annoyed face looming just outside the driver's window.

He knocked harder than necessary. I hadn't thought he'd be in too jocular a mood since he'd huffed a great sigh when he heard it was me on the phone and then made a grunt of displeasure upon the news of my predicament. I assumed the word of my knife-wielding admirer would have gotten more of a reaction, but there was just the grunt. I assumed it was displeasure. He could have had gas. And, frankly, as a victim, I had been hoping for more ginger treatment. Minus, of course, any lectures about women on dark roads at night. Or, god forbid, the assumption that it had something to do with the cases and starting on yet another hissy fit. At minimum, I deserved a brief inquiry about my physical or emotional well-being. Or a side hug.

I got out of the car, shutting the door a bit harder than necessary. Okay, I slammed it. He held his hand out and when I shrugged, he grabbed the flashlight from me.

"Manners much?"

"Willa, I was busy, okay? Remember the ongoing federal investigation you stomped your way into? I didn't need to come out here to help you fix your car when someone else was willing to do it."

Of course. The one time he doesn't pay attention is when I'm telling him someone tried to kill me. "What exactly did you hear me say, Seth? I said a guy stopped and pretended to help. Pretended. He attacked me with a knife instead. I fought him off."

He finally looked up from the engine compartment. In the dark I couldn't see his face but I was sure he wore an expression of disbelief. "You were attacked?"

"Yes, Seth. A guy rolled up behind me with no headlights, interior light of his car off, and trying his damndest to be unheard. Then he pulled a knife on me. Are you up to speed now?"

"Shit, Will. I'm so sorry. I just missed the … It doesn't matter. You're okay?"

I flipped my hand to open the baton and raised it up. "Just fine. Although he's probably regretting taking up attacking women on the side of the road as a hobby."

"You know that's illegal, right? The baton, I mean."

"Seriously? That's what's on your mind? The legality of my defensive weapon? Gosh, I hope he doesn't call the cops on me."

"Of course not. I don't know why … Let's start over. You said you're fine. You're sure?"

I nodded. "He didn't even get within a foot of me. Finally, these stupid overly long arms came in handy."

"Did you get a good look at him?"

"Good enough. I flashed him in the eyes with the flashlight when his intentions were clear. Not that it'll help much. He was pretty generic."

"Well, talk it out. Maybe something will pop while you're remembering."

I closed my eyes and tried to remember anything useful from the second I'd had to look at him. But I had tried that exercise while waiting for Seth to arrive and had gotten nowhere.

"Average height, average build but running a bit to fat, short hair. A tattoo on his neck, I think. Maybe. T-shirt and jeans or work pants. Not office work, manual labor. There's something else. I can't quite get it to gel yet."

"Concentrate on the tattoo then."

I put my hand over my eyes, pressing my thumb and middle finger into my temples. I dug them in a little harder, the pressure allowing me to focus better.

"It might have been a shadow, Seth. I flipped the light up to his face and swung. I don't know anything for sure except I made contact. It was enough to get him to take off."

"Okay. That's fine. Did he speak to you? What about his voice?"

"Ugh. Yes, he was gross. Called me little lady. His voice was greasy-sounding. I know that doesn't make any sense. But it was smug and one of those voices that puts your teeth on edge. Like Mr. Barlow."

I knew he'd remember the calculus teacher that didn't teach so much as berate and humiliate. His voice matched his weasely personality.

"Makes perfect sense. *Greasy* captures it perfectly, if you've heard it before. What about the car?"

"No back plate. I never saw the front. Dark. Early model small commuter box. Maybe a Corolla or a Hyundai. No damage from the view I got of it as he floored it out of here."

Seth put his arm around my shoulder and gave me a squeeze, gently pulling me along to the bike.

"We need to examine the scene. Maybe he dropped the knife." I eased away from him, taking the flashlight and aiming the beam at the area around and behind the bike.

After a few seconds he reached down and grabbed the flashlight. "Will, we won't find anything tonight and the reality is there's nothing usable. The side of the road like this is awash with trace." He handed me his helmet and got on the bike.

"This is your helmet. You need it," I said.

"Willa, please, for once in your life, don't argue. Put the damn helmet on."

# CHAPTER

## 16

**SETH OPENED THE DOOR** to the apartment. "Can I get you something to drink? A soda? Or I could make you some tea. Maybe." He looked at the door to the kitchen as if he wasn't really sure what he would find in there. "We might have some left over. I...I might have some, I mean," he said.

I suspected Seth was regretting the decision to bring me here. I felt it, hanging between us. Michael. The promise I'd made to never get involved with his brother. I was sure he'd extracted the same promise from Seth too. And we'd both broken our word just hours after the memorial service.

"Why don't you sit down and I'll see what I can pull together, okay?"

I allowed him to gently drag me over to the couch, where I flopped down. Gracefulness was not my gift. Coordination had been gained by years of practice, but it was beaten out by a bone-deep weariness and the chemical cocktail of adrenaline, serotonin, and dopamine. It was all I could do to keep upright.

I tried to play it cool, but we both knew I wasn't close to cool. Or calm. Or collected. A perverse part of me thought, for a moment, that Ben seeing me like this might have been a good idea. Nothing better to convince him that being a private investigator was a bad career choice than his big sister scared to the roots of her hair. And I was. It wasn't every day someone tried to knife me. I'm sure plenty of people have thought about giving me a good smack, some maybe even half seriously. But the guy with the knife was very serious. The feeling that there was something about him that I knew but couldn't place came back. It was frustrating.

I felt the couch dip down next to me. "I couldn't find any tea. Sorry."

I opened my eyes and giggled. What the hell? I was not a giggler. Except, he was holding a honey bear. He looked down at the container and smiled.

"I have no idea why I brought this out with me."

This was a Seth I hadn't seen in a very long time. Nostalgia made me lean my head against his shoulder.

"Don't read anything into this, okay? I'm still pretty pissed off at your cover. He's a rude jerk and him kissing me like that earlier wasn't okay."

Awkwardness tended to bring out my mean side but since I was making an effort to not push his buttons, I thought a joke would be a good idea. Also, I wanted to distract him from the lecture I was sure he was gearing up for regarding my personal safety.

"So let me see if I understand you. I shouldn't read anything into you leaning your head against my shoulder. Am I supposed to read anything into the fact that you specifically mentioned Undercover Seth's manner of kissing you?"

My mind blanked for a second. Why had I put it like that? Why did my mind come up with the worst possible way to phrase things? And that wasn't even a phrasing problem. That was just a flat-out dumbass thing to bring up. I kept my head still and hoped he'd think I'd fallen asleep.

"So if I kissed you right now it would be okay since I'm not him?"

No dice. He'd clearly not fallen for my Scooby-Doo ploy, genius investigator that he was. I had to just cross my fingers and hope that I wouldn't get myself further into trouble.

"I'm not sure what I meant. And I don't think this is a good time to figure out what I meant." Honesty. Huh. It hadn't even hurt too bad. In fact, I felt pretty great except for my arm, sore from the baton making contact with the assailant's body. "You know, I whacked that guy pretty good, Seth. I could have broken his arm. You might think about alerting the hospitals."

And I had gotten myself back into the other mess of talking about something I hadn't wanted to get into with him. My brain was on a ten-second delay.

"Will? Look at me."

I reluctantly dragged my head up off his shoulder.

"You're really okay, right? You'd tell me if you weren't?"

"No, I wouldn't. Mostly because I'm an idiot and I don't like to admit weakness. And I just can't listen to you talk at me anymore about my safety. But I really am okay." Heck, telling the truth seemed to be my new game plan. At least, the game plan of my brain-to-mouth filter.

He just looked at me with an expression that wasn't amusement but also wasn't annoyance. The two most common expressions I was used to with him.

I laid my head back down on his shoulder. I figured I could close my eyes for a minute or two.

"After this case is over we're revisiting the whole mess between us, Willa. Count on it."

I nodded, trying and failing to stifle a yawn.

We must have fallen asleep because a loud clunk shocked both of us awake. Seth was clearly more startled than me because I found myself bracketed under him on the couch, his eyes wild and unfocused.

"Whoa, Seth, it's okay." I looked up at him, his eyes scanning the room. It was as if he hadn't heard me. "Seth, listen to me. Everything's all right. It was just my phone falling off the couch."

His gaze sharpened. He glanced down at me, his skin blooming pink from under his shirt and up his neck.

"Sorry. That, uh, startled me. I just reacted." He eased up off me and offered his hand to help me up. It was clear from the way he refused to make eye contact that he didn't want to talk about what had just happened. I didn't push it. We all had our secrets. I knew enough to know that he'd done some work in the Army that was pretty dangerous. I was sure he had some bad memories. Lots of bad memories, if his reaction to a dropped phone was any indicator.

He bent over and grabbed my phone, handing it to me, still hiding his face. "Maybe now *is* the time to settle all of this. I don't know if I can do this otherwise," he said.

I just stared at him, not daring to open my mouth. I eased back, realizing how close we had been standing to each other. I cursed my hormones, which seemed to draw my body to his whether I chose to or not. Feeling like a smart coward, I fled to the bathroom. I just needed a moment and a door closed between us.

Seth was right. My safety was an issue. My emotional safety. I didn't hate the warm fuzzies I had allowed to flourish as much as I wanted to. How he wasn't sure he was going to be able to get through this case without figuring out what would happen with us. If I wanted to be with Seth, the only thing keeping us apart was my fear. Was it wrong that I wanted him to spell it out for me instead of the vagueness he kept offering? He'd just reappeared in my life after years. Years in which I'd gotten sporadic letters and emails. Years in which he'd kept alluding to what he felt, but never in a straightforward way, never in a way I couldn't dismiss as his standard surface flirting. I'd never challenged it. Michael hadn't wanted Seth and me to get together, so I had just ignored it. Years where I'd felt safe because I could ignore it.

Feeling safe with Seth seemed stupid in light of the big, mean guy wielding a knife at me on the side of the road.

My legs started to shake and I sat down on the edge of the tub. I didn't know if it was training, instincts, or dumb luck that had caused me to take that baton out with me. Sitting in the bathroom staring at the door made me want Seth to continue to fight me about staying on the case. Part of me—the dead-tired, scared-spitless, emotionally empty part—really wanted a hero to come swooping in and make everything better. It was a small part but it seemed to be winning. So I planted my feet and stood up. I locked the bathroom door. No way I was letting that weak bitch out to ask to be rescued. I gave myself a few more minutes before I headed back out to the living room.

Seth was on the phone when I got back to the couch. I heard him give some final details to the person on the other end of the call. It seemed he agreed that getting a description of my attacker out to medical facilities was a good idea. He ended the call and turned to me.

"I hope you did break the bastard's arm."

"It'd be nice to get our hands on him so quick, huh?"

His eyes were hard and angry. "It'd be nice to get my hands on him so I could beat him unconscious. Sorry, I know you don't want me doing that, being all protective. It just kills me that you were alone on the side of the road and some asshole tried to hurt you," he said.

"No, I get it. If anyone's going to kill me, you want it to be you."

He stared at me for a second and then laughed, shaking his head.

"Come on, Anderson, gallows humor. Besides, you'd never be able to pull it off. I've seen you fight. You're all posture and overly ambitious. That takedown at that garage was some weak shit."

"Any time you want to get on a mat, you let me know, Pennington. I learned some things in the Army." He had stepped into my personal space aggressively, proving my point.

"I'm sure you think you did but you've forgotten that I've trained too. What's say when this is all over we throw on some gloves and I take your ego down a few notches?"

That certainly had distracted him from the guy with the knife, but not as I intended. The space between us pulsed and swirled. Ben's ringtone broke the tension slightly and I looked down, out of the reach of Seth's searching gaze.

"Hey, Benjy."

"You gotta come home the Horowitzes are here their house is on fire."

In his excitement, the words had run all together. It was a bad habit we couldn't break him from but we'd all learned to translate.

"I'll be right there, Ben. You stay in our house. You don't go out to help. Fifteen minutes."

I disconnected the call and jammed the phone in my back pocket. I snatched my jacket up and shoved my arms in the sleeves, then turned around in circles looking for my keys, forgetting entirely the previous events of the evening. Seth grabbed my hand and tugged me to a stop.

"Will, what's wrong? What are you looking for?"

I yanked my arm out of his grip. "The neighbor's house is on fire. The one whose granddaughter was living with Joe Reagan."

Random things happen randomly sometimes. This? So not a coincidence. Not a chance. The whisper of memory floated through my head again. I clenched my fists, frustrated at how it flitted away just as I tried to grab it.

"You got another helmet? Get it now."

He didn't even blink, just turned and headed into his bedroom. He was gone no more than a minute and reappeared holding a helmet and a pair of leather gloves. He tossed the gloves at me and pulled open the front door.

Seth's driving took my breath away. As we sped to the house I wondered if he always drove like a madman. I concluded that he did. Of course he did. Like everything else in his life he pressed the throttle and leaned in. That was why it was so annoying when he accused me of doing it. He wasn't any different. He just got clapped on the back for it because he was a man. Even my parents, proclaimed feminists, had always admonished me to use care, be cautious, look before I leaped. That guy on the side of the road wouldn't have approached Seth so casually. It pissed me off.

Lost in my thoughts I barely noticed when we turned into the neighborhood. The scream of a fire engine's siren broke through my musings. We swerved around the slowing truck, almost clipping the bumper. I tightened my grip around Seth's middle, squeezing a bit tighter than necessary. I hoped he'd get my message. ATF Seth didn't need Undercover Seth getting noticed by the cops.

I hopped off the bike and yanked off my helmet, getting a deep breath of smoky air. A gust of wind blew water droplets into my face. Hot and cold at the same time, smoke and water, controlled chaos. The fire seemed to be under control, dying under the assault of the hose.

"Stay here."

Seth made to dismount too and I planted my hand on his shoulder. I didn't need anyone getting twitchy and a situation escalating. With the cops, the firefighters, and Seth, we'd have testosterone overload if they all got edgy at once.

"I said, *down boy*. I don't need your cover getting mouthy and inviting questions neither of us can answer. Boyd will be here sooner or later. We'll talk to her together. Until then, discreet and inconspicuous. Okay?"

"Your wish is my command, your majesty."

He had an annoyed purse to his lips. I had to gently smack him back down.

"Hey, all I'm asking for is a few minutes of patience. Think you can manage that, Ace?"

He nodded. A clipped little gesture, so I knew backing down cost him. As I walked up the path, I mentally patted myself on the back. I won the round without either of us yelling. Yay me. The cop at the door was one I knew slightly from a training workshop. He was well over six feet tall with a baby face that belied being in his early thirties. I remembered he was conscientious if a bit too trusting. But that workshop was years ago and even though I could remember his personality, his name eluded me. I squinted at his nameplate in the dim light. Lynch.

"Officer Lynch, I don't know if you remember me. I'm Willa Pennington. I live here."

"Of course I remember you. Good to see you again even if it's under these circumstances." He turned and opened the storm door for me.

I was inexplicably nervous passing over the threshold. The idea of David and Susan converging with Boyd and me in my home set my nerves loose. I stepped back to gesture to Seth, who was staring resolutely at the house.

"Officer Lynch, my friend on the bike will be sticking around. Can you let the others on scene know so they don't think he's a lookey-loo, please?"

"Will do."

My legitimate stall tactic spent, I entered the house and headed into the kitchen, where I knew Ben would have the Horowitzes. By now he'd have plied them with tea and cookies, Susan's currency of comfort. For a split second, I wished Ben was the adult. He was better at it than I was. He got his social graces from Nancy, whereas neither of my biological parents were what you'd call personable. Charming, yes. At ease in social settings, not even close. In crises, Leila would fall apart, fluttering around and trying on accents like she could put on a new identity; Dad reverted to cop mode, interrogation and deduction. It would never occur to either of them to offer tea and cookies. I doubted Leila could even make tea. I knew she couldn't make cookies.

Sure enough, Ben, David, and Susan sat at the table, steam swirling up from tea cups. On saucers. With cloth napkins. And sitting across from them was Boyd.

"Detective Boyd. You got here quickly." That sounded more like a challenge than I had intended. "Sorry, that came out wrong. I just meant I only found out fifteen minutes ago and I was nearby. You beating me here is pretty impressive."

She smiled at me. "No offense taken, Pennington. And nice save, by the way."

I walked over and gave Susan a little shoulder hug. "I'm so sorry this has happened. Were you able to get out your photo albums and mementos?" I knew those would be the only things truly important to them. Their family photos. Their memories.

Susan nodded, her eyes swollen, unshed tears shining. "We did … and … we just couldn't stand out there and watch anymore."

Ben pulled me aside. "The EMTs gave them the choice of hospital or our house. The cold and, you know, emotional stress."

I turned and gave him a look that said *thanks* and *get lost* at the same time. He knew me well enough to not be offended.

"Mr. and Mrs. Horowitz. Detective Boyd. All this excitement has worn me out so I think I'm going to go to bed now. I have school early in the morning," he said then disappeared into the back of the house.

"Wow. That is some kid," Boyd said.

"We think he was switched at birth with some government experiment to create the perfect forty-year-old infant," I said.

That got a genuine smile from both David and Boyd. She quickly sobered. "The arson inspector will make an official ruling, but we're fairly convinced this was arson."

I pulled out the head chair and sat. A position of power couldn't hurt. I was unsure how a chair with arms made me more powerful than someone sitting in a chair without arms, but whatever.

"And you think it's connected to the murder too, I assume."

"Considering the timing, I can't help but think that."

"Detective Boyd, do you have a full statement from the Horowitzes at this point? They should probably get some rest too."

The look she gave me told me she was clued in to my desire to have them out of the discussion and that she agreed. "Absolutely, and if we have any more questions, we can contact you later. I'm sorry for everything that has happened to you, Mr. and Mrs. Horowitz."

They looked lost. I couldn't imagine how they felt. It was all so overwhelming, all the events of the last week coming one right after another.

"We don't have anywhere to go. I suppose we could call a taxi and head to a hotel out by the mall."

I frowned. I hoped I hadn't given them the impression that I was kicking them out. "David, of course you'll stay here tonight."

I led them down the hall and got them some basic overnight supplies. I should have been nervous leaving Boyd alone in the house. Once invited in, anything in plain sight was fair game, but I had nothing to hide and I had fairly well ruled out the idea that she had her sights set on me or any of the Horowitzes for the murder of Joe Reagan. No matter how many years she'd been on the job, I couldn't see her being so cynical as to think a young woman would burn down her own grandparents' house to set up a fake suspect.

And I had a surprise guest I needed to invite in from the cold. Literally. Despite the fire the temperature outside was dropping rapidly and Seth was already annoyed.

Seth sat down across from Detective Boyd, his lips pressed together. Clearly, he'd kept warm by using his annoyance at me as fuel. The man at the table was somewhere between Undercover Seth and Agent Seth. He'd need to dial that down several notches to make any headway with Boyd. Unless he was taking over the murder case from the police, he needed her. And even if he decided to take the case over, she'd demand to stay on so he was stuck with her either way.

I poked him in the arm. Hard. He turned his annoyed expression on me, the real culprit, and just stared for a minute then softened a bit and nodded.

"The three of us have a great deal to talk about but first, I think under the circumstances, the Horowitzes need to get out of town for a few days," I said to Boyd.

She nodded. She was curious about Seth but I didn't bother looking at him. If he thought they had any information about his case, he'd have talked to them already anyway. And he wouldn't have asked for my input.

"Okay, now that we're all in agreement, I think introductions are in order. Detective Boyd, this is Agent Seth Anderson of the ATF."

# CHAPTER

# 17

THE NEWS WENT OVER like a clichéd lead balloon. She couldn't possibly know the circumstances that had brought Seth here, but it was obvious that she felt I'd been keeping information from her. Which was valid.

"Okay, both of you need to remember that I am the person between the rock and the hard place here," I said, pointing at each of them in turn. "You have jobs to do that require certain confidences to be kept and I have tried to honor that. Detective Boyd, I haven't revealed any information about your murder case except things that I have been personally involved in. Not even the walk-through of the crime scene—"

"What walk-through?" Seth asked.

I looked at him. "The walk-through I didn't tell you about, Agent."

Boyd smiled. She was not pleased about the ATF butting into her case.

"Agent Anderson came to me when your murder case crossed into a case he's working. He was concerned because of a personal relationship we have."

That was certainly a soft-peddle of the facts. I didn't want to elaborate or give her the chance to use her imagination. Based on her impressive eyebrow cock, she'd already started.

"Our families have been friends for years. In fact, our fathers served together in the Army."

She nodded with a look on her face that I could only describe as bemused—a word I hadn't fully understood until I saw her make that face. I wondered if I had been deluding myself into believing that I was good at hiding my feelings. And then I caught her line of sight to Seth. He looked like he'd been boiled. His face was flushed all the way up from under the collar of his motorcycle jacket. It wasn't anger I saw, it was embarrassment. Maybe it wasn't me who had to worry about masking emotion.

"When Joe Reagan's name popped in the system, Seth saw the alert and my name as the sole witness on scene. He came to ascertain how much I knew about his case, if anything."

*Ascertain?* I had fallen easily into the overly formal cop-speak. I sounded like I had been caught at a scene and forced on camera. I guess I should have been grateful I hadn't used the word *allegedly*. And she wasn't buying it even a little bit. If Boyd left her eyebrow like that it was going to get stuck.

"As I said, we've been friends since childhood and he was worried about me."

"I can see how worried he is about you," she said.

Okay, so we weren't going to play nice. "Fine, we can do it this way too. Anything outside of the case that has happened between me and Agent Anderson is, frankly none of your business. I have asked him repeatedly to loop you in so you'd see how Joe Reagan's murder was tied in with his case. And, yes, my loyalty to Seth is personal but I have tried to be honorable with little to no leeway. You want to be pissed, be pissed. But here's the thing, he takes over the murder and you lose the collar. If we work the cases together, you both come out winners."

I looked back and forth between them. Both wore stubborn expressions. "Or turn it into a pissing match for all I care. My real concern is Violet, and she's off the hook either way. And I'd prefer to not have someone trying to murder me."

"What?"

Boyd had lost her mulish look. I shot a glance at Seth out of the corner of my eye. His ire had risen again. Nothing like giving people a common enemy to make them forget their own grievances.

"This evening I was approached on the side of the road after my car broke down."

"Sabotage?" asked Boyd.

"I suspect so," Seth said.

Now he suspected sabotage. He must have felt guilty or my body language betrayed me because he wrapped his hand around mine, heedless of Boyd's presence.

"You said he tried to murder you. You're okay?" Boyd asked.

Seth's hand tightened on mine. If he kept doing that I'd be unable to move it after a few more sentences. "Well, my sangfroid is a bit bent. Just a little anyway."

She gaped at me. I wasn't about to confess to her that I had a serious case of the nervous nellies. I hadn't even delved too deep into that territory with Seth and I'd had his tongue in my mouth a few hours ago.

"Yes, I'm fine. Not a scratch. It was not an enjoyable experience, but I can't really dwell on it right now. I didn't get a decent look at the guy but I've got this feeling I know something about him or he reminds me of someone. I can't get my brain to focus on it."

"I have to assume that this guy is aware of the connection between you and the Horowitzes, Willa," Seth said. "That means this isn't a safe place for you to stay. Or Ben. I know you'll fight me on this but if you recognize that Ben has to be protected then you have to admit you aren't safe, either."

A jab-cross-uppercut combo slammed into the pathetic argument I had been about to make. Seth knew I'd never compromise Ben's safety. And if I sent Ben away, I'd never be able to argue that I could stay.

"I think you should pack a bag and I'll take you both over to bunk with the Colonel and Barbara."

My jaw dropped. He wanted me to have a sleepover with his parents. Was he out of his mind? I would have rather made my parents come home before I stayed at that house. And why was he suddenly calling his mom by her first name?

"No way in hell. Ben can go to John's house and I'll stay at your apartment."

The second the words were out of my mouth I realized how badly I'd been suckered. Boyd actually snickered. Had I been on the top of my game he never would have been able to get that little trick past me. Almost getting killed had taken a toll on the waning mental skills I possessed lately.

I glared at him. "You tricked me."

He shrugged without a trace of remorse. "Either way I win because you're protected. This way I'll be able to keep an eye on you myself."

I pushed back my chair, scraping the floor loudly. "You two compare notes. I have a bag to pack."

While I stomped down the stairs I kicked myself for walking into Seth's trap. I should have expected it. He'd warned me that he was the boss and this fit right in with controlling my every move. I resisted the urge to just throw whatever I found into a bag and reviewed my clothes, trying to figure out what I'd need. I didn't have that many options. When your work clothes are a uniform, you tend to have super casual and super dressy with nothing in between. Super dressy was exactly one item—the black dress for the memorial service. It was still balled up in the corner of my closet where it had been since I'd stripped it off in the weak light the morning after. I'd been on a plane to Santa Fe before noon.

I reached up into my stash of junk food to find it empty. I was embarrassed to find that was the final blow. My chest felt like a weight had settled on it. I threw the box across the room and sucked in air, hard. I wasn't crying. I was not going to cry with Boyd and Seth sitting upstairs reviewing the case. I was a grownup and I could handle this. My dead best friend, having to stay with Seth, my former colleague looking at me with knowing eyes, my neighbors and their fluffy granddaughter, finding a dead body, the guy with the knife, suburban gun runners. I could take it all. I just needed a damn candy bar to do it. Was that too much to ask?

I would even have been willing to take a poke or two from Captain Average's knife in exchange for some potato chips. Or a cupcake. Wait, there had been cookies upstairs. Where Boyd and Seth were talking. Crud. I trudged back up the stairs, duffle slung over my shoulder. Back in the kitchen, my two new partners were chatting amiably. I wasn't sure which one I hated more at that moment. I considered. Seth won. I hated him most because he'd tricked me.

"Are there any of those cookies left?" I scanned the counter but didn't see any. The cabinets were likewise empty. I turned and narrowed my eyes at the duo. Boyd looked guilty but Seth leaned back in his chair.

"Ben came back out and took the last two," he said.

Cool as a cucumber the man lied to my face. And threw my baby brother under the bus in the process. He'd tricked me earlier but this one wasn't even a good attempt.

"Ben? Ben ate the rest of the cookies? Health nut Ben?"

Seth nodded. He didn't even blink. No fidgeting. I was looking this time. Studying him for any signs of lying. Not a flinch. He'd have to have been pretty well trained by the ATF for this case. He could display all the signs of honesty but his chosen lie still wasn't believable because Ben just did not eat sweets.

"Hey, Will. Did you try the cookies? They were pretty good. Coconut," Ben said, walking back into the room.

Seth had the decency to look away. Or the good sense. He knew I wasn't about to go off on Ben but there was a line of fire and he was most certainly in it. And now I had to tell Ben he needed to go stay with John until this whole mess was resolved. I knew it wouldn't be a problem with John's mom. She adored Ben. He and John had been best friends since kindergarten. She'd be more than happy to take him for as long as I needed.

"Um, no, Benjy. Listen. With all the stuff that's come up, we think it's better if you're out of the house."

When I saw he was starting to protest, I cut him off. "Me too. I'm going over to Seth's for a bit. Just as a precaution. We don't know who did this to the Horowitzes, so better safe than sorry, right?"

He looked over at Seth for confirmation. Did my brother just check out my story?

"It's true. I tricked her into it."

They fist bumped. I wanted to hit something too, but it wasn't someone's fist. They both ignored my glare. Once upon a time, my glare could cause Ben deep fear. Now he was bigger than me. That truly sucked.

"Yeah, you're both hilarious. It was actually my concern for you that allowed me to be tricked, Benjamin. His first idea was staying with his parents."

My smug pronouncement was met with a big smile.

"That would have been cool too. Me and the Colonel could play Hearts of Iron more often."

Right, I forgot. Ben ate cookies, the Colonel played something called Hearts of Iron. I looked over at Seth and he shrugged.

"Fine, great, everyone is growing as people and trying new things. Fantastic. Please go pack to spend a few nights at John's house. I'll call his mom tomorrow. It's too late to decamp tonight. Plus we've got the Horowitzes in the spare room."

As one they all turned and looked in the direction of the back of the house. Ha! I was the only one who hadn't forgotten the houseguests.

After a little more back and forth with Boyd culminating in all parties deciding to start again in the morning, Seth insisted on staying. He wasn't about to leave a house full of people with an arsonist on the loose. With the spare room occupied by the Horowitzes and Ben's room full of Ben and his servers, the only options for Seth were my parents' room or one of the couches.

Seth chose the couch in the basement. His argument that David or Susan might feel uncomfortable if they came out to find a strange man clad only in his boxers on the couch was valid. I agreed in principle, but in practice *I* was uncomfortable coming out to find him in his boxers on the couch. But I had already seen him naked. Which I was loathe to remind myself of when I found a need to use the bathroom in the middle of the night. On the other side of the basement. Past where Seth lay in his boxers on the couch. He'd turned on the gas fireplace and to say there was a distinctly romantic movie scene ambience choking the air would have been an understatement.

"Are you all right with just that blanket?" I whispered to break the silence as I crept by. Super casual, not edgy at all. "It's kind of cold down here."

He sat up and the firelight flickered on his face and chest. The planes of his face glowed. Seth wasn't just good-looking. He was pretty in a strong way. Unfairly so. And the kiss from earlier. He'd done it for his cover, but he'd wanted to kiss me. And I hadn't minded. Not even a little, despite my protest later. He wanted me and I wanted him. Even if my brain told me it was a bad, terrible, horrible, no good idea, my body wanted me to fire up the engines, kick the tires, and get that sucker launched. Seth was that person for me. That perfect, so-wrong-it's-right person. And my heart didn't know whether to listen to my brain or my libido. Because all I saw was disaster ahead. Titanic, Hindenburg, fire at the Cocoanut Grove disaster.

"I'm fine. Are you okay?"

I nodded. Not okay. So not okay. I was really tired of pretending to be okay. But I kept nodding like an idiot. "I just needed to go to the bathroom. Can I get you anything?"

"From the bathroom?" He laughed. I was glad it was dark where I was standing and he couldn't see me blush.

"No, I just meant in general. While I was up. I could go to the kitchen to get you some water or something. So you don't have to wander around in your boxers."

*Shut up, Willa. Shut your stupid mouth right now before you say something so ridiculous you will have to step in front of a trash truck to end the humiliation.*

"You could sleep with me tonight," I offered, then bolted.

I scurried off to the bathroom and avoided looking at myself in the mirror and then at the couch on the way back to my room. My room was dark compared to the harsh florescent light in the bathroom and the gentle burn of the gas fireplace. So dark I didn't see Seth. I slid into the bed to find his warm body in my spot.

Seth scooted over toward the wall but the space he'd vacated was warm from his body heat. I laid on my back with my arms tight against my sides. He'd said he wanted to settle what was happening with us. He probably assumed that was my intent in inviting him into my bed. Had I actually thought before I spoke I would have known that.

"Thanks for sharing. It is warmer in here. The fire can't compete with the cold flooding in through that sliding door."

"Dad keeps meaning to fix it but he's not that good with home repair stuff."

"I'd be happy to look at it."

We lapsed into an uncomfortable silence. I wanted to stay mad at him for tricking me into having to relocate to his apartment, but I just wasn't. I had acted like us sleeping together after Michael's memorial service had taken me by surprise, but it had actually felt inevitable. It hadn't been a delayed reaction to grief or any of that crap about reaffirming life. We knew what we were doing was the result of years of holding back, of taking the higher road, of thinking of someone other than ourselves.

I rolled over onto my side to face Seth. He'd been on his side facing the door and we were almost touching. He'd brought his own blanket in with him and had lain down on the comforter. I shimmied free of my covers and slipped under his.

"What're you doing, Willa?" His voice was soft but it was the uncertainty in it that made me reach out and place my hand on his chest. "If this is about earlier, my remark about the kiss, I—"

"Someone tried to stab me tonight," I said.

"I thought you weren't scared." His voice was teasing.

"I'm not. And that scares me. Seth, what would you do after that memorial service?"

He brought his hand up and grabbed mine. "Don't say that."

"Where would you go? Who would you drink with? Who would know you then? It was always just the three of us and then you left us."

He raised my hand to his mouth and kissed it. "We grew up, Will."

I slid my leg in between his. "You grew away, Seth."

"I'm here now." He kissed me gently. "I thought you said this wasn't a good time to figure out—"

"I wasn't that drunk. I knew what I was doing," I said, interrupting him.

He reached up and used his phone to light us up. I shifted my eyes away and covered the phone with my hand. I had only started talking because he couldn't see me.

He dropped the phone on the bed. It still wasn't dark enough but if he wanted to hear what I had to say he'd have to do it my way.

"It wasn't grief. Not really. I was mad at him. He'd died and … he'd left me alone and you'd already left me and I wanted … someone back."

"Someone?"

"You."

"You know I didn't mean any of the things I said the other day. It's not just anyone. It's you." He kissed me again.

No one came in to interrupt us and I didn't stop him. I kissed him back.

# CHAPTER

# 18

**I WOKE WITH SETH'S** arm thrown over my rib cage and the rest of him pressed against my back. Memories of the morning after Michael's memorial surfaced and I thanked several gods I didn't believe in that at least I wasn't hungover too. Why hadn't I thought of the morning before I invited him into my bed? But I knew that if I had thought about it I wouldn't have done it. And I'd wanted to. I hadn't wanted to talk it all out. I knew what would resolve that particular tension.

It was too late for self-recrimination—a game I was exceptionally good at—so I tried to squeeze out from underneath his incredibly heavy limb and ease out of the bed. He tightened his grip and let out a sigh that tickled the hair on the back of my neck. Well crap. The domestic bliss of the scene was starting to make me itch.

"Seth? Wake up."

"Fifteen more minutes."

His hand inched lower and he pressed his stubbled chin against my shoulder.

"What you want will take longer than fifteen minutes," I said.

"You underestimate my determination, Sunshine."

"It's not your determination I'm questioning, Seth."

I got my arm free enough to send a glancing blow to his rib cage. He coughed hard and rolled off me. I sat up and smiled down at him. He grabbed his torso and put on an exaggerated expression of pain. I hadn't actually hurt him. I had barely touched him and I knew exactly how to use that move to cause real injury.

"I don't have time for your antics, Agent. Can you amuse yourself while I make some phone calls?"

He smirked at me. "I'm sure I can find something to keep busy with."

"Ew, perv," I said, laughing. "Maybe get cleaned up. You look rough."

I dressed hastily and called John's mother while Seth showered. She was more than happy to host Ben for as long as it took. I'd given her an abbreviated version of events, leaving out the murder and gun ring entirely. That with the fire investigation and commotion, I felt Ben should be away from the whole mess so he could focus on school. I didn't have to worry about him treating this as a vacation. John's mother would be on him worse than ours.

The Horowitzes had gotten up and were feeling less overwhelmed. The fire had been put out pretty quickly thanks to the fire crews and the house was salvageable. It was a mess but they'd already spoken to their insurance company and Susan's sister in Rhode Island. They were going to drive up and spend a week or two with her family in Providence. Four hundred miles away seemed like a good idea. I had no proof, but I was pretty sure Providence was where they had sent Violet off to when she called them the first time.

I had Ben and the Horowitzes squared away, so now I could focus on the intertwined cases. Seth came up from the basement just as I was ending my call with Boyd. She would be back at the house mid-afternoon, which gave all three of us some time to get settled into our respective new situations. Seth probably needed to check on his cover business and update his boss on the case's new elements.

When he entered the kitchen, I fixed myself a cup of coffee, two sugars and cream, downing it hastily. I had pulled out a second mug for him. He grabbed the cup and poured his own serving, black.

"I read somewhere that drinking coffee black indicates psychopathology," I said.

"And what does it indicate if you only drink milk and sugar with a dash of coffee?"

"I was just making conversation to avoid telling you that you smell like strawberries. Pretty girly, if you ask me." I shrugged. "But I'm sure your cover is enough of a badass to pull it off."

He groaned. "I have badass manly shampoo at home, you know."

"I can go see if Ben has anything you can borrow. Something that smells like tools or beer."

"Are you making fun of me?"

I nodded. "I'm a wicked, wicked girl."

"You don't need to remind me, Sunshine. It's only been a few hours."

I turned away from him, to the sink, dumping the dregs of my coffee. I didn't want he see me blush. Which was silly considering what we had done.

I turned around and leaned against the sink. "Okay, ground rules. We cannot be like this in front of Boyd. Or Ben. Or anyone."

He nodded. "Agreed."

"Once this is all done we'll decide how we want to handle … whatever this is. We both need to keep our wits about ourselves. What's our plan for the morning before we meet Boyd again? I did some short stakeouts on Reagan's known associates. I think we need to expand those."

He came toward me. I didn't like the look on his face. He slid his hand into my hair, running his thumb on my cheekbone. "Sunshine, after last night I thought you'd realized that our deal was off."

I pushed him away hard, sloshing his coffee on my shirt. "And why would I have realized that? Were you under the impression that after we screwed I was just going to hang out and, what, bake you some damn cookies while you saved the day?"

He looked incredulous. "No, I thought after someone tried to knife you and set fire to the house next door that you'd have come to your senses. And if I had any idea that you hadn't I would definitely not have gone to bed with you."

"Did you think you were doing me a favor? Oh, I get it. You rewarded me for being a good girl and realizing my place."

He set the mug on the counter with exquisite gentleness. I could see the control in his taut forearm. "You're twisting my words. It was not like that, but I'm not going to apologize for trying to keep you safe. That is my job, Willa."

"No, Agent Anderson, your job is to bust a gun ring. Protecting me is your own personal crusade. And you think you can accomplish that by treating me like I'm some stupid little girl."

"I'm trying to get you to see reason."

"And I'm trying to tell you that you can't. I'm not reasonable on this. I was a damn good cop, Seth. Let me be that cop."

"Even if I have to watch you get yourself killed in the process?"

He left without another word. I just stood there as he gathered his things and walked out. I heard the motorcycle's engine kick over. I listened as he drove away, the roar of the bike fading.

———

My phone bleeped with a text.

I HAD YOUR CAR TOWED TO THE GARAGE. HAVE YOUR BAGS READY FOR WHEN WE MEET BOYD.

He wouldn't have had time to reach the shop, so he had to have stopped. Maybe for coffee. He hadn't finished the cup he'd poured. It sat there on the counter. I picked it up and dumped it down the drain then set the mug next to mine. I hadn't even noticed that I'd pulled down a pair of the His and Hers mugs my parents used.

I slipped back down to my room and changed my shirt then headed back to Dad's office to run some searches on the average guy with the average car. I accepted that it wasn't all a coincidence, that all the events were related—the murder, the guy with the knife, the fire—and that meant it was more than likely my car hadn't just conveniently sprung a coolant leak just at the right time. The guy must have cut the line when I was parked at the garage. A spark of fear for Seth flared up. If this man knew about me, he knew about Seth.

I had picked up my phone to text him before I realized that Seth being undercover meant the guy didn't know who he really was even if I had been trailed to the garage. I could have been there for any number of reasons, like the ones I'd listed just yesterday. There was no reason to think Seth wasn't safe. And even if he wasn't, he was a damn ATF agent with a gun and everything. Multiple guns, in fact. He could take care of himself. He didn't need me to rescue him and he didn't want me to either. Being a hero was his job.

The computer didn't pull up any prosecuted cases with the MO I'd input. There were a few cases of people victimized on the side of the road, but most were crash-for-cash scams or Good Samaritans being robbed when they pulled over to help someone. I added in sexual assault search terms just to be sure. My instinct was telling me this was all related, but that didn't mean the guy hadn't done something like this before. It was a pretty good plan for a criminal—tamper with a woman's car and then follow her until she breaks down. Plan it for a deserted area and you had everything you needed.

I was relieved when I didn't get any hits on those searches. I knew Boyd would have run similar searches trying to pull up offenders but with the description I had given, the results would have either brought up nothing or so many she'd never be able to narrow it down to a pool of suspects we could get through in the next year. That meant we had to find this scumbag through his relationship to Joe Reagan.

I grabbed the file and reviewed all the notes I had so far. I looked again at what Violet had told me about Joe's friends. I kept coming back to what she'd said about Mark. How he was creepy. How Joe seemed afraid of him and in awe of him at the same time. She hadn't said anything about tattoos but, then, I hadn't asked. I scrolled through my call log and found the number she called from. It rang without going to voicemail, which was typical for a burner phone. I really wanted to either add Mark to the suspect list or rule him out. I was pretty sure the guy from last night had a tattoo on his neck. I didn't see any Marks on the list I'd compiled of Joe's known associates.

Once I talked to Violet, I'd have something definitive to give Boyd and Seth. And a name, even just a first name, could yield us a much more manageable suspect pool. If we had a suspect for the attack that we all believed was connected to the murder, we'd have the door we needed to the guns. We might be able to get this case closed by the time my parents got back from the cruise. It'd be a nice start to my partnership with Dad to be able to tell clients we'd assisted the ATF on a major gun theft and the local police with a murder. I just had to solve it first.

Boyd arrived at three, sharp. I had just gone back inside after fruitlessly waiting for Ben's bus, having forgotten that he was at John's for the foreseeable future. I tried to play it off that I was waiting for her but, though she had the decency not to laugh, she knew it was a lie.

"He's a great kid but I can see why you mother him. He's too sweet. Too soft. He thinks he's older because he's responsible, but there's a difference between being an old soul and knowing the world. Knowing what it's capable of. How it can crush good people just as easily as the bad."

In a few sentences, she'd nailed why we all pushed Ben away from justice and toward college and computers and a safe desk job. He was too sweet, too soft, too easy. He truly thought the world was a safe, benign place. And if it wasn't, that people like me and Dad and Seth and the Colonel would make it a better place. I thought that way too once. That we made a difference. That we made the world a better place. And then my best friend had been blown to hell half a world away from home just six days before he was supposed to leave. And I didn't think that way anymore. I didn't think there was a way to stop bad things from happening to good people. I knew we were just holding the ugly brutality at bay. Like human sandbags against the rising tide of greed and need from people like Joe Reagan and his friend Mark. And one day, no matter how hard we tried, the banks of that particular river might rise too high and flood our whole world. I hoped Ben never realized that and I'd do whatever it took to shield him from it.

I didn't know how to put that into words without sounding like I was about to take a razor to my veins, so I just nodded. Boyd understood the fight better than I did. She'd been doing it a lot longer. And even if the tide was rising, there were people who deserved to be stood for. I knew she understood that too.

We were heading up the walk toward the stairs when Seth arrived. He was driving an unremarkable sedan that could have been found in any office parking lot in any city in the country. It was even beige. He got out of the car in a business suit, his hair slicked back into the semblance of a conservative style and wearing those mirrored sunglasses. He may have been driving his mom's car, but Seth couldn't disguise the way his body moved. Not from me anyway. Even in that suit I'd know him anywhere.

His appearance screamed Fed and he looked less like himself than I had ever seen him. If I barely recognized him, no one else would take a second glance. And it occurred to me that he had done this to make it appear to anyone watching that I was surrounded by the good guys. He was determined to protect me no matter how much it pissed me off.

"Another new friend, Willa?" Boyd asked.

She hadn't recognized him up close even after sitting across a table from him for an hour. He slid his sunglasses down his nose and peered at her with a wry expression. She shook her head.

"You clean up well, Agent."

I parked them at the kitchen table and cranked up a pot of coffee. Maybe Seth could stick around to finish his cup this time. I kicked myself for not remembering to get more cookies. I hadn't left Dad's office most of the day, but a quick run to the store wouldn't have killed me. Seth had told me to stay parked but I had a listening problem: I didn't. Listen, that was. I couldn't get in trouble for regretting not going anywhere. I could, however, twist the knife a bit. He'd scammed me and I was still feeling a little sore about it.

"Sorry there aren't any cookies but you finished them last night and I wasn't allowed to go to the store today."

I deliberately let the cups clank together as I pulled them down. I'd made sure there weren't any cute matching mugs being handed out.

"I can fix that." Boyd pulled a bag of butter cookies out of her voluminous handbag. I got down a plate because my mom would have known from an ocean away that I hadn't and would beat me raw when she got home if I let "guests" eat out of a bag. The coffeemaker gave an irritated beep.

When the coffee was poured and the cookies plated, I joined Seth and Boyd at the table. She had obviously gotten over the fact that Seth had managed to fool her so thoroughly. I decided to jump in with my research.

"I've been going over my notes and I think I found a suspect."

"Based on?" Seth asked.

I tried to determine if he was challenging me or just asking for more information. I decided that I needed to stop being so defensive.

"I had a conversation with Violet a few days ago. I asked her about Joe's friends. Any interactions she witnessed, things like that."

Boyd laid her pen down, carefully lining it up next to the notepad's edge. "You had a conversation with Violet a few days ago how exactly?"

She didn't sound pleased. That was fair since I hadn't told her I talked to Violet. Nor had I asked Violet to contact her.

"Um, I threatened Dave Horowitz that if he didn't have Violet contact me I would tell you that they were hiding her and that you'd jail them for obstruction."

Seth and Boyd both gaped at me.

"Jesus, Willa, they're like grandparents to you. How could you?" Seth asked.

"Exactly. They are like grandparents to me, which is why I did it. I told them over and over that they needed to trust me and Boyd and have Violet return to talk to the cops, but they decided that hiding her was a better idea. I did what I had to in order to protect them."

"So, it's fine when you do it but no one else gets that privilege?" Seth had gone furious in an instant.

Boyd held up her hands. "Thank you, Willa. In situations like this most people tend to want to hunker down and protect their own, even cops. I'm honored that you have that much faith in me."

Seth looked like he was about to say something, but instead he took a sip of coffee, deliberately breaking eye contact with me. Screw him. Those situations were totally different.

"We should probably get back to the possible suspect," Boyd said.

I avoided looking at either Seth or Boyd. I kept my gaze focused on the table then picked up a cookie and bit into it. When I finally snuck a look at her, she was holding her pen and waiting to take notes. Her face was clear of any anger or annoyance. I chewed and swallowed as quickly as I could without choking. A sip of coffee and I was ready to continue.

"Okay, Violet said she wasn't really allowed around Joe's friends much. He kept her sequestered upstairs when they came over, but there was one guy. I can't find him in any of the known associates for any of Joe's court cases. And all Violet knows is his first name, Mark."

Boyd laid her pen down. "And why do you think this specific guy is someone to look at? If we can find him, that is."

Her voice was even but I felt my cheeks heat up. I hated having to admit that it was just instinct. I knew Boyd made decisions based on her gut, but she'd been a detective for years. I hadn't even been eligible for the detective's exam when I quit. I had no facts to back up my conclusion.

"Violet said Mark was creepy. She saw him only once or twice and he made her uncomfortable. That he was mean to Joe. She said Joe was afraid of him, yet he stayed friends with the guy. That's something a teenage girl does when her friends go mean girl on her, not a grown man."

Boyd had started taking notes again. "It's a great clue, kid. I'm impressed. But without a last name we're in the same boat as we are with finding the guy who attacked you. We could talk to Violet again, maybe get more from her, but with the Horowitzes out of town ... can you contact them?"

"Sure. But they're probably on the road still and Violet's calling me in the next hour, so we could just wait until then."

Boyd rolled her eyes and muttered something under her breath that sounded like *of course she arranged for Violet to call her why wouldn't she have done so instead of having her call me and not only that but didn't bother to tell me* but could have just been a prolonged throat clearing. A very, very prolonged throat clearing. Maybe she needed to see a doctor.

"The scans I ran this morning pulled up nothing. We are nowhere with your attacker. We need to see what else we can get out of your call with Violet. Any other friends or if she can remember anything else about Mark," Boyd said. "Let's make a list you can use when you're on the call with her."

"Like does Mark have a tattoo on the left side of his neck." Then I remembered. "The guy."

Seth had slid down in his seat a bit, but that remark got his full attention. "The guy. What guy? You said the guy who came after you might have a tattoo on his neck. You think Mark and the attacker are the same person?"

"No. At Killian's. There was a guy. Give me a second."

I closed my eyes and tried to remember the guy with the dead eyes. *That* was the memory I'd kept losing grasp of. Ed's friend. He was the same height, same build as the guy on the side of the road. And I was positive he had a neck tattoo.

I slammed my hand on the table. "Dammit."

# CHAPTER

# 19

"It's okay, Willa," Boyd said.

"No, I had him. At Killian's."

"You're positive?" Seth asked.

I nodded. "The guy at Killian's is the same guy from the side of the road, and Violet first met Joe at Killian's. This is all connected."

I was pissed off at myself. I had that piece of the puzzle stuck in my head for days. We could have been that much closer if I had just remembered him.

"I'll have a uniform start a search to see if any large silver pickups are registered to anyone named Mark. I'll have him start in Fairfax County and pull photos on those hits. You can look at them and if need be we'll expand out to Loudon, Arlington, and Prince William." Boyd smiled. "This is good, kid. You did good."

I glanced at the time on my phone. It was about the time I'd asked Violet to call me. I hoped she would keep her promise now that she was off the hook. I was pretty sure her grandparents had called her the second they got into the spare room last night.

Seth drummed his fingers on the table. He was unusually twitchy. I wondered if it was about our fight earlier and then reminded myself that we'd agreed to deal with all that crap after the case was over.

"Seth, how did the ATF get on to Reagan being related to the gun thefts?" I asked. Having a little more background on the case couldn't hurt and it would keep us all occupied while we waited for Violet to call. He stopped fidgeting.

"We got a call from a guy whose girlfriend had bought a gun from Reagan in the parking lot of a bar. Things weren't going too well between them lately and he followed her that night. Apparently, he was a little worried about his girl having a gun handy so he called the tip in and gave us Reagan's license plate."

"Yikes, tales of love and romance in the real world sure are different than you see on TV," I said. "They fight, she buys a gun, and he snitches her out to the Feds. They're probably married now."

"Hey, snitches make my job easier. Without that call and the follow-up visit we'd never have traced that gun to the second theft. We had the gun, we had the seller, and then we just needed to get into his life. I was so close. We set up this operation fast but it was solid. I had the bike shop and I'd hired Reagan's cousin to get my intro. I had gained Reagan's trust and we were getting ready to pop him for the gun sale so I could turn him."

"So why would a coward like Reagan take a gun from the stash and sell it on his own? That seems really risky."

"For him, sure, but the buyer was the sister of a high school friend, so he probably felt like he could trust her. And we figure he was tasked with selling some of the guns. If someone was going to get arrested for the crime, better it was him than one of the higher-ups."

"But if one of the guns gets traced to the robbery then you've got a lead," I said.

"But only a lead. If we only get one gun, it's all still compartmentalized. That one gun and Reagan are the bait. So this group is smart enough to bait a trap but not smart enough to realize the ATF isn't going to snap up the small-time bait when they see it."

I hoped I wasn't stating the obvious but I couldn't keep my mouth shut. "They're amateurs. They managed to put it all together, but they're not real criminals. Not the ones that make a career of it anyway."

Seth nodded. "That's what I think too."

"So we've got a group of people who are smart enough to put together the robberies but not savvy enough to know that the ATF wouldn't pounce at the first gun. They're willing to take their time, so while they want the money they most likely don't need it right away. They make a slow start and spread it out just a bit," Boyd said.

My phone rattled against the table, the ringer on vibrate. I looked at the display and saw a number I didn't recognize with an out-of-state area code. I looked at Boyd and she smiled at me. Seth just nodded. With the stakes on this call riding even higher than last time, I was nervous. This wasn't a mostly slam dunk case of finding an alternate direction to get the cops off Violet as a suspect. We were really tracking a murderer now. One that had tried to put holes in my person. I picked up the phone and accepted the call.

"Willa Pennington."

"Hi, Willa. It's um … Violet. Horowitz."

"Hey, listen, no one thinks you shot Joe anymore so there's no reason to be scared."

I heard her let out a shuddering breath.

"Do you remember what I asked you to do for me the last time we talked? Just think about things and see if you remembered anything that was out of the ordinary or that you even think was weird. Nothing is silly, Violet."

"Yeah, but if the police don't want to talk to me anymore why does it matter?"

Her voice had taken on a whiny quality. As long as she was off the hook it didn't matter that someone was murdered? I had to push down the annoyance I felt with her.

"Well, Violet, listen. There's still a killer out there. And you want us to catch him, right? For Joe. I know you cared about him even if things weren't always perfect between you two."

I saw Boyd nodding her head.

"I couldn't really think of anything. Like I told you last time, Joe didn't even let me downstairs when his friends were over."

Her voice had gotten harder and angry as she spoke. I was losing her. She had started to remember that Joe smacked her around and that she hadn't liked it. But while her personal evolution was good for her, I still needed information.

"Right. I remember. So you don't remember much about any of his friends except maybe Mark. Let me ask you something about him, Violet. Did he have a tattoo? Like maybe on his neck?"

"Ugh. Yes. It was so gross."

"Do you remember what the tattoo was?"

"Oh yeah. He was really proud of it. Showed it to me twice. It was a skull with bones behind it."

"Like a pirate?"

"No, like an equals sign," she said.

"Where on his neck?"

"On the right. No, it was my right so his left."

"Violet, what did Mark look like? Tall, short, fat, thin? Anything you can tell me will help."

"He's just a regular guy. Nothing about him stands out. You'd look right through him if you saw him in a store. But his eyes can be really mean. And he's got that gross tattoo."

I glanced over at Boyd, seeing her write down my side of the conversation and anything I repeated.

"So, he's just average looking. Average height and weight? Hair color? You said his eyes can be mean but what color are they?"

"Yeah, he's not really tall but not short. About Joe's height. He looked like he was putting on weight. Like kind of doughy. He sure thought he was a stud. His eyes are blue but not a pretty blue. Like a shark. I guess that's why they look mean. They're cold."

"Okay. And do you remember if you heard his last name ever?"

"No, I'm sorry. Listen, I gotta go now. Bubbe and Nono are here. I hope I helped."

I smiled. "Oh, you were very helpful."

I put the phone down.

"Looks like Mark's our guy. Violet described him as all around average running to fat. Oh, and a totally gross tattoo on his neck."

"So we just have to hope that the scans the police are running pull something useful. Was Violet able to describe the tattoo?" Seth asked.

I pushed my chair back and grabbed my mug. The coffee had gone cold while I was talking and I wanted a fresh cup.

"Yeah, she said it was a totally gross skull with some bones stacked behind it."

"Shit!"

I turned to stare at Seth. His reaction about the tattoo seemed odd. Boyd's face had taken on a funny expression too.

"What are you guys so jammed up about? So he's got bad taste in ink. He's hardly the first."

"He's a neo-Nazi, Willa. That's one of their symbols. A neck tattoo's a big commitment so he's probably part of an official group. This could mean the small-time amateur robbers just became organized ideologues. Those guys are forming corporations and creating compounds. Some of them are planted in law enforcement and politics. Many aren't even bothering to hide their beliefs anymore."

Seth took a deep breath and motioned for me to sit down. "Why do you think he came after you?"

"I...I guess he saw me at Killian's and followed me." It sounded pretty stupid when I said it out loud.

"I met you here after Killian's, Willa. You know that no one was following you. I would have seen him."

Boyd looked at Seth and then back at me. "He most likely saw you here when he was watching the Horowitzes' house. He saw you and he remembered you."

A sour taste flooded under my tongue. I shook my head. "And he decided I was a good target. So he followed me, sabotaged my car, and tried to knife me on the side of the road."

Another look flicked between Seth and Boyd.

"Look, you two can just quit it with this whole *no one is saying what they think* crap. I get it. He wants me dead because he figured out that I'm half black."

Boyd looked thoughtful. "You're angry. I don't blame you, but now you're getting the idea of how this can end up being a great deal more complicated. I don't know if I'm going to be able to hold back on talking to the higher-ups in the department. I think to keep it with us, you're

190

going to need to officially take over the murder, Seth. You've got the justification. And because it's an ongoing op with ATF, you'll keep control of it. I'll help you, of course. If you still want me involved."

"I agree. You've already got the in because of the murder so you'll stay the public face of the investigation, Detective Boyd, and my case continues undercover."

"So it's settled, the band stays together," I said. Why was Seth shaking his head?

"If by band, you mean the three of us then the answer is no. You're out, right now, Willa. No more arguments."

I looked at Boyd and she wouldn't meet my eyes. I shifted my gaze to Seth. He had the stubborn look I knew too well, hated a great deal, and had spent a ton of time trying to break. He had on his hero face. The one that accompanied every cliché in the hero book. *It's better this way. This hurts me more than it hurts you. I'm doing this for your own good. One day you'll thank me.*

"Oh, hell no. I'm not having this argument again, Seth. I'm in and I'm staying in."

The stubborn look only intensified. "Are you kidding me? You're kidding me, right? You're being funny now?"

He got louder with each disbelieving sentence. I saw Boyd slide out of her chair and beat it for the dining room. If he thought I was going to back down because he got a little loud, he was deluded.

"Kidding? No, I am not kidding, Seth. I am so far from kidding you could even call me deadly serious."

"I'm so glad you termed it like that, Sunshine, because now I can remind you again that you were almost killed last night."

I opened my mouth, but he cut me off. "A man who we think has already killed at least one person came at you with a knife. If you hadn't had the baton, he could have murdered you on that shoulder and no one would have been able to help you."

I had no defense against his logic. He was right. I had gotten lucky. My instinct to take the baton with me out of the car had saved me.

"I told you last night that I'm not scared."

"You're not? Well, I am. I'm sick just thinking about it. I was minutes away from you and I wouldn't have known. You asked who'd know me, who I'd drink with, and the answer is no one."

He'd lost all pretense of polite conversation. He was frantic and desperate. I knew then that he hadn't lied when he said it wasn't anyone but me. And I felt awful. But not awful enough to let it go. I needed to see this case through. I didn't know how to do anything else.

"I'm sorry, but I just can't walk away."

He threw his hands up in the air. "Of course you can. Violet's off the hook now and, as I have reminded you before, you're not a cop anymore."

"Just because I'm not wearing a badge anymore doesn't mean that I'm not responsible for seeing this through. This is about me now too. Not just the Horowitzes or Joe Reagan. I'm a target too."

"Yes, actually, that's exactly what it means. It means that in the most basic and simple way. Cops solve crimes and catch bad guys. You are a private citizen now. Private citizens let cops solve crimes and catch bad guys. See how that lines up so nicely?"

The angrier he got, the calmer I felt.

"I need this, Seth. I need to see it through."

"Willa, you could get killed."

"It's who I am. This is who I am," I said.

He looked at me like I was asking him to cut off his own leg. "Please don't ask me to do this, Willa."

"I'm trusting that you'll keep me safe, Seth. The original deal. I don't make a move without you."

The defeated look on his face told me I'd won. I wished I felt better about winning, so I did the only thing I could to show him that I knew how much it was costing him. I put my hand over his and squeezed.

"We can do this, Seth. Together. And when it's over, I'll be safe. The faster we bust them, the faster I'll be safe."

He nodded but didn't look at me. I would be safe when it was all over, but I had the feeling that maybe I would be alone.

"Is it okay to come back now?" Boyd wandered back into the kitchen with a little smirk. I wondered if Seth had given her lessons the previous night. "If you two are done kissing and making up, I had a thought maybe you'd like to explore while I'm pulling those scans."

I let that one slide. It was a cheap shot but it was fair. She had no idea what was really going on between the two of us. I pulled my hand off Seth's, hating to break the connection.

"We've actually got a really good clue with that tattoo. You two should track down the local guy that does the ink for them."

Of course they'd need their own guy. It wasn't as if they could traipse into the local tattoo parlor like a frat all wanting the same shamrock on their asses. They'd need someone sympathetic to their cause. One of them. Which meant he wasn't likely to talk without some incentive. Or some fear.

"Finding him will be easier said than done. Getting him to talk will be near to impossible," I said.

"This prick tried to hurt you. If our tattoo artist is feeling a little shy then I'll jack him up if I have to," Seth said.

193

Boyd looked at him, a neutral expression on her face. "I didn't hear that, Agent Anderson. But if I had heard it, I'd have to remind you that while it's understandable, it's important not to cross that line. I'd also be obliged to report it. Since I didn't hear it, light up whoever you have to in order to get this asshole." She had lost her neutral expression and her eyes flashed with anger. I was definitely never messing with her.

She gathered her things and began to leave. She turned back to level another fierce look at Seth. "Whatever you do, you make sure your first priority is to take care of Willa. She's got great instincts but is too headstrong."

I wasn't even offended that she was talking about me like I wasn't in the room. I probably would have been if I hadn't been busy marveling that she admired something about me.

Seth dropping the phone book on the table brought me back to the task at hand. How old school. I was glad Ben wasn't around to make fun of us.

"Where did you even find this monster?" I asked.

"Nancy always keeps one on the floor of the pantry, in the back." At my look of confusion, he laughed. "So she can stand on it to get the cookies she hides on the top shelf."

# CHAPTER

## 20

"Okay, there are about a dozen tattoo parlors in Fairfax County. If we have to expand outside the county we will, but this list is enough for now. I threw out a few already. We don't need ones that serve the college crowd. And there's one in Annandale that's run by two sisters from the Philippines."

I looked at the list he'd printed. I couldn't argue with his toss outs. I didn't see the skinheads mixing with the frat boys and girls needing a belly button piercing. The Filipino ladies weren't even a question. The ones left on the list were unremarkable.

A quick search of the websites for the shops allowed us to cull two more based on staff diversity. At the end we still had five. Boyd had texted me that she was adding the tattoo to the scans. There were over forty hits for a silver pickup truck registered to anyone named Mark or a variation of Mark. Her team had pulled all the DMV photos.

"This is maddening," I said as I scrolled through the photos. I didn't see anyone that had a tattoo on his neck. The photos could have been ten years old in some instances because of the renewal policies. I was looking for a guy that was maybe a decade older by now, different hair style, maybe having shaved a beard or mustache, added a tattoo. I had no idea how anyone was able to ID a suspect from photos.

Seth stopped scrolling through the websites. "You're just looking for possibilities, okay? You don't have to pick any one guy and you don't need to be sure of your choice."

I pushed away from the table and paced the kitchen floor. "I've got to get out of this house, Seth. Let's hit the nearest places and see what we can shake loose."

"Okay, I'll make you a deal. We'll head back to my place so I can change back into my cover and while we're driving you'll look at the photos. I want you to give Jan at least three possibilities."

I gave him the up and down look. "You look ridiculous, you know. Like you're interviewing for a job as a substitute teacher."

"You wound me. I thought I looked debonair and professional." He covered his heart with his hand.

"You look like Barbara dressed you."

His face dropped. Something was definitely up with him and his parents. Seth had always been more aloof than Michael where their parents were concerned. He had reacted to them the way they'd parented. Like he did his duty and followed the letter of the rules rather than the spirit. As if his heart hadn't been in it. He hadn't been that way with Michael. Or me.

"She'd love that. Me in a suit and tie every day going to some boring day job. An hour commute in a little family box on wheels, a wife like her, two point five kids, a house down the street from them."

He sounded more angry than amused. Maybe we'd get to this one sooner rather than later.

"Outside of how creepy it would be for you to be married to someone like your mother—and seriously, I shudder—it's not shocking that she'd want you safe."

Considering she was down to one son, she probably wasn't keen on another memorial service. Just because she wasn't warm like Nancy was with Ben and me didn't mean she didn't love her kids.

He snatched the suit jacket up off the back of the chair. "It's not her life."

And maybe we'd shelve that one for later after all. He sounded pretty hot on the subject and I was not up for getting caught in the crossfire. I needed to save my energy for our own battle. He must have seen the look on my face.

"Sorry. I guess my parents are not your problem, right?"

"No, but it's not as if I don't understand how your parents are. And have you even met my dad? About five ten, balding, convinced I made the biggest mistake of my life quitting the force before I made chief?"

"Yeah, sorry, sometimes I forget how much time you've spent with the Colonel and Barbara. Shit, we don't have time for this, Will. We need to get to this list."

Which is how I found myself sitting on his couch, flipping through the basic cable channels, while he changed from spit-and-polish federal agent back into on-the-fringes biker with questionable morals and a heart of gold. Or could only hookers have a heart of gold? Daytime talk shows, soap operas, and infomercials flew by as I absentmindedly pressed the button on the remote.

"Ready?"

I looked up to find him fully converted back. Jeans clean but stained and a work shirt. I wished I could say it wasn't appealing but if I was honest, he looked a hell of a lot better than he did in that soulless suit. In the well-cut wool he had been a parody. This was the real Seth, hot as hell—and that was a train of thought that would get me into trouble if I didn't jump off before it got to the final station, which if I recalled correctly was on the other side of the door he stood in front of. I wondered what he would say if I gave him the fifteen minutes he'd asked for earlier. I wondered why I was bothering to wonder; he'd made himself clear earlier. Me being a fully independent person wasn't part of the deal for him. It was his way or no way.

"Yeah, let's go find us the tattoo artist to the scum."

"We'll take the bike. Showing up in that sedan will shut doors faster than a badge would."

I looked down at my t-shirt, jeans, and boots. I was clean and presentable for most occasions barring church or black tie. I could pass for a biker's babe. A plain one.

"You look fine, Will. Just let me do the talking, okay?"

"Um, yeah, I'll do my best on that one, sparky." I said it with a straight face, though I was sure I saw doubt in Seth's eyes.

———

The first place was only a few miles from the apartment, tucked into a series of detached buildings in an older complex of shops and businesses. There were only a few cars parked in what could have been termed an alley since it was too narrow to be a road. The half dozen spots in front of the shop were empty. This was one of the shops on our list that didn't require appointments and since it was the middle of the day, it appeared there wasn't much drop-in business. The guy at the front desk was, unsurprisingly, heavily covered in ink. It probably made me weird that I felt more comfortable with him than I did with the khakis and polo crowd.

"Hey, I'm looking for some cover-up work and I heard you guys are a bit more traditional than some of the other shops in the area," Seth said.

Cover-up work? Granted, the last time I'd been in a position to see the majority of his skin it had been dark, but I had gotten a good eyeful of most of it four months ago. He'd been sporting a few tattoos but none looked in need of covering or updating. Frankly, the work had been fantastic and I'd spent some very non-bleary moments touching them.

He lifted his shirt to show the guy a tattoo on his side that had not been there that night in June. It was terrible. It made me cringe it was so bad. The guy chuckled.

"I see your girlfriend's not a fan of it either."

Not a fan? I didn't think *hate* was a strong enough word for the abomination that was marring Seth's torso.

"Yeah, well, she's the reason I got wasted that night so she's partly to blame."

He turned ever so slightly and winked at me, but I could sense honesty in the statement. I knew his cover, aside from the fake record, was probably based on the truth as much as possible. It would make it easier to remember and easier to believe. He'd gotten inked after that night. I wondered who was to blame for taking him to a tattoo shop and letting him get that hideous thing. I'd like to have a few words with whoever was responsible for that awful mermaid on his beautiful body. A mermaid. Jesus.

"I mean, it barely looks like her. The eyes are close."

It was supposed to be me? Seth looked sheepish, an expression he'd mastered a long time ago. If that hideous thing was supposed to look like me, he had good reason to be embarrassed.

I snapped my gum and rolled my eyes. If I was playing a part, I was going for broke. Especially since I was positive I was never getting the opportunity to go undercover again. Seth would out me to my dad the second he got home. He'd know if he couldn't stop me, Dad would. I wasn't having to act my annoyance. First his heavy-handed insistence that his "woman" wasn't authorized by him to investigate anything he deemed dangerous and then a permanent commitment to that position on his damn body was a bit more than I was willing to overlook.

"Serves you right. Who gets wasted and lets their dumbass friends take them to get a tattoo, anyway?"

"She's sassy. I like her," the tattoo artist said.

I leaned on the counter, pressing my breasts into my arms to give me the illusion of cleavage. I was seriously lacking those kinds of assets but Undercover Seth's girlfriend was the flirty type. I saw him scowling as I beamed a smile at the guy. Good.

"Damn straight. Cool ink, by the way," I said, chewing my gum in a way that I was sure was disturbing my mom's relaxation somewhere across the Atlantic.

"Heh. Yeah, she can be a handful sometimes. I was thinking maybe a skull."

Seth seemed unamused at my contribution to our interrogation. Probably because I was supposed to keep my mouth shut. I had warned him. I wasn't backing down just because he had decided I was supposed to.

"A skull? Yuck. How about something cool, like a phoenix? You know that fiery bird from that movie about the kid who did magic? With the glasses? You know, Harry Potter?"

Seth blinked at me a few times while the guy laughed. "You want me to get a tattoo from Harry Potter? It's a kid's movie."

"It was sweet and the bird is totally badass. I like birds."

The guy's attention was totally focused on me now. Seth glared at me.

"You can do birds, right?" I asked.

"So about the skull," Seth said, talking over me. This amused the guy even more. And I was really starting to like Undercover Willa. She was hilarious.

"Excuse us for a moment." Seth grabbed my arm, more gently than I know it appeared, and hustled me over to the door. "What're you doing?"

"Building a rapport. I'm fun, hot cop and you're stick-up-his-ass cop who doesn't know when he's being overbearing," I whispered.

"I'm glad you're having fun but whatever this is you're doing is wasting time. We need to get him around to skulls, Willa."

"And we will, Seth, just as soon as he trusts us. Besides, he's so distracted by my quote unquote sassiness, he'll have no idea you're interrogating him, okay?" I smiled at him and snapped my gum again. "So what's it going to be, babe?"

We turned back to the guy, who I was pretty sure had been ogling my ass, and I tucked myself into Seth's side. The one not sporting the vilest piece of body art I'd even seen in my life.

The guy ended up being a bust. As did the next three shops. And my butt had begun to hurt from riding the back of Seth's motorcycle. He'd blown me off when I briefly whined about how uncomfortable it was. Granted, it wasn't my best tough-girl moment.

We walked into the last shop on the list, way the hell out in the farthest suburb in the county. The area was one long main drag with all manner of shops and stores in an eclectic mix of ethnic restaurants and pawn shops. I was sure that it was going to be another waste of time, but Seth thought we were about to get lucky, so to speak. The area had seen a lot of changes in the past twenty years and, while diverse, it was also sharply divided between old-time residents and newcomers. Immigrant newcomers. Making it the kind of place where resentments could fester. And that also made it a place where you were more likely to find a tattoo artist that catered to some specific wishes to create a symbol for a group committed to its right to a lily white, homogenous society.

Two seconds in the door and I knew Seth was right. I didn't want to think in terms like "redneck," but it was the first thing that entered my mind. The shop had way too many people for late afternoon. As if this were where people who leaned to a certain philosophical bent came to hang out, not feeling comfortable at the Starbucks around the corner. Or any of the bodegas, Korean markets, or Indian groceries.

There was no diversity. And an overload of testosterone and menace. *This was what a gazelle feels like when it wanders into a pack of lions.* A tendril of fear curled into my stomach and I pressed closer to Seth. I've never been more grateful for the ambiguously European melting-pot facial features I saw every morning in the mirror. I had never spent too much time feeling out of place—the neighborhood, my schools, the area was too diverse—and I was never ashamed, but this was definitely not a welcoming environment for someone like me.

Seth had picked up on my tension. His arm and shoulder muscles were taut, ready to throw a punch. It must have shown on his face that he wasn't the kind of man to screw with and the tension ratcheted down considerably. The men in the place may have been rough around the edges but they weren't stupid. And they didn't like strangers.

A man stepped forward from the group. "Can I help you folks?"

"I have a friend that got a nice piece done here and I was looking for something similar. A skull tattoo. I want to get this covered."

He lifted his shirt showing the mermaid again. I looked down at the floor when I heard some mutterings about "a nice piece" from the back of the group. The undercover thing had gotten a lot less fun since we'd arrived. Seth's arm was rock hard as he dropped his shirt and turned toward the group. Clearly, he'd heard the mutterings as well. The guy who'd stepped forward motioned to the group to go into the back of the long, thin room where there was an incongruously flowered loveseat set in front of a flat-screen TV.

"Whoever did that should find a new line of work. Did you have that done in the area?"

"Bangkok. I was drunk."

"Everything those chinks do is shit." The yell from the back of the room got everyone's attention. Right place, indeed.

# CHAPTER

## 21

AFTER MAKING HIS EXCUSES that he didn't feel comfortable with his girl being around, Seth told the man he'd come back later alone. The guy's nod of assent was absent of any suspicion or annoyance. I think he wanted me out of there as badly as we did. The drive back to the garage had us whipping down the interstate and weaving into tight spaces between the commuters who were distracted with thoughts of home on Friday afternoon.

I could tell by the way he was slamming the bike through the gears that Seth was more than pissed off. The contradiction between his apparent feelings about my treatment at the tattoo parlor and his seeming disregard for my safety on the back of the bike was the biggest indicator.

We pulled into the parking lot and he slid off the seat before letting me get off.

"Where are your gloves? Your hands have to be freezing."

I shrugged. I wasn't about to raise his hackles any more than they already were. I knew there was a lot tied up in his feelings of anger and possession at that moment and, not too long ago, I might have waded in to set those fireworks off, but I wasn't interested. He was hurting. His pride was hurting because those idiots had mouthed off about me and he'd had to just stand there. I was willing to take him down a few arrogant pegs when he was being a rigid, controlling ass about my job, but I didn't enjoy kicking him simply to kick him.

"Seth, it's a case. You did the right thing holding back. I know you wanted to beat the crap out of them. And you could have. Rage alone would have taken care of it."

He took the helmet from my hands and hung it on the handlebar, fixing the strap. "It scares me. The rage I felt. That I still feel. That they were looking at you and talking about you that way. What I knew they were thinking."

I put my hand on his arm, wishing I could feel his skin instead of leather. I was in so much trouble with him. I knew he didn't get it. I barely got it. The water had been churning between us for so long. When it finally broke on the shore, it had spread too far, too fast.

"Hey, I get it. I do." I hoped he could hear everything I wasn't saying. The stuff I didn't know how to put into words.

"But you can't accept it."

I knew that it was a question. I knew what he wanted me to answer. To make it simple. To make it easy. And safe.

"You wouldn't want me if I was able to accept it."

The metal stairs creaked and clanged under his heavy footfalls. I watched him walk away. That was as simple as it was going to get. If

I were willing to step aside, let him wrap me in a cocoon of normal, be like his mother, live in that house down the street from our parents, I wouldn't be me. If he wanted someone who was willing to sit on the sidelines and just watch, he wouldn't want me. I wondered if he really did want me or if he'd just wanted what he was told he couldn't have. I hoped he figured it out. I wasn't going to fight him anymore.

He was on the phone when I stepped through the office door.

"Yeah, that's the place. The usual package."

He eyed me as he listened to whoever was on the other end of the call and then disconnected without a goodbye. I always hated when they did that on television shows. It seemed so rude. He paced back and forth, coiled energy emanating off him, graceful and dangerous as a caged predator. It was unnerving and sexy as hell.

"Quit. You're making me dizzy."

And by dizzy, of course, I meant, he was making me want to fling myself into him like he was the damn ocean. Sex was never going to be a problem for us, that was for sure.

"Who was that on the phone?"

He stopped pacing for a minute and then started up again, slower. He was going to make me embarrass myself if he didn't stop. "Tim. He's putting surveillance on that last tattoo shop."

"The usual package, huh? Your agent speak is so sexy. It makes it sound like they're getting the fancy floor mats and undercoating."

I could see he was trying not to smile. He was mad and he wanted to stay mad. It probably made it easier for him. I should know, I'd been pulling that trick for years.

The computer on the desk beeped. Seth pulled up the email that had come in.

"Boyd sent over the full results on the three guys you picked from the DMV photos. Two don't look likely but the third could be our guy. She's sent over uniforms to interview him. Mark Ingalls."

I shivered. We'd been stalled unraveling the knot for so long and feeling it come loose scared and excited me.

"Hey, Sunshine, you okay?"

I nodded, not trusting my voice. The look of concern on his face hurt. I didn't want him to be worried. I wanted to lie down and sleep for a year when this was all over, Mark Ingalls, or whoever the bad guy was, tried and in prison. I was tired of being on alert.

"Do you mind if I bail on you and lie down for a bit?"

He nodded. "I got this under control. A nap will do you some good."

I wasn't the only one who needed some real sleep. He looked like he'd been awake for decades.

"What about you?"

"Well, and not that I don't appreciate the offer, but I don't think that cot's big enough for the both of us. Even if you are a slip of a thing, darlin'."

His John Wayne impression had gotten better since I'd heard it last. I wasn't sure if he was trying to put me at ease or himself, but I figured I could do my part. Him making innuendo and me insulting his manhood. Good times.

"But you're a little slip of a thing too, aren't you, sweet cheeks?" I let my eyes drift down to the front of his pants. Slowly and deliberately so there was no question of my meaning. "And it wasn't an invitation. It was a concern for your sleeping habits and whether the lack of sleep was going to cause you to get us both killed zooming along on that deathtrap of yours."

He clutched his hands to his chest dramatically and rocked back on the heels of his boots. "Ouch. Straight to the heart, Sunshine."

I settled my eyes on his crotch again. "That wasn't where I was aiming." Content that I had gotten in the last word, I turned and headed toward the back closet where the temporary bed was.

I laid down on the not terribly uncomfortable cot and tried not to notice that the pillow smelled like Seth's manly shampoo. Or how comforting the smell of him was. He'd been out of my life for years with the rare holiday appearance and yet he'd slipped into a spot I hadn't even known I'd been holding for him. And that was a lie. I'd fought against myself, hadn't wanted to hold a spot for him. Friend or foe, lover or not. It had scared me. Funny how all the stupid things I'd been afraid of had vanished after someone tried to kill me. I dropped into sleep quickly and dreamed of faceless men with tattoos chasing us through a burning house that had hundreds of doors, none of which would open.

I woke up in Seth's arms. He was shaking me, and the room was filled with smoke.

"Jesus, Willa, wake up!"

I was completely confused. It made no sense. How could I have fallen asleep in the house? We were running. Looking around, I saw the cinder block walls of the storage room. We were at the motorcycle garage. It had been a dream. Except the fire. I coughed. That was obviously real. I stumbled up from the cot, tripping into Seth.

"You scared the shit out of me. I thought you were dead."

I bent over coughing as he tugged me out of the storage room. The office air was cleaner. Or the area was bigger so it hadn't filled as quickly. Either way, it was easier to breathe. My coughing fit died down. He was pale. Fear or the smoke had taken a toll on him. I saw the sluggish look to his eyes and the desk chair turned over on the floor. He'd clearly nodded off looking at the computer. The main room started to get hazy, the smoke getting heavier.

"We've got to get out of here."

He looked at me, genuinely afraid. "The door's blocked."

"Come again? The door's the only way out?"

He shook his head, looking over to the high, narrow window on the back wall. My eyes widened. Our options were burn to death or take a two-story fall onto pavement? I hated both options.

I looked at the window and shook my head. "No way. No! The fire department's on the way. The building is cinder block. It'll hold off the fire long enough. And they'll put out the fire before it gets up here. We'll wait it out. I refuse to die here."

"Will, the smoke will kill us before they get the fire out. I'll boost you out the window and hold onto you. That way it's barely a one-floor drop. You can do it."

"We won't fit. It's too narrow."

"You'll fit. Just barely but you'll make it."

He outweighed me by seventy pounds of solid muscle. Even if I fit, there was no way he'd get through it. Not even if he broke the glass out. And he knew that. He was planning to drop me out the window knowing he was still trapped.

"NO! I'm not leaving you in here."

"Please, baby, please. This is the only chance we have. Once you're out you can get the door open. You'll be saving me by going."

He moved away from me and began dragging the desk over to the wall under the window. Without a word, I joined him in pushing it across the room. He climbed up on it and pushed the louvered window open. The cool fall air rushed in, clearing the smoke a bit. It wouldn't be long before even that little bit of fresh air was gone. I had barely noticed the temperature in the room jacking up. The fire must have been raging before Seth woke up. We were out of time. Me going out the window was the only chance we had.

He motioned for me to climb up beside him. When we were face to face again he wrapped his arms around me. His mouth was right by my ear so when he spoke it was like he was inside my head.

"Listen to me, Sunshine. All that shit I said, everything I've done...I'm sorry. So sorry. I lo—"

I pulled away from him. "Stop. We're not dying tonight."

He looked like he wanted to argue with me, but I set my jaw. I wasn't accepting any deathbed confessions.

He nodded. "I'll lean out as far as I can to give you a shorter drop. You can do this, Will. Just make sure when you land you don't go over onto your back. You can't risk hitting your head."

I nodded. Me agreeing to his plan was probably freaking him out more than the idea of dying. He'd never close his case. That asshole would get away with it all. Killing Joe Reagan, burning the Horowitzes' house, trying to knife me. He'd get away with killing us. Not a chance in hell I was letting that happen.

"I'm ready."

He smiled at me. "That's my girl."

He boosted me up. I grabbed the frame of the window and wedged my body through the opening while Seth held me tightly. I shimmied out the building slowly, the metal digging into my ribs. I pivoted slightly so I could face him, wrapping my hand around the frame. I had to get angled down to the ground but my ass was stuck on the bottom of the window.

"You have to push me. I'm caught on the window."

He tightened his grip on my arm and planted the heel of his palm against my hip. I kept my eyes locked on his as he shoved me free. He grabbed my wrist just as I started to lose my grip on the narrow ledge.

"I got you. I'm not letting go until you're ready."

My muscles burned. I was exhausted and drenched in sweat. It had to be even worse for him, holding all my weight. I let go of the ledge, grateful that the metal wasn't biting into my hand anymore. This was the hard part. Seth leaned out the window, dangling me above the ground. I looked down. I could barely see the pavement in the hazy dark. The blood was a loud thump in my ears but I could hear the sirens flying toward us on the parkway.

"Hey, Sunshine."

I looked back up at him, the angle making my neck ache.

"You're the biggest badass I know. This is nothing. A couple feet." He was lying. It was scary as hell. And at least fifteen feet. The sweat made his hold on my arms slick and I started to slip out of his grasp, my wrists feeling like they were coming apart.

"Let go."

He shook his head. The effort of holding my dead weight made the cords in his neck stand out. I imagined I could see the vein in his neck throbbing. I couldn't. The smoke was now pouring out of the window. I had to go.

"We're out of time! Drop me."

He still held me. I knew he didn't want to let go so I pulled down and away from him hard.

And fell.

# CHAPTER

## 22

SLAMMING INTO THE GROUND jarred every bone, feeling like they were all out of place at once, and I barely managed to stick the landing. I tried to hit on the balls of my feet, old cheerleading training kicking in years too late, so I didn't break my ankles. I ended up toppling over and hitting my butt. Thank god that was well padded. I scraped the hell out of my elbow, but when I assessed my body I didn't feel any broken bones.

The sirens were so loud at that point it was almost deafening. I could see the red lights bouncing off the walls. I got up and wobbled, tripping over my own feet a bit, and ran to the side of the building. The stairs shook alarmingly as I pounded up them. I got to the landing and saw that there was a steering wheel lock braced along the back railing and jammed under the handle. It would turn but the door was wedged shut. I could hear Seth kicking the door from the inside.

I slammed my hands against the door in frustration.

"Stay by the window, Seth!"

I had no idea if he heard me over the booming blows he was delivering. I needed a hammer or axe or something. I turned and almost tumbled face first down the stairs in my rush. I hit the alley and almost tripped again. The length of the building was no more than fifty feet, but I felt like I couldn't close the distance. Panic was sending tremors throughout my body. I could feel every limb tingling and my heart thumped like a bass line. It felt too big for my chest and I knew I had to pace my breathing so I didn't hyperventilate. I had to get something to get Seth out. I skidded to a stop at the first truck.

"The door's blocked. Axe!"

I sucked in air that felt like acid and it practically buckled my legs knowing that Seth was running out of air.

"Are you hurt, ma'am?"

A firefighter put his hand on my back. I worried he hadn't made out what I said. It had made sense to my ears but I had no idea what came out of my mouth. I needed some authority I sure wasn't feeling to get some action.

"I'm an LEO. The door is deliberately jammed shut and my partner is trapped inside. Bring an axe. NOW!" My *don't fuck with me* cop voice had kicked in.

He grabbed an axe from the equipment on the truck and followed me. He saw the stairs just as I pointed and pushed past me. I should have been impressed how he'd managed to outpace me in all his gear, but I was truly terrified he wasn't going to get Seth out in time. My footsteps had been loud when I'd run up the stairs but his were thunderous. I saw the first blow of the axe before I passed the stairs to turn the corner and look up at the window. I couldn't see Seth.

"SETH!"

I had lost track of how much time had passed since he'd woken me up. I developed tunnel vision. All I saw was that window and the smoke rushing out of it. I willed myself to not invent Seth at the window when he was the only thing I wanted to see. Screaming his name over and over so loudly, I eventually felt something give in my throat. His name was just a hoarse wail after that. I felt someone's arms go around me, trying to pull me away from the building.

"Ma'am, we need to check you out."

"No. Seth is in there. I'm not leaving without him."

The smoke and the screaming had robbed me of any semblance of voice and what came out was just a croaky garble.

I tried to shake off the hands holding me but I was bodily picked up. I struggled as hard as I could, all my strength gone. I sobbed into the shoulder of whoever carried me. I heard shouting all around me but it was far away. I was laid down and felt someone working on me. An oxygen mask slipped over my face, pressing into and slipping around the greasy soot that coated my skin. I heard someone asking me questions, but I didn't care. All I wanted was Seth.

Medical jargon was flying all around my head. Then my ears picked up a beautiful sound.

"Male, early thirties, smoke inhalation. No burns. Female, mid-twenties, shock, smoke inhalation."

He wasn't dead. They got him out. He was safe. I blinked, trying to clear my vision, but my eyes were so irritated from the smoke and crying that it was hard to keep them open. I pushed the oxygen mask away and my hand was grabbed.

"Ma'am, you need to leave that on."

I mustered my strength and pushed it off again. "Seth?"

I could barely make out the sound of my own voice in the commotion. The water roaring out of the hoses, people shouting out instructions, the equipment inside the trucks squawking and squealing.

"She's trying to say something."

"Seth?" The pain flared raw in my throat.

"The man? That's Seth? He's fine. Just rest while we look you over." The female EMT had a sweet but firm voice and tried to replace the oxygen

I shook my head, preventing her from getting it back on. "I need to see him."

"Let me just take care of you."

"Now."

"He's fine. I promise."

I grabbed her hand and stilled it. "It can't wait."

"You're not going to let me finish checking you out until you see for yourself, are you?"

I shook my head and tried to smile at her. I could only imagine what it ended up looking like, but she gave a little chuckle so I assumed it wasn't too monstrous. I felt the gurney bumping over the gravel and ruts of the parking lot.

The back of the gurney came up enough that I wasn't flat on my back anymore. That simple change helped clear the fuzziness in my head. My vision started to clear a bit too. I could make out the back of the ambulance, its doors opening and the lights inside shining out onto the dark ground. I could almost make out the features of the other EMT gathering equipment in the back but the bright lights behind him obscured more than revealed.

I pulled off the mask for the last time. "I don't need this. I'm fine. Water?"

A bottle of cold water was pressed into my hands. They shook as I tried to take the cap off, not recognizing it had already been opened for me. Some splashed out on my arms and the cold woke me up almost completely. I brought the bottle to my lips carefully, taking a small sip. The last thing I wanted to do was throw up.

"Good. Little sips. Your friend is still getting checked out. I know he was in there longer than you and took in more smoke."

I took another tiny sip. "He saved me. Put me out the window and eased me down."

The water had soothed my throat enough that talking didn't feel like swallowing razor blades, but my voice was well and truly trashed. I sounded like I had smoked two packs of cigarettes every day for forty years. And then gargled rusty barbed wire.

"Oh yeah? I heard you saved him right back. You both sound pretty awesome, if you ask me."

"Can I see him now?"

"Can I stop you?"

"Hey, Sunshine, nice dismount."

He was sweaty and covered in greasy soot but he was alive. That was all I cared about. I tried to get up to go to him but was gently pressed back down onto the gurney.

"Stay put. I still need to check you out. Smoke inhalation can be tricky."

I couldn't take my eyes off his face. He was alive. I scanned him for any burns or injury. He was dirty and his shirt was torn but he looked perfect.

"Her name is Willa. And, yes, she's always this much trouble."

The EMT leaned down to check my pulse. Her nametag read K. Barnes. "Well, your pulse is a bit elevated but considering the circumstances I'm not worried."

The relief on Seth's face made me realize he was only worried about me. The weight of that hit me.

"You put me out that window thinking it was the last time you were going to see me. That's why you tried—"

"It's fine, Will. We made it."

I shook my head and felt myself close to tears again. "No, it's not fine."

I had so much I wanted to say and no idea where to begin. Our fight that morning—hell, every fight we'd ever had—seemed so stupid. I knew how he felt. I felt it too now. The fierce determination that I would do anything, any way I had to, no matter how much it hurt me, or if even he hated me, so that he was safe. I hadn't understood. I had thought it was his pride, pumped full of testosterone and male ego. It wasn't pride. Or ownership. He loved me. There was the simple truth I hadn't wanted to admit. A tear slipped down my cheek.

I took another mouthful of water. I wanted to just look at him forever. I didn't care if we solved the case. I didn't care about anything except him and the fact that he was safe in front of me.

I wanted to tell him that. It came out differently than I had planned. "You were trapped and I thought that you'd … and now … I swear, if you ever die on me, I will kick your ass," I said.

"Only you, Sunshine." Seth began to laugh, which turned into choking coughs. The male EMT pushed the hand holding the oxygen mask up to Seth's face again. I got up, pressing past both EMTs to sit on his gurney. I twined my hand into the one not holding the mask and laid my face against his arm.

I heard the EMTs whispering to each other as Seth's coughing eased. He dropped the mask again. I couldn't look him in the eye. He rubbed the pad of his thumb on the back of my hand. "When you dropped it was the hardest second of my life since I'd heard Michael had died. I wanted to trust that you would be fine, that we both would, but all I could think was that I had failed again."

I watched the red light from the fire trucks bounce off the tree line across the road, the leaves already red and gold, looking like fire themselves. I had spent the entire time I'd known him—years, almost two decades—not understanding how I felt. I didn't even know if there were words to explain it. I got it now, I just didn't know how to express it. I tried anyway.

"You didn't fail me. You saved me tonight. And you trusted that I'd save you. You're my hero."

I snuck a look at his face. I needed to know if he believed me.

"I mean it, Seth. That was some serious hero shit you pulled in there."

He ducked his head but he was smiling. "We make a good team."

"This is sweet, but we need to get you both to the hospital to be fully checked and you're not both going to fit in the ambulance like this," the male EMT said.

Seth dug out his phone and keyed in a sequence to bring up a screen that showed his badge. Neat. He stood brandishing it at the EMTs like weapon. "My name is Seth Anderson. I'm a special agent with the Bureau of Alcohol, Tobacco and Firearms and I'm officially refusing additional medical care."

Both EMTs had begun packing up the second ambulance the second he'd flashed his digital badge. They'd obviously had enough experience with the Feds to know what he was going to say.

"Are you an idiot? Of course you're going to the hospital." I had words to express those feelings. Annoyance. Impatience.

He shook his head. "Willa, I wet down the sleeve of my shirt and tied it around my nose and mouth. I'm fine. But I need you to go. You could have broken something when you hit the ground," he said.

"Oh, hell no. You're not pulling that on me. If you want me to go then you get back on that gurney and let them take you too."

He crouched down in front of me. I could see the set of his jaw. "I have work I need to do."

"So you're shipping me off to the hospital and going back to, what?"

He took both of my hands in his and squeezed them. "Baby, I need to get this guy. He's dangerous."

While I understood it wasn't his ego that pushed him to protect me at all costs, it still chafed. I wanted to do this differently than we always had. I was definitely going to try after this case was over, but we didn't have time for the no-holds-barred screaming throw down it was going to take to negotiate a peace accord. Mouthy Willa was still on the job. I wasn't backing down on this.

"Wow, thanks for the news flash. I hadn't pieced that together on my own. I mean, the knife should have given it away but, you know, maybe I had a loose thread on my sweater. And the fire, well, maybe I looked cold. No shit, he's dangerous. And you need medical attention, dumbass, so get back on the gurney."

He had started to shake his head again and stand when I dropped his hands and grabbed him by the front of his shirt, yanking him back down so we were nose to nose.

"Get on the gurney. Now." Cop voice was back.

The EMTs watched us with interest. I could tell he was wavering.

"Ten bucks on the girl," said the male EMT.

"No bet there. She will totally win this one," K. Barnes said.

Seth sat back down on the gurney next to me. "If it will make you feel better that I get checked out ... "

"Shut up and get your own damn gurney, caveman."

# CHAPTER

## 23

AFTER FOUR HOURS AT the emergency room, people poking and prodding us, taking X-rays, and drawing vials of blood, and Seth bitching the entire time anyone touched him yet demanding more tests for me, we were declared probably unlikely to die from smoke inhalation and sent home. Either you got amazing service if you were a federal agent or the ER staff just got sick of all the complaining. An agent from Seth's office came to pick us up and the two talked shop in the front seat while I dozed in the back. I never fell asleep completely. The car would hit a bump or pothole and I would jolt awake, feeling as if I was falling away from the fire again. At two in the morning, the roads were empty and we were back at Seth's apartment in no time.

I stared at the door to Michael's room. I was so tired I was afraid that if I thought about it too much, remembering that Michael was gone and that I'd almost lost Seth too, I'd break down. Seth saw me hesitate and took my hand to lead me into his room. We hadn't been alone the whole evening once we got out of the building.

"I should probably get a shower. Wash this smoke off me."

"Yeah, right, of course. Let me get you some stuff to change into."

I stood in the doorway to the bathroom, waiting. I saw him pulling out clothes. He handed me an Army t-shirt and shorts from his dresser.

"I'm just going to …" I hitched my thumb over my shoulder

"Take your time. I'll get cleaned up in Michael's, um, the other bathroom."

As I washed the smoke and soot out of my hair a wave of fatigue swamped me. I got out of the shower as quickly as I could and pulled Seth's Army shirt on. I needed to get into bed. The scant hours of sleep I had gotten over the past few days had prompted my body to start demanding it. Had it only been last night that I had fallen asleep easily in Seth's arms?

I turned off the light, pulled down the covers on the bed, and collapsed against the pillow. I didn't care that my hair was wet and probably not as clean as I'd have liked. It probably still reeked of smoke. Not that I would have been able to tell the difference since that was all I smelled anymore. All I wanted was to close my eyes and sleep off the sore muscles and achy lungs.

Despite my utter exhaustion, I could not fall asleep. I had the same problem as in the car, and it wasn't my old insomnia. I'd start to drop off and my leg would kick out, feeling like I was falling. I heard the door latch disengage quietly. Seth poked his head into the room. Failing to see my brutal murder occurring, he pulled back and stopped only when he heard my voice.

"I'm awake," I said. "Come in."

"I just wanted to check and make sure you were okay. You need to rest." He began to pull the door shut.

"Wait. Stay."

"I'm not going anywhere tonight." He started to shut the door again.

"I mean, stay in here with me." When he hesitated, I continued. "Look, we both know you'll keep waking me up trying to check on me so if you're in here at least we'll both be able to get some sleep."

I felt him slip in beside me, gingerly, leaving a gap between us. I reached over and grabbed his arm, dragging it over me and scooting back into him.

"We'll just end up like this anyway." I could feel him smile against my shoulder.

I startled awake only one more time.

"I've got you. I'm not going to let you fall. I've got you, love," Seth said, pulling me deeper into his body, curving around me, shielding me entirely, his cheek against mine, his words a whisper on my skin.

———

It was late morning by my standard when Seth's phone started ringing. He got up to let in the other agent, who'd spent the night in the car as lookout. I tried to curl into the warm spot he'd left, but without Seth sleep eluded me.

I pulled on the shorts he had given me before I got in the shower hours earlier. They hung off me and I yanked the drawstring as tightly as it would go. I wasn't sure why I hadn't bothered with the clothes I'd packed. I hadn't thought of it and swimming in Seth's t-shirt made me feel small and secure.

In the kitchen, Seth handed me a cup of coffee without any smart remarks about how I took it, but I did notice that for a man who took it black he had sugar and cream available suddenly.

Agent Gordon and I had a stare-off over coffee. He hadn't spoken a word to me last night either.

"Is he mute with girls? Like that guy on the science show?" I asked.

Seth laughed. Agent Silent Treatment scowled at me. At least we knew he could hear.

"I don't bite. Well, I will if you ask nicely."

What was it about so many cops that made them sarcasm-impaired, humorless prigs? I'd been a cop for years and still didn't know why some of them, like Harrison, were such buzzkills. Lucky me, I got to have breakfast with one while I was wearing someone else's jammies. I smiled at the agent sitting across from me. It wasn't a pleasant one. In fact, it barely qualified as a smile. He lowered his eyes back down to his coffee cup. I didn't see any reason the guy couldn't try to engage in polite, superficial conversation. If I was capable of it after two attempts on my life, he could muster a little small talk.

"No, seriously, are you mute? Because if so, that's cool. All federal agencies have to meet disability hire quotas but I'm curious, how are you able to do the radio? Morse code or something?"

I heard Seth snort a mouthful of coffee.

"Is it me? Because I'm a civilian and you've just lived the life too long? You don't know how to relate? You should know, I was a cop."

"I know," he said.

"Wow, you can speak. I'm so impressed. Maybe now we can introduce ourselves already since, you know, I've been sitting across from you for ten minutes and I'm not wearing a bra."

The agent spit his mouthful of coffee onto the table.

"Are you two really crack federal agents who are supposed to keep America safe from people misusing alcohol, tobacco, and firearms? The word *bra* sets you off?" I stood up, taking my cup with me, and left the kitchen. That was the only silver lining to having a psycho hunting you: you gave up any pretense of giving a damn what other people thought. Gordon wasn't a guest so I didn't have to entertain him. Seth was smart enough to not follow me.

I grabbed my overnight bag from the closet floor and threw it on the bed. I yanked out a pair of jeans and tank top. I wanted my own clothes after all. Being looked at like a bug by Seth's Fed buddy had made me feel small in a way I didn't like. I'd be damned if some suit was going to look down on me.

My secret admirer, who was no doubt Mark Ingalls, was feeling the pressure we'd put on him. I called Boyd for an update. She'd barely said hello before I jumped in.

"Jan, do you have anything on Ingalls?"

"Wow, two days in a row someone tries to kill you and you're not even slightly off track? I don't know if you're the toughest person I've met or the dumbest."

"Probably both. Honestly, I just really want you to tell me that some SWAT guys kicked in his door last night and he's now in an orange jumpsuit." I paced around the bedroom. More than once I eyed the bed wishing I could go back to sleep.

"Sorry, kid. We haven't found him yet. We met Ingalls's uncle, who's also not a fan of yours. Called you a 'snoopy little bitch.' Said he saw you at the garage and then later spying on their house. Told Mark."

My lame stakeout of Reagan's known associates hadn't been so lame, after all. That was twice I'd been close to connecting the murder to Ingalls.

"Seth's okay? I got some second- and third-hand reports last night."

"Yeah. We checked out fine at the hospital and the ATF sent another agent to get us. Our new friend picked us up from the hospital last night and has spoken exactly two words to me."

Boyd was silent for a bit. I could hear noises that told me she was in her car.

"Jan?"

"Sorry, Willa, I was just thinking about that agent. Is it possible they're going to take you into protective custody? I know they won't yank Seth off the case—it's clearly too late for that."

It was my turn to be silent. I didn't want to think Seth would do something like that behind my back, but I couldn't deny he'd jump at the chance to get me locked down and safe. If his boss presented it to him, he'd even be able to convince himself, and try to convince me, that he had no choice. Then he'd pack me up and get back to taking down Ingalls and his associates while I sat in some federal safe house. The ends would justify the means. Bust, made; Willa, not dead.

"It might not be a bad idea," she said.

"Do you honestly think I'm going to sit watching talk shows while the ATF saddles up and gets their man? My man?"

"Ingalls has a serious thing for you. He had a wall with pictures of you. Some of them were as old as your high school graduation and there were even stories he'd downloaded from the Internet about your mother's drama festival in Santa Fe. He got all that in just a few days. He's not just angry with you. He's fixated."

A crazy ass murder wall was a real thing? I thought that was just something on TV shows. "Why is it the only men who are interested in me are emotionally unreliable?" I quipped, but my heart wasn't in the joke and my voice broke.

"This is almost over, kid. He can't hide from us forever."

*Almost over* was almost as good as *over*. I gathered back up the scattered bits of my stupid determination, which I was sure was her intention.

"We rattled some cages yesterday at one of the tattoo parlors. Seth had some surveillance set up for it last night. I forgot to call you in all the trying not to die."

"You really jumped out a second-story window?"

I laughed so hard I started coughing again. "Jumped like tuck and roll, all action movie? No. Dangled out and fell on my butt? Yes. My whole ass is purple."

"It was pretty impressive from where I was standing, Sunshine," Seth said from the now open door.

After a few more words with Boyd, I disconnected the call and stared at Seth for a minute. "Are you putting me in protective custody?"

"That was the plan," he said.

I might have let an expletive or two slip out. There was possibly something about cow excrement. I can recall a few compound curses involving his mother. He took it all just looking at me impassively.

"You done, Sunshine?"

I grabbed my bag off the floor. It wasn't the most authoritative stomp out I'd ever performed since I wasn't wearing shoes but I felt that my lavender toenail polish lent it a certain gravitas. Or it would have if Seth hadn't grabbed my arm. I was so outraged I barely felt his fingers pressing into the hideous bruise on my bicep I'd earned during our great escape.

"My turn."

I rolled my neck from side to side and nodded, waiting, planning my next attack.

"That *was* the plan. Then I changed my mind," he said. "Instead I asked for Gordon to be assigned to the case with me. Despite his lack of people skills, or maybe because of them, he's one of the best the ATF has at urban warfare tactics."

"You changed your mind? Just like that?" I was skeptical. Seth had been unwavering that he'd do anything to guarantee my safety, even going so far as to ruin any personal relationship we had. Protective custody at an ATF safe house seemed like a no-brainer.

"It may be the biggest mistake I ever make but when you said that I trusted you to save me, I realized I have to trust you to save yourself too. How's that for evolved?"

The way he looked at me lit a fire that shot down between my legs. It was totally inappropriate but if I wasn't able to resist it when I was mad at him, I wasn't going to be able to override that impulse when I was feeling the rush of victory and fondly remembering his skin on mine. Once we'd crossed that line there was no going back.

"I'm sure the answer is no, but if I offered you those fifteen minutes from yesterday morning now ... ?"

I shifted my weight. He locked eyes with me and I wasn't sure what he was going to do.

"As much as I'd love to take you up on the offer ... " He closed his eyes for a second and smiled faintly. "Timing, am I right?"

There was work left to do and, hopefully, plenty of time.

He inclined his head toward the door. "I think he's being standoffish with you because he can't figure you out. You have to admit, you're pretty casual despite almost dying. He sees you and can't picture what you did last night. You've got to admit, Sunshine, you don't look like the badass you are. But he'd take a bullet for you, which was the only condition I had for bringing him on."

Seth took a step forward but a knock on the door stopped him. He eased back from me and went to open it. I stayed put. After a moment I got up and wandered around the room. Gun still in its TV remote holster. I hadn't noticed during my B&E that the room still looked move-in ready. Seth had nothing that couldn't be packed in under an hour. No pictures on the walls, not even a poster of some underwear model that seemed de rigueur for the unattached male. Michael's room was plastered with them. Even Ben had a few.

I picked up one of the frames that was lying face down on the dresser. Michael. But this picture wasn't his service photo like from the memorial service. I hated that memorial photo. Those stupid pictures that they didn't let them smile in. Knowing that the last time some people would ever see him was that unsmiling photo of him in uniform had made me so angry. I wanted to remember him always like he was in this photo. Happy. Smiling. Full of life. I realized Seth must have them all face down for me.

He'd been doing those little things that I kept missing. Not so much ignoring but not *seeing* because I didn't expect them to be there. I didn't know exactly what to make of them other than he was trying. And he was doing it in ways that mattered. Not big gestures but the things that could go unseen because he wasn't making a big deal about them. Like the sugar and cream for my coffee.

A knock on the door and a beat of a wait saw the door open to Seth again. "We wanted to brief you about tonight if you're ready."

He held his hand out for the photo I was still holding. He stared at the photo for a minute, a faint smile lighting his face. He placed it back on the dresser, properly.

I followed him out to the kitchen where Gordon still sat, suit jacket off, sleeves rolled up, laptop in front of him. He looked up as we came in and gave us each a nod. Two words and a nod. Clearly, he was warming up to me.

Agent Gordon flipped the laptop around to face Seth. I caught sight of a document that looked like a blueprint. Seth studied it for a minute, nodding occasionally. I wondered when the briefing would start.

"Guys, I'm not sure if the ATF outfits its agents with brain chips that allow for telepathic communication, but I'll keep up much better if we actually do this out loud."

Gordon snorted. Was that a laugh or an aborted sneeze? I glanced over at Seth, who looked a little nonplussed himself.

"You're right, Anderson, she's funny. Most of this would be too technical for you to understand if we did a standard briefing, former cop or not, so I'll high-level it for you," Gordon said.

He had a really nice voice. Like one of those guys that did movie trailers. If I had a voice like that I'd be talking all the time just to hear it. Melted caramel with a hint of chocolate. Dammit, I was hungry and getting distracted.

I stood up and started to forage in the cabinets full of food that hadn't been there when I searched the place earlier in the week. The cream and sugar weren't outliers. The man had made a grocery run for me. That was even hotter than the half-lidded glances he'd been throwing me since I entered the kitchen. Not just the fact of the food he'd gone out his way to pick up but imagining him sauntering down the aisles of the store in his rough-and-tumble clothes searching for all my favorite foods. Gordon stopped talking. I turned around to find him looking at me with an annoyed expression.

"I'm hungry, but I can listen while I'm looking for something to eat. It's called multitasking, sparky."

That earned me another snort and a smile. I grabbed a package of cookies and handed them back to Seth while Gordon continued his explanation. I let the info sink in while I looked over the various cans and packages in the fridge.

I grabbed a soda, my favorite, and sat down across from Gordon again. Seth ripped open the package of cookies without taking his eyes off the computer and handed it over to me. I pulled a stack out and popped open the soda. I was reminding myself that grownups don't drool as I jammed a cookie into my mouth when I noticed Gordon had stopped talking again.

"Wha?" I mumbled around a mouth of cookie.

"You're actually going to ingest that?"

Seth looked up from the computer, his expression one of real fear. He knew how seriously I took my junk food. I could be civil. I mean, now that the sugar was coursing into my blood and I felt calmer.

"Listen, a racist psycho who's probably already killed one of his own friends has come after me twice. Failing both times, I may add. So if a handful of cookies and some caffeinated, colored sugar water makes me feel better, you can bet your ass I'm going to ingest it. I'd mainline them if it was possible."

Gordon just looked at me for a second, shook his head, and smiled widely. "You're a badass, all right. But we need to work on your diet."

I took another bite of the cookie and stared back at him with a blank expression. He could try, like my mom and Ben. He'd fail just like them. He could have my cookies when he pried them from my cold, dead, well-preserved hands.

He continued on with a bunch of boring details about warrants and exigent circumstances and imminent threat to civilian life.

"Civilian life—that'd be me, right?"

Gordon nodded. "Two attempts on your life in as many days constitutes imminent threat."

"It probably looks bad for your team if I get killed tracking down a murderer for the ATF, huh?" I winked at him.

Seth's hand eased over and stole a cookie from the package without even rustling the wrapper. I noticed Gordon was silent on Seth's cookie.

"Okay, so, the team's surveillance report on the tattoo parlor didn't get us any specific intel on the guns," Seth said, "but we did get what we needed to in order to get in, search the place, and get out without drawing any attention."

"Please tell me we're going in on wires like acrobats, *Mission Impossible* style."

"*We?*" Gordon asked. He looked over at Seth.

"Will, you can't come tonight. There's no way around it. Chain of evidence protocols. We'll go in and you'll stay home with a black-and-white," Seth said.

Gordon continued. "We're going to hit the tattoo parlor tonight and hope there's something more there that leads us to other locations. They've been so careful that this is our first real lead."

"I guess I'd better see what's on TV tonight then. Make sure you leave me some money for pizza and wings, Dads."

"Gordon, can you excuse us for a minute?" Seth grabbed my hand and walked me back to the bedroom. "You're pissed."

"I have to just sit home while you guys are out playing secret agent using information I got you? Yeah, I'm pissed. But I also get it. I'd rather drive a railroad spike through my hand using my forehead than let Ingalls weasel out of anything, so if you need me to stay home and knit you a damn sweater in order to take him down, I'll do it. I don't have to like it."

"You knit?"

"Do I look like I can knit, Seth?"

# CHAPTER

## 24

I FLIPPED THROUGH THE channels half-heartedly. I was bored and miffed. I knew why I couldn't be there with Seth and Gordon. It probably wasn't all that exciting anyway—just the two of them searching through a grungy tattoo parlor with its stashes of gross skin magazines and a porn collection alarming enough to generate a second investigation—but I still wanted to be there. These people had sold stolen guns to dangerous people not caring about the consequences. Mark Ingalls had killed Joe Reagan and had burned down the Horowitzes' house. He'd come after me. He'd almost killed Seth. And I wanted to see the cuffs being put on every last one of them. Especially Ingalls. I deserved that. So if it meant I sat quietly at home with asshole

Officer Harrison outside in a black-and-white at the curb and wait, then I'd do it.

I checked my phone for the tenth time since they'd left. Seth had sworn several times he'd contact me the minute it was over. He'd wanted me to stay at the apartment, but I wanted my own bed and my own things. When he brought me home, I had showered again, finally washing off all the smoke from the fire, replacing the burnt wood and chemical smell with strawberries. I had stayed in there a long, long time, only getting out when the water ran cold.

He'd sat on the bed, watching as I dropped my towel, not making a move toward me. I had dressed reluctantly, trying to drag out the time before he left, wanting to fall back into the rumpled covers with him, to forget about fires and knives and racists like Mark Ingalls. Seth had been right—we had crappy timing.

When I had finally pulled on the last of my clothes, he stood up and wrapped his arms around me. We stood quietly leaning against one another for as long as we could before he had to leave. He promised me one final time that he'd let me know when he was done and on his way home. I assumed he meant *home* was wherever I was and marveled at how quickly that had happened after years of stalled desire. How easy it was to be a team despite both our best efforts to push the other away.

I was tired and thirsty, something the nurses had warned me would be a near constant complaint in the days after jumping out of a fire-engulfed building. My head pounded. I turned the TV off and got up from the couch to get some aspirin and water.

I rounded the door from the dining room and had half a step and a heartbeat to recognize Mark Ingalls before he hit me in the face. I felt his fist glance off my cheekbone, clipping my brow and ghosting my eye. My teeth clacked together and pain exploded along my jawline.

My ribs slammed into the edge of the counter, and that was enough to distract me from my face feeling like it was splitting in two.

"You stupid bitch. You ruined everything."

Verbal skills notwithstanding, Mark Ingalls could throw a punch. I had gotten lucky that it was a glancing blow. If he'd hit me square, I'd have been in real trouble.

I lashed my foot out and kicked him in the side of the knee but I was off-balance and slipped down onto the counter, mouth first, lip popping open. Ingalls doubled over, grabbing his leg and yelling. I was happy to note I still held the remote, so I smacked him across the face with it. It was one of those old ones—big numbers, lots of buttons, and a half-dozen batteries. The compartment opened and they all flew out.

I took care with my footing as I pushed myself to standing and stumbled back out of arm's reach. I had caught him on the nose and he was having a hard time seeing me, his eyes watering, blood streaming from a cut on the bridge.

I was hurting and that first shimmer of fight-or-flight coursed into me. Adrenaline was my friend for now. I needed to keep it pumped up and I had to get my head into the game. Indulging in the pain could get me killed. This was Ingalls's third try at me and he was not screwing around. He was bigger, he was stronger, and he was angrier, but I was smarter and I had home-field advantage.

I backed into the dining room. My ear was starting to ring a bit. Ingalls was wild-eyed.

"Reagan was a traitor. He lied to me. Never told me his piece was a kike."

This guy couldn't stop being racist even while he was trying to kill me. Psychos really will talk at you about where it all went wrong and why they just had to do it—and it was always someone else's fault. I looked around hoping to find something I could use as a weapon. All

I saw was the cabinet full of creepy little figurines, which were about as dangerous as a nightmare. I thought about the knives in the kitchen and discarded the idea. I needed to keep him away from the knives. He could grab one just as easily, and I wasn't trained in knife fighting. Plus he seemed to like them. I turned away and got two steps into the room before my head snapped back, his hand tangled in my hair.

"No so fast. You're not smarter than me, you bitch!"

Creepy figurines it was. I kicked out, breaking the glass in the cabinet. There were a few that had a decent heft to them. I'd dusted them enough times to know which ones. Sorry, big-eyed couple on the swing. I pushed through the broken glass and closed my hand around it. I swung around, pulling my hair out of his hand. Shit, that hurt. The ceramic smashed into his temple. I pulled free completely and vowed not to turn my back on him again.

Ingalls panted, a dazed look in his eyes. The powdery remains of the tchotchke dusted his face, mixing with the sweat and blood. He was more out of shape than I had figured. I eased to the right, trying to put the dining room table in between us.

"You don't deserve to breathe the same air as righteous white men, you worthless mongrel. When I'm done here I'm going to kill your boyfriend. Does he even know you're a half-breed? Shame he has to die just because you're a lying nigger."

Jesus, he was super-no-doubts-about-it-capital-*I* insane. Maybe if I could keep him talking.

"This is not going to help you, Ingalls. My boyfriend is with the ATF. They're on to your group. You need to get the hell out of here."

He lunged at me, uninterested in self-preservation. I shoved the small table hard, hoping to knock it into him, take him down. The damn thing had been in the same spot for fifteen years and the legs had made deep divots in the carpet that held like glue. My side of the table tipped up as I powered my muscles into the shove and it flipped up on its side. It didn't even knock into Ingalls, but it provided the distraction I needed. I kicked the chair over, trying to give myself another layer. If he couldn't run after me I had a better chance of getting to the back of the house. To the gun safe in the master bedroom.

The muscle-deep bruise on my arm screamed at me. It had nagged all day but the table had woken it and it was fierce and angry. I reminded myself that being dead would be worse.

Dad had a revolver in the office. The lockbox would be easier to get to than the gun safe. But that door was behind Ingalls. Dammit. I feinted to the left like I was going for the living room and he moved to the outside of the table just as I moved back to the right, pushing the table as hard as I could again, hoping that flipping it onto its top would distract Ingalls enough to slow him down.

I raced into the kitchen, fighting every instinct that screamed at me to get the butcher block full of knives. I already knew he liked knives, so I didn't even glance at it and took the corner to the hallway, clipping my shoulder on the edge of the wall. I heard his heavy work boots pounding after me on the linoleum. But he was slowing. I deliberately swiped my hand on the painting closest to the back hall. A little misdirection could only help. I knew the master bedroom door was closed. He'd think I slipped in there to hide.

Back on the carpet my steps were muffled but my breathing was another matter. I was sucking in air too hard. I had to slow it down, be quieter, so I wasted a second taking a deep breath. My lungs clenched and I couldn't stop the cough, only barely muffling it by keeping my mouth closed.

I eased into the office and gave myself another second I didn't have to acclimate myself to the dark. I slipped around the side of the desk and down into the chair well. It was a terrible place to hide but I wasn't hiding. The desk was old and cheap with exposed drawer slides. I palmed the side of the top drawer and slid it open carefully. The lockbox was in the back of the bottom drawer. I could reach in and grab it without having to move out from under the desk.

I clicked open the suitcase lock, flipping the code by memory. Dad's badge number. I pulled the loaded revolver out.

Ingalls had enough time now to find out I wasn't in the back of the house. He'd be coming for the office any second. I was out of time. And I wasn't running or hiding anymore. This was my house. This was my life. And he'd taken enough from me already. He wasn't taking any more.

I stood up and walked out of the office into the dining room. Ingalls was standing in the kitchen holding the butcher knife.

He took a step. Then another. He was no more than ten feet from me. Even though I was armed and had the table between us, my stomach gave way to terrified spasms.

As a cop, I should have given a warning. But I wasn't a cop anymore, and he'd had plenty of time to stop. To leave. To not hurt me. To not try to kill me. He wanted me dead. He'd made that clear.

I'd been well trained for situations like this. My mind tunneled. Just Mark Ingalls. Just the expanse of gray cotton stretched across his pudgy torso.

Squeeze, don't snap.

Squeeze, don't snap.

I forced my mind clear of the pain and noise and panic. Then I planted my feet, let my knees relax, and swayed slightly forward at the hips. Perfect shooter's stance. One deep breath then another.

Squeeze, don't snap.

Squeeze, don't snap.

The bullet hit him center mass. He grunted. In pain or surprise, I didn't know. He looked surprised. Another bullet just to the left of the first. That one stopped him. He dropped to his knee and just lay down on the kitchen floor. It was almost graceful except for the blood.

My tunnel vision was clearing. The dining room was destroyed. I couldn't imagine how I would clean it all up, fix all the stuff that had been broken, make it okay to have my family in here. How would I ever sit at the table and eat Thanksgiving dinner again knowing I had shot a man over it? How would I have breakfast with my family in the kitchen with all that blood on the floor?

Shit. There was blood on the floor. I shook my head. Mark Ingalls was bleeding on the floor and I was worrying about family holidays. I needed to call 911.

I couldn't find my cell phone. It must have fallen out of my pocket somewhere in our fight. I didn't have time to look for it. I glanced over at the landline hanging on the wall. Mom had insisted we keep it. It hadn't seemed like a good idea before I shot someone. The problem was I had to walk past Mark Ingalls lying on the floor to get to it and I really didn't want to get anywhere near him.

I stared at him for what felt like hours but was probably only a minute. I kept the gun aimed at him. I was practically sitting on the counter, sidestepping to the phone. I couldn't take my eyes off his face. I was waiting for him to lunge up at me like the horror movie monsters did.

From far away I heard hammering on the front door. I had forgotten the black-and-white. There had been a cop outside the whole time. How had Ingalls gotten in? He wasn't supposed to have been able to get to me. That was the damn point of the security detail. Why the hell was Ingalls bleeding on my floor if I was being protected?

Then I remembered Seth's comment about some cops being neo-Nazis too. Could Tony Harrison have helped Ingalls?

I looked away from Ingalls only long enough to grab the phone handle and lift it from the cradle. I saw that my hand was covered in blood, oozing from a dozen little cuts. With a shaking hand I punched in the numbers and eased away as far as the phone cord would allow.

"911, what's your emergency?"

"I've been attacked in my home. I'm hurt. I shot him."

"What's your address, dear?"

"I'm a ... I, uh ... I don't remember." An address I knew by heart was just gone from my mind.

"It's okay, dear. I've got the address. I'm dispatching help to you right now. I need you to stay on the line with me until they get there. Can you do that?"

I nodded, forgetting that she couldn't see me. I coughed hard again. My heart tripped in my chest. The adrenaline was overwhelming my system.

"There's a cop here already but Ingalls shouldn't have been able to get past him. I don't know if I should let him in."

"Let him in, ma'am. He's there to help you."

The lady's voice was so calm but my heart was drumming in my head. "Are you sure?"

Knocking on the kitchen window startled me and I dropped the phone. I heard the 911 operator's voice calling out to me. Harrison was yelling at me through the glass. "Pennington, open the door."

I looked down at Ingalls again and then at the phone swinging on its cord against the wall.

Blood from my hands smudged onto the emergency phone number list taped to the surface. I looked away from it. The latest perversion of my mom's orderly house.

239

I didn't know what to do. I stared at Ingalls. At the holes in his shirt, blood spreading out from them, running into the logo on the fabric. I tried to focus on the logo.

"PENNINGTON. Let me in."

Of course Harrison wasn't working with Ingalls. I rushed to the hall and twisted the deadbolt before turning the handle and pulling open the front door. It bounced off the wall but stayed open. I still had a ton of adrenaline flying through my blood. Harrison's face stared at me.

"What the hell happened, Pennington?" he asked, easing the gun out of my hand.

I led him to the kitchen and Ingalls on the floor. He kicked the knife away from Ingalls's body.

I reached for the phone receiver and it slid against my hand, slick with blood. "I'm back. I let him in."

The operator talked to me in soothing tones and I heard sirens in the air. The neighborhood association was probably flooded with complaints about all the noise this week. I wondered why I cared. And then the house was full of people. I forgot to say goodbye before I hung up the phone.

The paramedics worked on Mark Ingalls, trying to stop the blood, get a regular heartbeat. I could barely tear my eyes away. I was responsible for those injuries and I knew the men working frantically to save him. I had worked car accidents with them. I wanted them to stop. I wanted to tell them what kind of man he was, what he had done, what he had tried to do. I wanted to scream that he was a monster. I said nothing. They would do their jobs no matter their feelings.

"Pennington? Can you tell me what happened?" Tony Harrison stood in front of me. The house I had grown up in was now a crime scene. There was blood on the kitchen floor.

"Um, I shot him. He had a knife."

He looked at me like he was seeing me for the first time. "Are you okay?"

I nodded. A racist who had tried to kill me was bleeding out in my kitchen. Could I tell him what had happened? I could barely figure it out myself.

"This was self-defense, Pennington."

I nodded again even though it hadn't sounded like a question. The trashed house and bruises blooming on my face were a pretty good indicator that we'd been fighting. And the knife that had been lying next to Mark Ingalls. I covered my eyes with my hands, barely feeling the black eye. I just needed a moment to gather my thoughts. Harrison needed a timeline.

"I was thirsty. I wanted some water."

He waited, a patient look on his face. It struck me that he was doing a good job pretending he didn't hate me. Was that how he was with victims? Was I a victim? A man had broken into my house. He had hit me and threatened me. He had told me he was going to kill me. He'd tried twice before. Harrison was going to put my name down in the victim field on a form.

"My brother is staying with a friend tonight and I was waiting for him. No, not him. Seth."

Ben could have been here. That bastard could have hurt by baby brother. My sweet, brilliant, just-becoming-a-man baby brother. "How did he get in, Harrison? How did he get past you?"

If he was embarrassed that Ingalls had gotten past him, he didn't show it. "Wilkes said the door in the basement was open."

Goddamn broken sliding glass door.

I saw Harrison turn away to talk on the phone.

I was suddenly exhausted, the adrenaline wearing off. It had been a really long time since that morning. I just wanted to lie down. It was probably a bad time for that. I slumped against the wall.

"Pennington, I need you to sit down, okay? Boyd's on her way. She'll want you to tell her the story yourself." He had me by the arm and was leading me over to the wrecked dining room, away from the commotion in the kitchen. There were so many people. It seemed like dozens but I didn't remember that many people arriving. He picked up the nearest chair and gently settled me into it.

"The ATF is doing a search right now. Or maybe it's over by now. I don't know. I can't remember. Is it still today? Seth can tell you."

Something swam in my head. It slid around like oil on the surface of water. I pushed myself up and moved toward Ingalls and the paramedics.

Harrison tried to push me back toward the chair. "You don't need to see this, Pennington."

"His shirt. The logo, Harrison."

He let me by and held me up as I leaned over the paramedic who'd cut the shirt down the middle to access the wounds.

"I need to see the logo."

Harrison nodded at the EMT and the man flipped the shirt flap up off the floor. Just like the truck I'd seen during the stakeout. There had even been one in the parking lot at Killian's. I hadn't even thought twice about them. Those trucks were all over the county.

"Harrison. You need to call Boyd. Tell her Farley Brothers Construction."

He looked at me uncertainly. "Willa, you've had a big shock tonight. You're not making sense."

"Harrison, please call her now. She'll understand."

He pulled his radio off the shoulder holster and began talking.

I tried to keep my thoughts straight but they were impossible to hold on to and it was hard to keep my eyes open. I was so tired.

I looked up at Harrison talking to Boyd on the radio, but he was taller than I remembered. I couldn't see his face. I couldn't see anything above his neck. It was just a gray blur. I wondered how his face could be gone if I could hear him talking. He was saying something but his words were like bees buzzing around my ears. I didn't understand how his words could be bees.

And then I knew. "I'm going to pass out now."

My body gave out from my control and all I could hear was his voice, sounding so far away, yelling, "Officer down."

# CHAPTER

## 25

**I HATED HOSPITALS. I** hated the smells and the fake cheeriness. The room looked standard issue with crappy linoleum and a TV bolted to the wall but there was no other bed. How had I rated a private room with no insurance?

I didn't hate the drugs. Those were pretty awesome. I didn't remember much about my second visit to the ER in as many days. I had gotten much better drugs this trip, which probably explained my sketchy memory. I knew Boyd had been by and that John's mother had brought Ben to see me. I vaguely remembered threatening to take a hammer to Ben's computers if he called our parents. The nurse had told me a bunch of cops had been in asking about me. I wondered if that meant Seth. I couldn't remember if I'd seen him.

My back ached from lying flat so I adjusted the bed up. I tried to turn on my side but the compression bandage reminded me that I had broken ribs. I couldn't get comfortable. Considering my injuries, that wasn't too surprising. I decided being a martyr wasn't helping anyone, so I pressed the button. The nurse had warned it would take a few minutes for relief to kick in, so I began to count slowly, evening out my breath like she'd advised. I had gotten to two hundred when I felt the hair on the back of my neck stand up. I opened my eyes and saw the woman from Killian's glaring at me from the doorway. Head Bitch. Her dark green eyes were staring daggers at me.

"I recognized you when I saw the cops hauling out the pictures from his room."

The pictures?

"He'd still be alive if you'd kept your nose out of it."

She was talking about Ingalls. She'd seen the cops hauling out the murder wall.

I watched her edge just slightly into the room. Her coat was over her arm, pulled tightly against her stomach.

"He wasn't a bad person. They're making it sound like he was this awful person on the news."

I motioned to the stitches in my eyebrow. "He did this to me. He hit me in the face with his fist."

Her face hardened. "It wasn't your business. You should have stayed out of it."

"He killed his friend. Shot him in the chest and then rifled his pockets. He did that before I even laid eyes on him. That makes him a bad person."

She looked away. I could feel the blurry edges of the pain medication pushing in. All my limbs felt warm and heavy but my brain struggled against the darkness. I couldn't let myself fall asleep.

"He was my son. I'd have known if he was like that."

She was Mark Ingalls's mother? Alarm shot through my numbed body. What was she capable of if she had raised him?

I grabbed the call button and pressed it three times quickly. I just had to keep my eyes open until the nurse got to the room.

"He came at me with a knife," I said. "He blocked me in that motorcycle shop and set the fire." My tongue was thick and the words dribbled out. I pressed the call button again.

"You're lying." Her image began to sway.

Where was the nurse?

A voice rang out from the hallway. "Who are you? What are you doing here?"

Seth.

"She killed my son! He's dead! My baby is dead. She killed him!" Head Bitch was screaming and crying.

I couldn't keep my eyes open any longer. But it was okay because Seth wouldn't let anything happen to me. I let myself fall but there was no building, no smoke, just darkness.

————

"Will?"

I cracked open my good eye. Seth was standing at the foot of the bed, his hand hovering over my foot.

"Good morning, Sunshine," he said.

"Hey, super spy." My voice was hoarse. I watched as he sat down in the chair next to the bed and then glanced around.

"Nice digs, huh?" Seth followed my eyes around the room. "Courtesy of your friendly neighborhood ATF field office."

"Seth." I scooted my hand over toward the edge of the bed, close to him. He didn't move toward me. Instead he looked up at the heart rate monitor.

"It was the least we could do. The least I could do. I almost got you killed. I'm so, so sorry."

I tried to push up off the bed and my torso screamed at me to lie the hell back down and be still. I ignored the pain and pushed on. Seth jumped up, reaching his hands out to assist. I grasped his bicep and squeezed as hard as I could. My wrist protested but it had been through worse so I ignored it too. My wrist and ribs could start a whiners club together. I pressed my cheek into his chest while I tried to wrap my other arm around his waist. Not the best hug I'd ever given him but I was sure he'd forgive me, considering. He wrapped his hand gently around the back of my head.

"Seth, you are not to blame for this."

He let out a deep breath and I felt his chest rise and fall against my face. I liked it. It felt like safety.

"You scared the shit out of me, Will. When I saw all those alerts from Boyd, I freaked out. Gordon just pushed me into a car and told me to go, that he'd get a ride. When you weren't at the house ... God, I thought you were dead, Will. I thought this asshole that I hadn't stopped had killed you."

"I'm fine. See?" I pulled away slightly. "Near perfect. Slap some makeup on me and no one will be able to tell."

He laughed and sat back down, keeping hold of my hand. The smile dropped from his face. "I'm serious. I know you're tough but this asshole was not messing around. He wanted you dead in a bad way. Your dining room is wrecked."

"That was mostly me." I gave him the best fake smile my bruised face could muster. The right side of my mouth didn't want to lift. I probably looked like I'd had a stroke. "I put anything in his way I could get my hands on. Mom's going to be pissed that I destroyed most of her creepy little figurines."

Seth looked like he wanted to smile at the image of me cartooning ceramic tchotchkes at Mark Ingalls. My near fatal beating seemed to put a damper on his humor. Understandable.

I gave his fingers a fluttering little press with mine. "I know it looks bad, but I am okay. I promise. It hurts like shit and I'm pretty sure I won't ever play the piano again, but I will live to piss off another lunatic."

"Of that I have no doubt. Can you promise me that the next time you don't cut it quite so close?" He gestured at my face.

I knew it was bad. My eye ached bone deep. Even blinking hurt. Anything more than that glancing blow and… well, I didn't want to think about it.

"Harrison said Ingalls got in the sliding door. He must have come through the trees from the next street over when he saw that patrol car."

Seth's eyes flashed angry. "Harrison. I almost killed the asshole. He was sitting out in the car while Ingalls was beating the crap out of you."

"It's not his fault, Seth. He didn't know Ingalls would be crazy enough to sneak in the back with a cop sitting out front."

"I should have made you stay at the apartment."

"You're determined to take the blame for this, aren't you? No one is to blame but Mark Ingalls."

He cleared his throat. "I don't know if you remember. His mother was here earlier. You were pretty out of it."

I nodded. "I was calling for the nurse but you rescued me instead."

"You were still asleep so I went to the lobby to make some calls. I didn't want to disturb you. It took longer than I thought. I'm so sorry, babe."

"You have to stop apologizing."

"You could have died."

"But I didn't. Ingalls did."

I tried to harden my heart. Mark Ingalls was not a person who deserved life. He had been a horrid human being, full of hate and rage. I understood feeling hate and rage, but not the cause of it. The color of someone's skin wasn't a reason to hate them. I also understood feeling helpless. But I couldn't understand feeling so lost that you took it out on others, hurting them to make yourself feel better. I hadn't ever gotten that deep in the abyss. I would never understand that.

I didn't know how I felt. I knew it was a righteous kill. He'd broken into my house. He'd hurt me. He was trying to kill me. I just got to him first.

But.

But his mother had loved him. She'd called him her baby. He'd been a baby once. He'd been innocent once.

"Yeah. He died on the operating table. Listen, you did what you had to. He made the choice, not you."

I nodded. I tried to swallow down the lump in my throat. I had gotten used to doing that. I refused to cry but I did gasp. I didn't think I was going to be able to hold it in anymore. This was exactly why I quit the force. I didn't think I could survive having killed someone, having to knock on someone's door and shatter their world, when I knew first-hand what it felt like being on the other side of that door.

I had killed someone.

I made a sound I had never heard before. The breath was leaving me faster than I could suck it in. Oh god, my lungs didn't work anymore. I couldn't breathe. I felt Seth's grip on me tighten.

"Will! Listen to me. You need to breathe slower. You're hyperventilating."

I locked eyes with him. I tried to focus them. Blink and breathe. One, two. In, out. I don't know how long we sat like that with me just breathing. It helped focusing on his eyes. His pale green eyes. It was like they belonged to me. It got easier and then my chest no longer felt like wet cement. It was just me and Seth, him rubbing my hand, the other on my leg, grounding me.

"You're okay. I'm not going to let anything happen to you ever again, babe."

At some point I had closed my eyes. Being sixteen sheets to the wind on painkillers will knock the piss and vinegar right out of you.

"Still with me, Sunshine?"

I nodded carefully, trying not to jog loose any bones that were holding on with a wing, a prayer, and a double shot of bubble gum.

"So, I think I made the emergency room staff real nervous in my gear. I bet I have some footage from my vest cam if you want to see. You'd think they'd be harder to scare, given their jobs."

I tried to laugh without causing internal bleeding but that proved difficult so I sputtered out and lay back against the pillows, staring at him. "Uh huh, an angry man in a bulletproof vest storms into the ER. Sure. It must happen five times a night."

"I wasn't angry. I was concerned. There is a big difference. And my gear does have 'ATF' all over it."

"I'll bet you looked like a stud too. All sweaty and hero-like." My split lip didn't like all the talking I was doing and began to seep against the stitches. Those had been a bitch going in even with the drugs so I didn't want to have them redone.

He rubbed his thumb over the back of my hand, avoiding the IV line and grabbed a tissue to press against the leaking blood on my chin.

"Shut up, already, would you? I want to tell you about how you solved the case. And yes, I looked like Colin Farrell in *S.W.A.T.* coming through those automatic doors."

I nodded, trying not to chuckle. Seth was way better looking than Colin Farrell. I definitely wanted to hear about the raid. Ingalls's words came back to me. *Mongrel bitch.* I didn't want it to hurt as much as it did. He'd been a loser full of ignorance and rage, but he wasn't an outlier. There were more than a few people that thought anyone different was an affront. People who believed the word *abomination* was applicable to a biracial child. Those twisted ideologies never died. They just crouched down low and hid, waiting for the right audience. The right time. The right victim.

"Farley Brothers Construction. Jesus, Sunshine. I've been working this case for months and in a week you found the link. Gordon led an ATF team into their warehouse out in Chantilly at six. They never saw the team coming. They busted in and half of them started blubbering like they'd been sent to the principal's office. Those wannabe badasses running a gun ring in the suburbs cried. They had the guns hidden in boxes of toilets, for god's sake. The team is matching up the weapons to the lists from the gun store robberies. We know some will be missing but we're hoping most are recoverable."

"*They?* I don't understand. You weren't there?"

He gave me a confused smile. "I was here waiting for you to wake up."

My eyes filled. "You missed your own raid? Are you stupid? That was your bust, Seth. You should have been there."

He reached up and brushed his fingers across my unbruised cheek. "I was exactly where I wanted to be. With you."

I choked down a sob. His fingers squeezed mine. He'd stayed with me. I let out my breath and just focused on how the rough, callused skin of his thumb felt rubbing across my palm.

He rubbed my hand a little harder. "I know your dad wants you to get your license and work with him, but I was hoping maybe you'd see your way to joining the ATF. You're a hell of a cop, Will. My boss was blown away by what you'd figured out with just those crappy PI databases. They'd fast-track you."

I hadn't considered going back to the badge. And certainly not a different badge. The ATF. Working with Seth. My confusion must have shown on my face because he smiled.

"Think about it later. We'll talk more when you're feeling better. Just rest for now."

My face ached. My wrist throbbed. All the little cuts on my hands were beginning to sting. The drugs were wearing off again. I had a sudden rush of empathy for drug addicts. All I wanted was to push the button to get relief but the clarity was better.

"You told your boss I was the one who'd tipped you off to Farley? You missed your own raid *and* you told your boss a civilian figured out where the guns were being stored?"

I looked at him harder than I ever had ever since the first time we met. He wasn't that shy fifteen year old I remembered when they first moved here. He'd moved past the guy who flirted with every girl to hide that he was the shy new kid. The football hero who had a smile that never quite reached his eyes. The winner who never let anyone get too close. The man who'd accepted medals and honors with the conviction he hadn't really deserved them. Jesus, he'd given me credit for his case and acted like it was no big deal.

And he looked like hell with dark circles under his eyes, pale skin, his uneven shave. Like he hadn't slept for weeks. He probably hadn't, worrying about the trouble I was getting myself into. The trouble he'd been trying to steer me away from. And when that failed, he'd risked his case to keep an eye on me.

"Seth, I'm sorry." I shifted in the bed, uncomfortable. Injuries I hadn't known about were battling for my attention. I gritted my teeth and realized that even those hurt.

"Don't."

"I should have listened. I didn't want to be left out. I wanted to prove to you that I was a good cop. And I didn't think of the risks."

"It's probably not a good time to say that I told you so, is it?"

"It's probably the only safe time to say it," I joked.

"You challenge me. I need that even if I don't like it. You make me better, Sunshine."

"Me too, Ace." I closed my eyes and let my body relax against the hospital bed, exhausted.

He stood up and leaned over to kiss me gently on the side of my mouth free of sutures. "You need to sleep, love. I'm not going anywhere."

## The End

# Acknowledgments

The idea for this book, which was very different at the beginning, began a decade ago. It was a long time before I was brave enough to tell the idea to another person. He informed me it was a story that needed to be written and that I had to be the one to do it. He was with me every word, every page, every chapter; being my sounding board; being my cheerleader; being my mentor. Without Matthew V. Clemens this book would not exist. Thanks, Matt. You don't suck.

Jessie Lourey, Maggie Barbieri, and Wendy Watson were generous enough to read the first draft of this story, and I am profoundly appreciative of the time and energy that took and for the excellent comments and suggestions they made.

Many thanks to Sherry Harris, who always makes time to lend an ear and share a cup of coffee and who did me the great honor of recommending me to her (now our) agent.

Extra special thanks to Terri Bischoff, Amy Glaser, Nicole Nugent, and the entire Midnight Ink team.

Dru Ann Love is the most aptly named human being. She is the personification of everything you could wish for in a friend and somehow manages to be even more than you could ever think to ask for. I am grateful every day she decided she wanted to be my friend and help be a part of the making of this book.

So many people have contributed to this journey by providing support, advice, cheerleading, and butt-kicking. I am so grateful that I have the chance to thank all of them here: Joelle Charbonneau, Mollie Cox Bryan, Heather Webber, Jessie Chandler, Dana Fredsti, Eleanor Cawood Jones, Alan Orloff, Kristi Belcamino, Dorothy McFalls, Sally Goldenbaum, Ellery Adams, Karen Fraunfelder Cantwell, Nancy Parra, Shannon Baker, Catriona McPherson, LynDee Walker Stephens, Eileen Rendahl, John Talbot, and Tracy Kiely.

My undying devotion and gratitude to my husband, who upon hearing me say that I wanted to quit my day job and write full-time after completing my first manuscript (that which you hold now) and not even having sold it yet, replied, "I'm in." It was a gift I can never repay, that unconditional faith. Thank you every day, my love.

Finally, I set out to do this because I wanted to show my daughter that if you work hard and are brave, you can accomplish what you set out to even if it takes longer than you thought it would. Thank you for being the inspiration for everything and the reason I challenge myself to do hard things.

## About the Author

Aimee Hix is a former defense contractor turned mystery writer. She's a member of Sisters in Crime. *What Doesn't Kill You* is her first book.

Visit her at www.AimeeHix.com.